For the Love
of Jazz

Look for these titles by *Shiloh Walker*

Now Available:

For the Love of Jazz

Shiloh Walker

A Samhain Publishing, Ltd. publication.

Samhain Publishing, Ltd.
577 Mulberry Street, Suite 1520
Macon, GA 31201
www.samhainpublishing.com

For the Love of Jazz
Copyright © 2008 by Shiloh Walker
Print ISBN: 978-1-59998-830-6
Digital ISBN: 1-59998-675-2

Editing by Heidi Moore
Cover by Scott Carpenter

First Samhain Publishing, Ltd. electronic publication: October 2007
First Samhain Publishing, Ltd. print publication: November 2008

Dedication

Hugs and kisses to Renee. You always liked this one best. And to Pam, for helping me stay sane one very long afternoon.

Mom, you're allowed to read this one.

And to Sherry...just in case you're reading this...do you see it? Do you remember? It's blue.

Chapter One

Spring 1987

He ached. From head to toe and back up again, he ached. His jaw throbbed where that sonovabitch had clobbered him across the face the first time. His ribs hurt, his gut hurt, his head hurt, but most of all, his hands hurt. His hands were torn, bloodied and bruised, his knuckles raw and scraped, and every single mark was a battle scar.

Yet he had a smile of satisfaction on his face.

Jasper Wayne McNeil Jr., better known as Jazz, had fought back for the first time in his young life. And he had given it good. He hadn't meant to, certainly hadn't planned it, even though he had dreamed of it, time and time again. But when he walked in on that bastard beating his Mama again, he'd lost it.

With the speed of youth and the advantage of surprise, Jazz had taken a swing at the man the law called his stepfather, and broken his nose. Big for his age, and smart, Jazz was an eerie echo of the man Beau Muldoon had hated his entire life. With his father's eyes and his father's derisive smile on his young face, Jasper McNeil Jr. had stood up to the man who had been beating both him and his Mama for the past six years.

"You sure you don't wanna go see the doc?" Alexander

Kincade asked. With his gilt-edged hair and sky blue eyes, Alex looked like a golden angel mending a fallen one.

"Shit, no," Jazz snapped, curling his split lip in a sneer when all he wanted to do was whimper. The sneer hurt like hell, but he couldn't exactly cry like a baby in front of his best friend, could he? "He didn't get me that bad." The sad fact was that Jazz spoke no less than the truth. Beau had laid into Jazz before and a time or two had put Jazz flat on his back for a week. This beating, much as it hurt, wouldn't slow him down more than a day or two.

He sucked in a breath of air when Alex doused his burning knuckles with alcohol.

"Sorry, man. Gotta get it clean." Spoken like the son of a doctor. Born to one of the most prominent cardiologists in the south, destined to go to medical school himself, Alex had spent a good amount of time doctoring up Jazz's battered body over the past few years. But this was the first time Jazz had come swaggering to their private haunt wearing his bruises like battle scars.

Tonight, Alex was filled with pride and fear. Pride that his bud had done the damage he'd done, fear that Muldoon would retaliate in the worst possible way. "If you say so, man," he replied, shaking his head as he eyed the ugly, red cuts on the backs of Jazz's hands. "You look like you're hurt, that's all."

Hell, yeah, he hurt, Jazz thought. But if the local social worker found out he'd been beat again, he'd be in a home for sure this time.

There was no way in hell Jazz was going to let that happen. He wasn't leaving his Mama. He didn't want to, but even if he did, he couldn't do it. If he left Mama alone, Beau would end up killing her.

℘

At the tender age of fourteen, Jazz became a man, fighting his way into manhood as he hauled his stepfather off the battered body of his mother. At sixteen, he stood in a sullen rain, watching as her casket was lowered into the ground. The sky was leaden gray and the downpour had started late the night before, soaking the earth so it turned into mud. The few people who had bothered to come to the funeral stood in their Sunday best, soaked to the bone, shoes covered with mud, and most of them still in a state of shock over what Delia McNeil Muldoon had done.

Stone-faced, Jazz stared at the headstone and wondered who'd taken care of it. Somebody with a decent amount of money. Jazz suspected it was Alex's daddy. The name engraved into the pale pink marble read *Delia McNeil, beloved wife and mother.*

The Muldoon name, thankfully, wasn't anywhere on the stone.

In his pocket, he had the note she'd left on the kitchen table, along with a locket Jazz's daddy had given her years ago.

Please don't hate me, Jazz, she had written. *But I can't take it any more.*

She had loaded up the Smith & Wesson Jazz's daddy had gotten her years earlier. Then, Delia had waited in the tiny kitchen of the shack they lived in, waited for Beau Muldoon to return from his trip to Lenny's, the bar he always visited after his weekly beating of his wife.

When he had crossed the threshold and looked into his wife's bruised eyes, she pulled the trigger, sending a bullet into her second husband's surprised face. Then she turned the gun on herself, no longer able to live with the shame. She had done this, placed herself and her son in a home where they were beaten regularly. The guilt and shame she'd lived with ever since Beau had started beating her and her son had eaten her alive and she simply couldn't live with it anymore.

Rain running down his face, Jazz thought, *I could never hate you, Mama.*

She was with Daddy again. After ten years of living without him, Delia McNeil had found her Jasper again.

Only problem was, she'd left her son alone.

"I'm real sorry about your Mama, Jazz," a quiet little voice said from his side. Turning his head, he met the wide, green eyes of Anne-Marie Kincade, Alex's baby sister and general pain in the backside. Fourteen years old, she was already a veritable shrew. She was bossy, she was a know-it-all, and Jazz loved her dearly. Next to Alex, there wasn't anybody in the world he cared for the way he cared for Anne-Marie. He was as protective of her as Alex was, although he had a bit more patience. For a while, he'd suspected she'd had a crush on him and while it usually amused him, he couldn't deal with the adoring way she watched him right now.

He couldn't deal with anything.

He started to mumble something, but then she tucked her hand in his, and tugged. Dutifully, he lowered his head to hers.

"I know how awful bad it hurts, Jazz. I missed my Mama so much when she died, I wanted to die too. But Daddy told me that Mama had done her job here, so she got to go be with God. We all have a job to do."

Rising on her tiptoes, she brushed Jazz's cheek with a feather-light kiss. Then she whispered in his ear, "Your Mama's job was done, that's all. Now she's with your daddy again, and she's happy."

With that, she turned around, daintily side stepped a

puddle in her shiny, black patent leathers, then joined her father, who stood by watching. Desmond watched him with sad eyes. His voice was soft and gentle as he said, "Time will help, Jasper. I can promise you that."

Closing his eyes, turning his face heavenward, he wished he had been the one to empty the lead into Beau Muldoon. His Mama would be alive, and safe, and free.

Now he had all the time in the world to regret he hadn't been the one to do it.

July 1991

It was hot that night in late June, their last summer as kids. Come fall, Alex was heading north to the University of Kentucky, and after that, medical school.

At eighteen, Jazz was heading for the Marines. After spending the last two years with the Kincade family, he knew he had to do something to make Desmond Kincade proud of him.

Going into medicine wasn't in his future, though. He was smart enough, Jazz guessed. School was ridiculously easy for him. But he had issues with blood. Alex was the only person on God's green earth that knew it, and if his friend ever breathed a word about it, Jazz would kill him. Issues with blood aside, Jazz had no idea what he wanted to do and if nothing else, the military was a good way to kill time while he figured it out.

That night, the air was thick and heavy with the scent of coming rain. A storm was brewing, both inside the car and out. Hands drumming on the steering wheel, staring straight ahead, Alex drove in silence. Taking a sip from the icy soda, Jazz waited, knowing the fallout would come shortly.

Something was eating Alex up inside but asking what the

problem was wouldn't do a damn bit of good until Alex was ready to talk. So Jazz didn't waste his breath. The tension in the car got heavier and heavier and when it finally broke, Jazz breathed out a sigh of relief.

"Maribeth is pregnant," Alex blurted out.

"'Scuse me?" Jazz asked, sticking his finger in his ear and wiggling it. He studied Alex and hoped like hell this was some kind of trick. It wasn't, though. Alex's face was pale and his eyes were miserable. He wasn't much of an actor. "Sorry, bud. Did you just say Maribeth was pregnant?"

"That's what I said." His voice was grim, his eyes wild and scared. Impossibly young.

"Shit," Jazz muttered, shoving his hand through his thick black hair. His eyes were wide and dark, the color of melted chocolate, and as he stared at Alex, they narrowed. "You two broke up a few months back. She ain't saying it's yours, is she?"

"Sure as hell is."

Glaring out the window, unsure of what to say, he remained silent. The words *I told you so* danced around his head, but he didn't give voice to them. He had warned Alex, time and again, Maribeth Park was nothing but trouble. She might not be an abusive bitch, but other than that, Maribeth was the female version of Jazz's dead stepfather. Cut from the same cloth, Maribeth and Beau believed in only one thing and that was to get as much for themselves as they could, without actually having to work for it. Maribeth looked at Alex and dollar signs all but gleamed in her eyes.

But the last thing Alex needed right now was a reminder about how many times Jazz had warned him about Maribeth. So instead, he stayed quiet for a minute, thinking. "Seeing as how you two ain't been together in months, she's gonna have a hard time getting you in any trouble."

Alex looked away, his eyes guilty. "Well, you see, the thing is... Remember graduation? We were all at the river that night and Maribeth and me started talking."

"Talking, my ass," Jazz muttered, blowing a breath out between his teeth. No talking, and no thinking either, at least not on Alex's part. "So the baby could be yours."

His voice soft, Alex said, "I don't think there is a 'could', Jazz. I got a feeling that baby is mine." Not just a feeling, but a bone-deep certainty.

Silence once again fell.

"What's the old man said?" Jazz asked, as Alex took a sharp curve going near sixty.

"Before or after he skinned me?" Alex asked with a faint grin. "He told me that I had made a mistake, but he'd be damned before he saw me marrying somebody like her. He's going to get a lawyer."

"A lawyer? Why in the hell do you need a lawyer?"

"To get custody of the baby," Alex replied calmly. "I am not going to see that woman, or her mother, taking care of my baby. Shit, I wouldn't trust them to take care of a stray cat."

"Alex, you're eighteen years old."

"If I was old enough to be screwing her, then I'd better be old enough to deal with the consequences." He was quiet for a minute and then he murmured, "You know what Maribeth is like. You warned me about her more times than I can count. Do you honestly think she could love a baby? Hell, forget love. Do you think a baby would be safe with her?"

Jazz sighed and rubbed at the back of his neck. He had a vicious headache all of a sudden and he suspected it was going to get worse before it got better. "Maribeth isn't capable of loving

15

or taking care of anything."

"Then you understand why I can't let it happen." He tapped the steering wheel with his hands, a habitual nervous gesture. When Alex was nervous, being still was impossible. "Dad thinks we're going to have to pay her money—between her and her mother, they're greedy enough they'll take the money and be thankful they don't have to take care of some kid."

"You really ready to be a dad, Alex?"

Alex looked too damn old for his years as he replied, "Doesn't matter if I'm ready or not. It's going to happen. But I can handle it." With a trace of his normal good humor, Alex slid Jazz a sly glance. "I'll name you the godfather, bro."

In the process of sipping from his soda, Jazz choked on a laugh. "The hell you will," he replied, good-naturedly smacking Alex on the head.

಄

Three weeks later, there was no baby. Maribeth lay in her bed, glaring up at the beautiful young man at her bedside. Thick, wheat-blond hair fell over a lightly tanned face, eyes bluer than the noontime sky, a mouth straight off the mold of a master sculptor. Already, he had his father's build, long, rangy and powerful.

It wasn't fair, a man looking like he did, being as smart as he was, and rich to boot. And the bastard wouldn't share it with her.

"I got rid of it," she said coldly. "Me and Mama went into town and I got an abortion."

"You bitch," Alex whispered, his hands shaking with rage. "How in the hell could you do that?"

Across the street, Jazz rose from the porch where he had been passing the time with Sandy Pritchard. The skin on the back of his neck rose as he listened to the porch swing creak behind him. "What's wrong, baby?" Sandy asked softly, rising to go wrap an arm around his waist. He only shook his head.

Staring at the silent house, his gut churning, Jazz waited. He'd waved at Alex when his friend pulled up. Jazz and Sandy were supposed to go to the drive-in, although he was wondering if he could talk her into someplace a little more private. Another week, Jazz was leaving and he wouldn't be back for a long while.

"Something wrong, Jazz?" Sandy asked again.

Jazz shook his head. "I don't know." Alex had acted as if he hadn't seen Jazz when he waved and there had been a look on his face that Jazz didn't like one bit. Sandy stood silently next to him, her mink-brown curls pulled into a high ponytail. Laying her head on his shoulder, Sandy's eyes drifted to the house across the street.

Off in the distance, thunder rumbled. The sky held the dark promise of a summer thunderstorm and the air felt heavy and thick with it. Staring at Maribeth's ramshackle, little house, Jazz felt like the air was weighing down on him, but it had nothing to do with the quicksilver change in the weather.

Voices rose and although Jazz couldn't make out the words, he recognized his friend's voice. Alex wasn't the kind to yell much. Too laid-back, too easy going. When Alex yelled, people were better off to just shut up and get out of his way, because it took a lot to make him lose it.

"Something bad's going down," Sandy murmured, stroking his rigid back with a soothing hand. "Awful bad."

Inside the house, face gone white with fury, Alex closed his hands into tight fists, dragging a deep breath of air into his lungs. The curtains fluttered in the window, a small fan busily whirling in the open frame. The scent of ozone drifted in on the air and in the distance, there was the ominous rumble of thunder.

"That was my baby," he said, his voice gone hoarse with emotion. "Mine!"

Sneering at him, Maribeth said, "How do you know? I didn't even know if you were the father. Besides, it was my choice."

"A baby isn't a damned choice!" Alex shouted. "Why in the hell did you do it?"

In a calm voice, she replied, "Because you wouldn't marry me."

"I said I'd take care of the baby. I would have taken the baby," Alex said. The rage inside him boiled and simmered, ready to strike out.

"No wife, no baby," Maribeth said, shrugging her shoulders. "Me and Mama talked it out. And I wasn't going to sell you my baby to live in your fine house on the hill, so it could grow up rich, while I spend my life in this hell hole."

Without even realizing it, Alex started to reach for her. Her lovely gray eyes widened only slightly and a smile flirted with her mouth. "Go ahead," she offered. "I should get something out of this, at least."

Shaken, Alex pulled his hands back, jammed them deep into his pockets. "You'll regret this," he said, his voice quiet. And then, he turned away and left the room.

In the living room, he came up with Maribeth's maker. Her mother, a sly, cunning woman with cold eyes, blocked his path. "If you're wanting this to stay quiet, we could use some money around here," Eleanor said, smiling up at him, her mouth an obscene red.

"You're not getting a penny from me," Alex said, brushing past her.

Eleanor took a slow drag on her cigarette and smiled. "The town of Briarwood isn't going to like to hear the story of its favored son's downfall." He'd break, they always did. Passing a hand down her heavy fall of platinum blonde hair, she waited.

But the young man who turned to look at her had a backbone of pure steel. "I was ready and willing to take the baby and raise it. I *wanted* it. Do you think anybody who knows me will give a rat's ass what you say?"

She batted her eyes at him. "Oh, they'll believe me," she murmured. Then she closed her eyes and when she opened them, she looked at him through a blur of tears. She made her voice quiver as she whispered, "You raped my baby girl, got her pregnant, and made her get rid of it." As easy as she had brought on the tears, she blinked them away and smirked at Alex.

But he didn't look at all worried. In fact, the arrogant brat actually *laughed* at her. He laughed—then he threatened her. "Ms. Park, you feel free to say whatever you want to say. But, before you do, you might want to remember that it's my Aunt Sarah that owns the beauty parlor you work in. And Jed Stokes, down at the bank, well, he and my daddy grew up together. You have a mortgage on this house, don't you?"

Fury flooded her and she hissed, "You wouldn't dare! Damn it, I'll tell the whole town what a bastard you are."

He laughed, tucking his hands in the pockets of his Levi's. Spread-legged, a mean grin on his face, he looked at her and shook his head. "You honestly think anybody in this town is going to take your word over mine? Besides, do you really think I give a damn what a piece of trash like you says?"

Her hand flashed out but he caught her wrist before it

connected with his cheek. He held her wrist so tight it hurt as he leaned down and looked at her eye to eye. Alex whispered, "I could make your life a lot rougher than you could make mine. So I suggest you think long and hard before you go and do or say something you might regret."

Shaken, Eleanor watched him leave and it wasn't until the door slammed behind him that she dared to move.

Out on the sidewalk, walking blindly, Alex plowed straight into Jazz. Catching him by the arms, Jazz took one look at Alex's face and swiped the keys from him. "C'mon, buddy."

"Get the hell away from me," Alex snarled, shoving Jazz away from him. "Just stay the hell away."

"You wanna pound on something, you might as well pound on me," Jazz said, jamming the keys in his pockets. Jutting his chin out, he stepped closer, until they stood toe to toe. "You got a need to hit something, go ahead and hit me," Jazz offered. "But I don't think this is the place for it." He turned his gaze onto the porch of the house Alex had just left, to the woman watching from the door, and the girl watching from her bedroom window, the younger with a cat's smile, the elder with rage in her eyes.

Hands clenched into impotent fists, he stood there, quivering with rage. Without saying a word, he moved past Jazz and climbed into the passenger seat.

"She got rid of it," Alex said as Jazz slid behind the wheel. "Went into Frankfort and had somebody cut the baby out. She killed it, all because I told her I wasn't going to marry her."

Jazz remained silent, unsure of what to say. With a flick of his wrist, he started the car. The Mustang's powerful engine came to life with a roar, quieting down to a purr as Jazz shifted into gear and pulled away. As they drove off, he could feel the gazes of the two women they left behind.

Across the street, Sandy rubbed her hands over her arms, chilled despite the thick, hot air. Her eyes met the furious gaze of Eleanor Park before returning to watch as the taillights grew smaller on the horizon.

Come back, she thought desperately, not knowing why. *Please come back.*

&

"I was going to take care of her, Jazz." They ended up down at the river with Alex killing the better part of a case of beer. They'd liberated it from Alex's cousin who was conveniently out of town. Desmond Kincade would skin them both if he knew they had the liquor but right now, Jazz was more concerned about Alex than the old man.

"I know." He knew Alex wasn't really listening to him though. His friend had been going on for a while now and it didn't seem like Alex was going to stop any time soon. Guilt sat in his gut like a heavy stone, because he couldn't help but wonder if he wouldn't be relieved, if he was in Alex's shoes.

"Was I wrong? Should I have been willing to marry her?"

Jazz shot Alex a glare. "Hell, no. She fucked around on you when you two were together and she'd do the same if you got married. She treated you like shit half the time, treated your dad like shit half the time and treated Anne-Marie like shit all the time. Only person she doesn't treat like shit is herself—do you really think that would change just cuz she was going to be a mother?"

Alex turned away, his hands jammed inside his back pockets, head down and shoulders slumped like he carried the weight of the world. "I wanted that baby."

Now that was something Jazz didn't know how to answer. He couldn't even imagine being a dad. Much less wanting to be one. Wasn't like he had the best role model, not after his dad died. Beau sure as hell wasn't a good example. Jazz couldn't remember ever holding a baby and he knew there was a lot more to it than just holding one. Especially if there wasn't a mom in the picture. Maribeth wasn't going to be the kind to change diapers. It would have messed up her manicure.

So instead of trying to say something to make his friend feel better, he just laid a hand on Alex's slumped shoulder and squeezed. Alex wasn't much in the mood for comforting. He shrugged Jazz's hand away and stalked down to the river, staring into the murky, slow-flowing waters. After a long time, he looked back at Jazz, eyes dark and turbulent. "Why did she do it, Jazz?"

"I dunno, Alex," he responded honestly. "That girl only knows one thing, buddy. Just like her Mama, she looks out for herself and herself only."

"It was my baby, too." Tipping his head back, Alex sighed. He closed his eyes and muttered, "It ain't right. Women's rights be damned. It was my baby, too."

"I know, buddy. I know."

Hours later, they sat on the hood of the car. The beer was easily half-gone, maybe eight or ten cans left, and Alex was drunk out of his mind. Still madder than hell, though. And hurt. It was the hurt that bothered Jazz the most. Nothing was going to help that but time.

Listening with a sympathetic ear, Jazz made all the right sounds and agreements as Alex rambled on. Jumping from Maribeth to her mother to the doctor in Frankfort, to Roe vs.

Wade and back all over again, he spoke, his words making sense only to himself.

Lying back, head pillowed on his hands, Jazz stared up into the dark sky. The moon, full and bright, danced in and out of clouds, casting its silvered light on the land. The music of the night sang in his ears, crickets, birds, occasional squeaks and squeals as the night predators caught their prey.

"Yeah, I know, buddy," he responded when Alex said his name, knowing what he agreed to really didn't matter, not when Alex was in this shape.

The keys hung forgotten in the ignition as Alex decided, "I oughta go knock her silly."

That caught Jazz's attention. "No way, buddy. You ain't gonna go hitting a woman."

"Ain't no woman. She's a cold-blooded little bitch."

"Bitch or not, she's still a woman, and you don't go beating up women." Even though Jazz wholeheartedly agreed that Maribeth Park had something coming her way.

"We could always sneak into her house while she's sleeping and shave her bald," Jazz suggested. "Put coconut oil into her bath stuff."

"Maribeth's allergic to coconut, gives her hives."

"Exactly," Jazz said, smiling as the edge started to leave Alex's voice. "Or try putting some of that hair remover stuff, what's it called? Nair? Try putting some of that in her shampoo."

"Where the hell'd you come up with that one?" Alex asked, grinning as though he was considering how Maribeth would look bald.

"Anne-Marie," Jazz replied, shaking his head. "That sister of yours has a devious mind. She read about that little trick in

23

some magazine she shouldn't be reading."

A laugh echoed in the air and Alex flopped back on his elbows. "Yeah, that's an idea. And we could pay Anne-Marie to do it, so we don't end up in trouble. Even if she got caught, Daddy wouldn't say much. He'd be too busy laughing."

"I know. We'll tell everybody ya'll broke up after she slept with some guy in Lexington and got crabs. No guy is gonna touch her for weeks."

"But it won't bring that baby back, Jazz. Nothing will." He buried his face in his hands. "I wanted that baby, Jazz. I really wanted it."

Sitting up, Jazz laid a hand on Alex's shoulder. "I'm sorry, bro. God, am I sorry," he whispered, squeezing tightly. When Alex's arms closed around him, he just sat there, staring into the night, grieving for his friend, the brother of his heart, as Alex cried himself hoarse.

∞

He came awake when the engine roared to life beneath his sleeping body. Dazed, staring up the star-studded night sky, it took Jazz a minute to figure out where in the hell he was. A quick glance told him that Alex had finished off the rest of the Miller and empty beer cans rattled under his feet as he slid to the ground. "Alex, what in hell are you doing?"

Judging by the amount of empty beer cans around them, Alex hadn't sobered any. And from the dim light of the moon, Jazz could see those wild eyes as Alex threw the car into gear. "Damn it, Alex, what in the hell are you doing?" he shouted.

"Goin' back into town," Alex said, his voice grim, eyes shadowed.

"You're drunk as a polecat, and you wanna drive into town?" Jazz demanded, stomping around to the door. "Gimme the damn keys. I'll drive you." But Alex didn't even seem to hear as he reached for the gearshift again, jamming it from reverse into first. With a curse, Jazz grabbed hold and leaped into the car right as Alex planted his foot on the gas and left it there.

It was Lawrence Muldoon, a county deputy and brother to the man who had married Jazz's Mama, that was first on the scene. The vintage Mustang had been turned into a pile of twisted metal and smoke, the driver a bleeding mess behind the steering wheel. After pulling him from the car, Larry stared into the torn and bleeding face of the county's golden boy, watched as he breathed his last.

Then he turned his eyes to the dark-haired, dark-eyed bastard who was responsible for helping to put his brother in the ground. Didn't matter not one bit that he was just a kid, and it didn't matter that the bastard's Mama had pulled the trigger.

Jazz was alive—Beau wasn't. Black and blue already, the boy lay some fifteen feet from the wreck. When the car had flipped, he had been ejected, and that had probably saved his life. The thick, coarse grass that lined the country road had cushioned his landing considerably.

One boy dead, the other unconscious, when the deputy rose and made the call to the desk, there was nobody there to dispute him.

☘

Three days later, Jazz woke in a hospital, gazing at the white ceiling overhead. They had told him the previous night that Alex was dead. A uniformed guard stood at the door.

25

They'd told him that he was to blame.

He'd killed his best friend.

"Jazz?"

Closing his eyes, he turned his face away from the door. He knew that voice. And it was the last voice he wanted to hear. Full of tears and grief, just like her eyes would be.

"Jazz?" Anne-Marie asked again, her voice a little louder this time.

Turning his head, he stared at Anne-Marie. Her father, his eyes full of grief and rage, stood at his daughter's side, his hands on her shoulders. "Hey, Annie," he whispered, staring past her and her father, unable to look at them.

"Is it true?" she asked tearfully. "Were you driving?"

"I dunno, Annie."

"They say it's your fault he's gone," she told him. She closed her eyes tightly, pressed her lips together and tried not to cry. "Is it your fault?"

That, he did know. "Yeah. I guess it was," he responded, turning his head away. Why else would he feel so guilty? "Dr. Kincade, I know it doesn't mean anything, but I'm..." His voice trailed away and tears blinded him.

"I know, son," Desmond Kincade said quietly, sighing. He shoved a hand through his salt and pepper hair, staring down at the battered body of his son's best friend. How many times had he heard, *Alex will come to no good, hanging around that McNeil boy. Muldoon done went and ruined him.*

How many times?

If he had listened, would Alex be alive today?

Taking Annie's hand, he led her out of the room, away from the boy who lay silently crying on the hospital bed.

Chapter Two

The day was overcast, which only seemed fitting. Crouched by the gravesite, Jazz studied the pale gray headstone with troubled eyes. "Why did you have to go and die, Sheri?" he whispered. Even though nearly two years had passed, he still couldn't quite believe she wasn't going to be lying in bed next to him in the morning. They had been married less than two years when Sheri was diagnosed with a brain tumor, an inoperable one.

She was dead less than six months later, and all the treatments in the world couldn't have saved her.

It seemed so unreal. Bawdy, loud, lovable Sheri with her wildly curling mass of blonde hair and her gamin grin lay under six feet of cold, dark earth. And her widowed husband was left alone, again, to raise their little girl. Mariah was almost three when her mother died and now, two years later, she hardly remembered the woman who'd given birth to her, although Jazz kept a picture of Sheri by Mariah's bed.

He could see something of Sheri in Mariah's grin—hear the echo when his little girl laughed, and that hurt almost as much as it helped. He hadn't planned on loving Sheri. They'd gotten married because of the baby. Both of them wanted a child, they liked each other well enough and had planned on that being enough.

It would have been, too. If Sheri hadn't died. Jazz had fallen in love with her, slowly, day by day. The woman made him laugh like he hadn't laughed in years and for a while, he stopped taking life so seriously. Then life took Sheri from him.

"I miss you, Sheri," he whispered, closing his eyes.

Though he had known her less than four years, and married her only because of an unplanned pregnancy, Sheri Robertson McNeil had been the focus of his life. The loneliness that ate at him had disappeared when he had met Sheri at a party, only to return in full force now that she was gone again.

As the clouds overhead opened, a heavy downpour falling, Jazz opened his eyes and stared at the headstone, his lean face etched with despair. "Damn it, Sheri. You were all I had. How in the hell could you go and die on me?"

Blowing out a harsh breath, he rose and stared down at the gravesite one last time. In the morning, he'd bring Mariah by one more time to say good-bye to her mama, and then they were heading south.

After sixteen years away, Jazz was finally going home.

A voice from the past whispered in his ear, *You're cursed, boy. Everything you touch is destroyed, and everybody you love dies.*

Cursed.

⅋

With one hand pressed to the small of her back, Anne-Marie stretched work-stiffened muscles. Chasing after toddlers and preschoolers all day was hard work, she didn't care what anybody said. Ear infections, pink eye, runny noses, head lice and all, she wouldn't trade it for anything.

She couldn't even comprehend why a person would want to be an adult doctor. What was the fun in that? Her father, God love him, couldn't understand why she had chosen pediatrics. She linked her hands together and stretched them high overhead, before sighing with relief. Her nurse and best friend laughed as Anne-Marie bent down to touch her toes.

"You look like you just finished an aerobics class," Jackie Smith said, taking her stethoscope off and tossing it on her workstation.

"I feel like I just finished an aerobics class," she replied. "Let's call it a night—oh, hell. Did Shelly forget to lock the door again?"

Behind the frosted glass window, a tall, dark shadow stood at the sign-in desk. "Can we kill her yet?" Jackie asked, a hopeful light in her eyes. "Please?"

"Be nice," Anne-Marie replied. She picked her lab coat up and slid her arms back into it. Pasting a pleasant, and completely false, smile on her face, she walked up to the window and slid it open. The words *Can I help you?* died on her tongue as she got an eyeful of the most delicious man she had ever laid eyes on.

Tall, broad-shouldered with hair as black as sin, eyes the color of dark, melted chocolate, and a mouth that would have made a nun blush. High cheekbones and a hard, chiseled chin with a dent right in the center.

If his face looked like that, what kind of body did he have? If it was half as good, her heart would give out before she reached his abdomen. If it was a match, she just might start stripping out of her clothes right there.

Torn out of her trance by Jackie's elbow in her side, she focused her eyes back on his face, on that sculpted mouth. But for the life of her, she couldn't understand a word he was saying. Her heart had suddenly started doing this odd little jumping-around-in-her-chest dance and her knees were getting weak.

A soft little voice piped, "I got a owie."

Anne-Marie shook her head slightly, frowning, feeling as though she had just come out of a trance, pulled out by the sound of the tiny voice.

The demigod bent, lifted a child that looked more like a cherub than anything. "She busted her head open," he said, holding a blood-soaked pad on the child's forehead. "Tripped over a box and hit the corner of the coffee table. I was taking her to the hospital when I saw your sign, the lights. It hasn't stopped bleeding."

The sight of blood and the distress in his eyes cleared the lust-induced fog long enough for her training to kick in. "You've not been here before?" she asked, motioning for Jackie to put them in a room. If he had, then he must have seen Jake because Anne-Marie would have remembered this guy.

Those dark eyes were familiar, the square jaw, the sculpted mouth. Where had she seen him before? Other than in her wildest fantasies, that is. The way her heart was racing and dancing around and leaping with joy—she had seen some seriously good-looking guys before but not a one of them had caused this kind of reaction. Of course, up until a few months ago, Anne-Marie had been too busy with medical school, her internship and everything else required to get licensed to practice medicine. So maybe all the guys had just slipped under her radar and she was too busy to notice.

Then again...maybe not. Something about the way this particular guy made that radar scream had Anne-Marie thinking this was a one-time occurrence—or at least a one-man occurrence.

"No. We just moved here and hadn't gotten settled yet," he said irritably. "Can you take a look at her or not? I can pay up front, if that's the problem."

Well, shit. He looked that good, Anne-Marie should have figured there was going to be some kind of problem. Gorgeous or not, it seemed he had a chip on his oh-so-delectable shoulders. *Have mercy, don't all the good ones have some kinda problem,* she thought disgustedly as his insinuation that she was only in medicine for the money came through loud and clear. She'd only been in practice a few months now, partnering up with Jake midwinter, but the innuendo wasn't an uncommon one, not even in town where she knew half the population.

"I'm not concerned about the money just yet." She kept her voice pleasant, even though that tone of his had already put her back up. "Come on inside and I'll take a look."

As head wounds went, it wasn't bad, shallow and skinny, right near the hairline. "We need to clean this up a little, Jackie. Can you soak it for a minute or so? I need to take a closer look at it."

While Jackie tended to that, Anne-Marie hunted up the paperwork she needed. Which took considerably longer than it should have. Anne-Marie was certain that Shelly LaCrosse had some good points, some excellent qualities, but secretarial skills were not among them. Which was odd, because talking on the phone was one of her finer abilities.

She made appointments and forgot to enter them into the computer. She scheduled five-year-old check-ups before the patient's fourth birthday. She expected the doctors to give answers to patient questions when she couldn't even remember to write down the question. She scheduled prenatal interviews for a mother who had already delivered. She showed up on Sundays, but forgot to come to work on Mondays. And she had put the paperwork for new patients in a file that generally only held information on deceased and/or released patients.

No, Shelly was not medical receptionist material.

But she was Anne-Marie's second cousin, and Anne-Marie was too nice to fire her simply for being stupid. At least, she had been. With a soft growl, Anne-Marie rose, staring at a phone note from a potential partner that Anne-Marie and Jake Hart had been waiting on. It was dated from three days before. It, too, had been filed away with charts belonging to former patients.

"Three more days, three more days," she chanted. "Then Jake and Marti are back, and chaos will end. Three more days. Three more days." *Three more days and I can fire my empty-headed cousin.*

"Three more days to what?" Jackie asked, stripping off the gloves as she slid the door shut behind her.

"Until Jake and Marti are back. And I'll never let them take a vacation together again."

"They're married, hon. That won't work," Jackie said, grinning.

"So we'll have them get divorced and all our problems will be solved." She waggled the forgotten phone message in front of Jackie's nose. "Wednesday! He called Wednesday."

Glancing at the note, Jackie turned her eyes on Anne-Marie and smiled beatifically. "I told you we'd be better off hiring a for real temp."

Giving Jackie a quelling look, she muttered, "I don't need to hear the *I told you so's.*" Anne-Marie grabbed a clipboard from the wall just as the exam room door slid open, revealing the late-night patient and her surly father.

"Are you going to come in here any time soon, Dr. Hart?"

Too irritated to correct him, she thrust the patient forms at him. "We need these filled out, sir," she said as she pulled on a pair of gloves. Anne-Marie was proud to discover her insides didn't quiver as she walked past him.

At least, not much.

"Can't it wait?" he demanded, tossing the paperwork an incredulous glance.

"Unless it's life or death, I'm not allowed to treat your daughter without consent and some basic history. This isn't life or death and even then, I would at least need a verbal consent to treat. Medical history is always nice—medication allergies, history of seizures, whether or not she's lost consciousness. Little things like that." Already aggravated by the addition to the long day, Anne-Marie was in no mood to put up with a surly, temperamental jerk.

No matter how good looking he was. Mouth wateringly, heart stoppingly good looking. Nope, never mind that.

She'd been up since four a.m. when the hospital called about a newborn with breathing difficulties. Added to that was the irate family she had dealt with earlier. Imagine, they weren't pleased to be released from the practice simply for an unpaid debt of $862.91. And, of course, having to deal with Shelly's ineptness all day hadn't helped.

Across the room, Jackie's eyes widened but she continued laying out the supplies without a word.

"You have consent. She has no allergies, no history of seizures and no loss of consciousness. Anything else?"

"Is she allergic to latex?" Anne-Marie asked, keeping firm hold of her temper.

"No. She's not allergic to latex or anything else, to my

knowledge. Any other questions, doc?" he replied, narrowing those dark eyes.

"Not at this moment, no." *Yes, I do want to know one more thing. What bug crawled up your very excellent ass and died?* she thought sourly as she soaked a cotton ball with saline and pressed it against the sullenly oozing cut.

"Y'know, if this is too much trouble, we can go on to the hospital," he offered sarcastically when Jackie murmured an apology and whispered, "I'll have to get some more supplies."

"A good place to keep them would be the cabinet, wouldn't it?" he snapped, glaring at Jackie's retreating back. She paused for one brief second, causing Anne-Marie to hold her breath, but then she kept going without a word.

Keeping her voice pleasant was getting harder with every second that passed. *Of course, it's to be expected, I suppose. As good looking as he is, it was only fair for God to skimp out on something. Something like common courtesy.*

"Good and clean little cut, there," she said. "Aw, sweetie, you're such a big girl."

"I know," the little cherub replied, piping up for the first time since announcing her wounded condition at the front desk.

"What's your name, honey?" Anne-Marie asked as she exchanged the bloodied cotton ball for a fresh one.

"Mariah," she said, smiling sweetly. She reached up and brushed her hand across Anne-Marie's chin. "You're pretty."

With her free hand, she pinched Mariah's nose and said, "So are you. Does your head hurt, Mariah?"

"Uh-uh. Just when I fell down. Not anymore. I didn't cry hardly at all, did I, Daddy?" she asked, smiling at the man who stood breathing over Anne-Marie's shoulder.

"No, sweetheart. You're a big girl."

That same sweet, angelic smile on her face, she turned her gaze back to Anne-Marie. "Daddy cussed, bad. He said all sorts of bad words, he said the 's' word and the 'd' word and the 'f—"

Chuckling, Anne-Marie said, "I get the point. I imagine you scared him quite a bit."

"That's what he said," Mariah said. "Do you know what the 'f' word is?"

"Yep. It's fudge," Anne-Marie said, smiling as the little girl's eyes rounded.

"It's not fudge. It's—"

"Fudge, I absolutely promise you. That's what my daddy always told me the 'f' word was. Fudge."

Mariah giggled and whispered, "Fudge," when Anne-Marie dabbed some peroxide on the shallow cut. "Am I going to get stitches?"

"Maybe one or two," she said with a sympathetic smile.

Mariah made a dramatic little gulp. Then her lower lip started to tremble. Her voice was a small, terrified whisper as she asked, "Will it hurt?"

Gently, Anne-Marie brushed back a lock of hair from the girl's face, tucking it behind her ear. It was pierced and the small silver unicorn in the girl's lobe made her smile. Unicorns had always been her favorite—even now, she had little pewter unicorns dancing across the top of her desk at home. "The stitches themselves won't hurt because I have special medicine. That special medicine won't let you feel any pain at all."

"Really?"

Big brown eyes gazed up at her and the trust Anne-Marie saw there made her heart clench. "Oh, absolutely." It was amazing, dealing with kids. The trick, though, was to be honest. A lot of people in the medical field still treated kids like they were less than people, never answering their questions, talking over them, about them, but never really to them.

Anne-Marie was big on being honest with her patients. If they were old enough to ask a question, whenever possible, she was going to answer the question as best as she could. Behind her, she could hear Jackie. A minute later, a gloved hand held out a small gauze square and Anne-Marie took it, cleaning the laceration a little better. In a low voice, she told Jackie the supplies she needed and then she leaned back and waited for Mariah to look up at her. "Do you think you can be a brave girl for a little longer, Mariah?"

Solemnly, she nodded.

Anne-Marie gave her a reassuring smile. "That's a big girl. Now I have to tell you about the special medicine."

That lower lip started to quiver. "Will the special medicine hurt?"

From the corner of her eye, she could see the father moving closer and Anne-Marie held up a hand. Too many parents expected a doctor or a nurse to lie about shots, which was half the reason so many kids freaked about coming to the office. The vast majority wouldn't hate the doctor so much if they didn't have grown-ups lying about it. "It will hurt—at first. A little bit of a pinch but it only lasts a few seconds and then it's done. After that, you'll feel me touching you but it won't hurt."

Mariah looked at her father and then she looked back at Anne-Marie. She took a deep breath, one that made her thin shoulders rise and fall, then she looked down, tucking her chin against her chest. "Do I have to?"

"Well...no," Anne-Marie said slowly, pretending to think about it. She took another gauze sponge and wiped at the blood. It was still oozing, although it was slowing down and Anne-Marie could tell it was starting to clot. She didn't have to tell the little girl that, though. "We could just wait here until it stops bleeding. Might take a while. But I can't let you go anywhere while it's still bleeding."

As if on cue, Anne-Marie heard the little girl's belly rumble. She pretended she didn't hear as she glanced up at the clock. It was pushing seven. "I don't know about you, but I'm pretty hungry." She dabbed at the cut again and sighed theatrically. "I sure hope it stops bleeding soon."

"How long will it bleed?"

Jackie leaned around Anne-Marie and studied the cut. "Hmmm. I dunno, Doc. I think it's going to take a while."

They fell silent. The kitty cat clock on the wall ticked away the seconds and it seemed to get louder with each one. The cat had a yellow and blue tail that swung back and forth with the second hand and Anne-Marie counted thirty before Mariah looked at the bloodied gauze in Anne-Marie's hand. "Is it still bleeding?"

Solemnly, Anne-Marie nodded.

Another huge sigh left Mariah's lips and she whispered, "Okay."

In less than twenty minutes, sporting a bright pink Band-Aid on her uninjured hand and a wide smile, Mariah inspected her "owie" in the fun house-style mirror that hung on the far end of the wall. Behind her, the dad was finally doing the paperwork and Anne-Marie and Jackie cleaned up the bloodied gauze and the remnants of the sutures. The clipboard landed with a clatter on the counter behind her and Anne-Marie hissed out a breath.

She reached for the clipboard and gave it a cursory glance. "Mariah, I need to speak with your father a moment. Jackie can show you where we keep the suckers and stickers. I think we've got some unicorn stickers somewhere."

Mariah squealed. "Oh, *stickers!*" She went skipping out the door and as she disappeared from view, Anne-Marie leaned back against the exam table. Slowly, she removed her gloves and folded one into the other. She tossed them into the trashcan and then looked at the man still glaring at her.

One black brow lifted arrogantly. "Is this going to take long? We've had a rough day."

Her temper jerked at its chain and to give herself a minute, she pushed off the table and went to the cabinet hanging over the sink. There was an info sheet on head injuries and she pulled one for him. "You need to keep an eye on her for the next few hours. Any sign of confusion, she goes to sleep and is hard to wake up, you need to call right away."

He took the sheet. "I've had a few hits in the head. I know the drill. Does she have a concussion?"

"A mild one, probably. Give her some ibuprofen when you get her home. She's probably going to have a headache. Now... Generally, we make allowances for distraught parents. When your child is injured, it's natural to be upset. However, I will not tolerate rudeness to my nurses."

His brows arched up. "Was I rude? Sorry, but when a doctor's office doesn't have the needed supplies to take care of a hurt kid, it's my place to question it."

Anne-Marie narrowed her eyes and let some of the irritation she felt edge its way into her voice. "This is the end of a very long day for us and we generally restock on Mondays before the office opens. It's a Friday night, well after hours and it took Jackie all of two minutes to grab some gauze. I will not tolerate somebody insinuating that I do not feel like doing my job or that my nurses are inept. Furthermore, I can't provide medical care without knowing some basic information. Such things are vital in providing safe care."

"You really needed to know if she takes her vitamins every damned day before you can look at a cut?" he snapped, jamming his hands in his pockets.

"No. But it is useful to know, oh, say if she has any latex allergies. A latex allergy can be fatal and allergies to latex are not at all uncommon. If she had one, and I unknowingly used the gloves we normally use, it could have caused you and your daughter some severe problems. Or an allergy to lidocaine, since I had to use that to numb her up before we did the stitches."

She tucked the clipboard under her arm. "We can bill you for today's services. The receptionist has already left. I'll want to see her back in a week, check and see if she is healing well. Remember to call if any problems arise, blurred vision, severe headaches, nausea, vomiting, anything at all unusual, or any concerns." On her way out the door, she gave him a card that had the answering service phone number on it.

"Dr. Hart?"

"Dr. Hart is my partner. He's not in the office this week. I'm Anne-Marie Kincade," she responded. They kept forgetting to update the sign out front. In a town as small as Briarwood, most everybody knew Anne-Marie had accepted Jake's offer to join the practice so they weren't in a big hurry. She headed to the door and glanced at the paperwork without really seeing it.

A drink. Just a nice glass of white wine and something to eat, she thought. *And my chair*, she wished longingly. *I want my chair. And chocolate...I really need chocolate.*

"Annie." The word was a whisper, a question almost too faint for her to hear.

Her eyes fell on the patient's name. Mariah Delia McNeil. The mother's name seemed to leap off the paper. Sheri McNeil— Deceased.

And the father's name.

Jasper Wayne McNeil Jr.

Jazz.

Oh, dear Lord, she prayed, as her heart started to pound in a slow, deep rhythm.

Dazed, she turned around and met the black eyes she had dreamed about for a good part of her young life. The years since he had left fell away and she could see the boy she knew. His lean, lanky body had bulked up a little and filled out. Broad shoulders strained at the seams of his worn button-down and the denim jeans clung to legs that looked long and powerful.

Staring into those black eyes, Anne-Marie suddenly understood her body's weird reaction when she'd seen him standing at the check-in window. Her body had recognized him, even if she hadn't. He looked so different—harder, harsher—and tired. Very tired.

Jazz McNeil, back in town. "Jazz, I didn't recognize you," she said, congratulating herself on her smooth, level tone.

"Me, neither." His eyes roamed from her head to her feet and back again. Every inch between seemed to burn. "You've grown up."

Her eyes filled with tears, remembered grief making her throat constrict. The awful night her father had woken her up and they had cried in each other's arms.

"Jazz, they say it's your fault he's gone. Is it true?"

"Yeah, I guess so."

A steel gray coffin lowered into the ground, next to the mother she had lost to cancer at the age of eight.

The night she learned Jazz wouldn't be prosecuted, there had been tears of relief. Then tears of grief came three days later when Jazz left town for good. Angry and as bitter as

Desmond was, Jazz's leaving had done the surviving Kincades more harm than good. Desmond lost two sons with that accident, and Anne-Marie had lost her hero.

Now, standing there, looking at him, she wondered how badly his armor had tarnished.

"It's been a long time," Anne-Marie said quietly, tucking her hands into the deep pockets of her lab coat. "I hadn't heard you were back in Briarwood."

"Just got here a few days ago. Annie, I'm sorry about the..."

"Attitude? Why, because we know each other?" she asked, inclining her head. "If you're going to be sorry, be sorry for treating me and my nurse like shit, Jazz. But...you are forgiven, whatever the reason for the apology."

"It's no excuse, but the past few days have been rough. I just can't stand to see her hurting." His eyes were still the color of melted chocolate, and just as addicting. Over the years, his voice had deepened to a whiskey-smooth southern drawl that warmed Anne-Marie clear down to her toes. Shifting from one foot to the other, he looked uncomfortable, the way a boy would look when summoned to the principal's office.

"No parent enjoys seeing a child suffer. We try to keep that in mind here." An uncomfortable silence spread out as they stared at each other. She finally turned away, busying herself with the chart.

Quietly, Jazz asked, "Do you hate me, Annie?"

Taking a deep breath, she took in the familiar scents of candy, alcohol and disinfectant. Opening her eyes, she stared at the framed caricature of dancing mice on the pale blue wall in front of her. She closed her hands around the chart to still their trembling.

Hate you? Anne-Marie thought silently. How could she tell him hating him would be like hating herself? He was a part of

41

her, every bit as much as Alex and her father.

Cautious, Anne-Marie turned and looked at him, studying that face, looking for remnants of the boy she remembered. With a sad smile, she answered, "No. No, Jazz. I don't hate you. I never did. I miss Alex, and I always will. But, Alex is gone because that is how it was meant to be. Some lights burn so brightly, they can only burn for a short time. And Alex was as bright as they come."

His eyes, so dark and unreadable, met hers. "I've never had another friend like him. Not a day goes by that I don't think of him." The simple cotton button-down shirt stretched tight across his shoulders as he jammed his hands in his pockets. "Not a day goes by that I don't wish I could undo that night."

Tears burning her eyes, she turned her head. A lump in her throat made speech nearly impossible. "Jazz, I don't have anything that I can say to you that will change things. I can't offer you absolution. But I don't hate you, and I've never wished you ill."

Without another word, she left.

℣

Little Annie, all grown up. And damn, but did she grow up nice. He hadn't recognized her, not that it was too surprising. It had been more than fifteen years. And she was already a doctor—Jazz did the math in his head and figured she'd probably graduated early. Not too surprising. Annie had skipped second and sixth grade, and that was before Jazz disappeared from her life.

No telling how many grades she'd skipped in high school, or how fast she'd managed to get through college. Briarwood was a small town and their school system wasn't equipped to handle kids as smart as Anne-Marie had been. So instead of accelerated classes, Annie skipped grades. Alex had been like that too, although Jazz suspected Annie pushed harder. Would explain why she skipped grades as easy as some kids could skip stones, and why Alex had only skipped the fourth grade.

As he drove down the two-lane highway, Jazz realized coming home was going to be harder than he had thought. It might have been easier if Anne-Marie had looked at him with hatred instead of sadness. Hatred was so much easier to deal with than disappointment.

"She was pretty, wasn't she, Daddy?"

Glancing in the mirror, he smiled at Mariah's reflection. She sat in the patterned, pink booster seat with her favorite pink T-shirt splattered with blood and probably some ketchup from the hotdog she was chowing down on. "Not as pretty as you are," he told her and he meant it sincerely. Thick spiral curls tumbled down her back, around her face, curls the color of midnight. That inky black came from him but the curls came from Sheri. Her eyes were bluer than cornflowers and her skin was all ivory and peach. Those eyes and her complexion were another gift from her mother. Jazz's skin was swarthy and dark and it had nothing to do with time spent out in the sun.

His pretty little girl looked like a china doll. How something that beautiful had come from one brief, rowdy affair with a friend of his high-class editor was beyond his comprehension.

Giggling, Mariah said, "You always say that."

"And I always mean it."

"Am I gonna be ugly now?" she asked mournfully.

Muffling a chuckle, Jazz told her, "Honey, you could bump your head two hundred and sixty-two times and never be ugly."

"'Kay," she said, a yawn stretching her mouth wide. "Miss

Jackie gave me a sucker. And she said Dr. Anne is the best."

"I bet she is," he said absently.

"Is she gonna be my doctor now?"

"I dunno. Maybe," he said, stalling. He wasn't so certain how Annie would feel about that, though. She wasn't going to want to take care of the child of her brother's killer. Not even sweet Saint Anne-Marie.

"Is that what y'all were talking about?"

Glancing down the highway, he moved into the opposite lane to pass around a slow-moving farm truck. "She was telling me how to take care of your pretty little head." Jazz didn't see how a parent could be a parent without telling little white lies from time to time.

"I hope she is my doctor. She smells nice." Her voice was getting slower and softer, and in the rearview, he saw her eyes drooping closed. *And lucky me*, he thought wryly. *I have the pleasure of waking her up every couple of hours now.* He'd willingly wake up every two hours for the next ten years to make sure she was okay, but it was going to make for one long-assed night.

Jazz was faintly surprised that toddlers and preschoolers could even suffer head injuries. Their heads seemed rock hard. At least, Mariah's did.

Passing by the bright lights of the Shell station, he flicked on his turn signal and took the turn that led to their new house. Bought outright, with money he had hoarded over the years. It was going to require a lot of work to make the house look the way he wanted. Built at the turn of the last century, it needed a new roof, needed new paint inside and out, and the wraparound porch was going to have to be completely redone. Not to mention the plumbing was outdated, and probably the wiring. It needed work and it was going to take time and a lot of money.

As fate would have it, Jazz now had plenty of both.

Jazz had always planned to come home, home to Briarwood, to face his past. He wasn't going to fail on those plans, even if the local townsfolk decided they didn't want him around.

He just hadn't expected his reckoning to come so soon. He hadn't expected to come back for a few years yet. He had wanted to settle himself a bit more, maybe have another baby with Sheri. But then her headaches had started, severe ones that nearly blinded her. By the time she had gone to the doctor about them, the tumor had grown to monstrous proportions. Surgery was out of the question and the chemo had failed. Within months, Sheri was dead, leaving Jazz alone with a three-year-old. Jazz and Mariah were the benefactors of a surprisingly large life insurance policy, along with a college fund Sheri had started.

Two years after she'd gone, Jazz woke up one morning and found himself staring at the condo they'd shared and he realized he hated it. He hadn't liked it much when they picked it out, but it was close to the city and although Jazz could work from home, Sheri couldn't. He looked around at the stark, sterile rooms and realized without Sheri there, the place felt empty.

It wasn't a good place to raise a little girl. So here they were, the owners of a ramshackle, falling-down excuse of a house that needed more work than a ghost town needed ghosts. With a sigh, he pulled into the rutted excuse of a driveway. The driveway needed work, too. But first, the house.

Oh, man, the house. What in the hell had he been thinking? Even if he didn't have to worry about the roof, the wiring, the painting or the porch, there were still the bathrooms, the carpet and the basement—oh man, he didn't even want to think about the basement. Walls had to come down in some places and go up in others, and the kitchen was totally outdated.

In the faint moonlight, he studied the century-old farmhouse. Yeah, it was going to take a long time and a lot of sweat to make this place work. But, once he got going, it would be a sweet reprieve over the way he'd spent the past few years. When he wasn't chasing after Mariah and being both Mom and Dad, he was trapped in front of a computer, facing his nemesis, Vance Marrone.

Vance Marrone, ace detective, lady's man and general jackass, was the creation of Jazz McNeil's mind, and his own worst enemy. Man, he hated Vance, hated writing about him, hated making money off of him. It hadn't been so bad when he first started, plunking out that first story while recovering in a VA hospital when a training op had ended badly. Badly as in him nearly losing his leg and having to spend three weeks in the hospital and six months in rehab.

Back then, Vance had kept Jazz sane, but he made the big mistake of sending the book off to an agent. She sold it almost instantly, landing him his first modest advance. The second book hit a little better and each one garnered more and more readers and he ended up signing more and more contracts. By the fifth book, he was tired of Vance Marrone, but he still had four more books to fulfill his contract.

He would have been done with those five years ago and he had plans to write something else, but then—well, life happened. Sheri happened. The baby came along and then Sheri got sick. All the money in the world wouldn't have been able to save her, but he'd tried anyway, agreeing to five more books. Sad thing was by the time he got the first part of the advance, Sheri was already dead.

He was now on the last book of that contract and he suspected it wasn't going to go over well. Jazz was going to kill Marrone off. Maybe then he'd have some peace and quiet and could write something worthwhile. He even had a contract—a smaller house, one that focused on sci fi and fantasy. They couldn't pay him anywhere close to the advances he'd gotten used to but he could write the story he wanted to write, instead of what he had to write. Every new Marrone book seemed to take longer and longer to write and he spent hours each day in front of the computer, obsessing over a character he hated and not focusing as much as he'd like on the one important person in his life.

Now that he didn't have to worry so much about the money, he was going to take the time to write the book he wanted, take more time to be the father he wanted to be to his little girl and work on the big old farmhouse, making it into a home for her.

With a sigh, he shut off the engine and climbed out of the Escalade. He slung Mariah's bag over his shoulder and released her from her booster seat.

"Are we home, Daddy?" she asked sleepily, rubbing at one eye with a closed fist.

"Yeah, honey. We're home. Your head okay?"

"Uh-huh. I'm sleepy, though."

"Going to bed right now, girl," he promised, shifting her to his right arm so he could dig out his keys. The door creaked loudly as he pushed it open, and that jumped to the top of his list of things to fix tomorrow. That and the leaking faucets in the kitchen and bathroom.

"Where are my jammies?" she asked.

"On your bed, where we left them this morning."

"Are they dirty?"

"Not until tomorrow. We'll go find some place to wash them then," he told her, rolling his eyes. He couldn't have had a messy child. No, he had a little lady from her head to her size six feet. She might spill stuff all over her clothes but the minute she did, they had to come off and clean clothes put on. Added up to a lot of laundry. Which was why getting a washer and dryer was one of the next things on the list tomorrow.

"What 'bout my bath?"

Sniffing loudly at her neck, like a puppy, Jazz announced, "Smell good to me. We'll take a bath in the morning, okay?"

She nodded sleepily again. "'Kay. I'm sleepy, Daddy."

She was out before he even got her buttoned into her Scooby Doo pajamas.

Resigning himself to another sleepless night, he headed for the makeshift office he had in the little alcove at the end of the hall. Might as well get some work done. As the computer booted, he jogged downstairs and started some coffee. Pausing in the doorway of the kitchen, one hand curled around the cup, he surveyed the mess spread out before him.

What in the hell are you doing here?

It wasn't the first time he had asked himself that. Jazz doubted it would be the last and he still didn't know the answer. He only knew the night sixteen years earlier haunted him, the lack of memories of that night haunted him. He needed some answers.

He prayed that in trying to find them, he wouldn't cause Desmond and Anne-Marie any more pain.

ත

"Daddy?"

Desmond laid down the medical journal he had been studying as he looked up to smile at his only child. It only took one look for his smile to fade. "You do look terribly serious standing there, Anne-Marie," he mused, studying his daughter. Her eyes were dark and turbulent. "What's the matter, honey?"

"Jazz is back."

Jazz.

Immediately, Desmond could see the boy Alex had befriended, tall for his age, sulky, defiant, with anger burning in those dark eyes. It had been sixteen years since he'd last seen Jasper McNeil. How many times had he thought of that boy over the years?

"Is he now?" he murmured, leaning back in his chair, folding his hands over a belly he kept flat with rigorous exercise. It wouldn't do for a cardiologist not to be fit. He had people drive from all over the south to see him and he took that responsibility seriously. If he was going to lecture them on the benefits of a heart-healthy diet, then he could also follow his own advice.

If he snuck some doughnuts every now and then, a cigar here and there, well, every man was entitled to a few vices.

"Is he really?" he murmured, thoughtfully tugging at his lower lip.

Knowing he was not asking for confirmation, she remained silent, seating herself in the leather wing chair by the window. She studied her neatly trimmed and buffed nails, the small capable hands that had tended Mariah McNeil's head wound the night before.

"You've seen him?"

"Last night. He has a daughter now," she responded, explaining how he had come to the office after hours—and how Shelly how forgotten, again, to lock up when she left.

49

"Anne-Marie, I know that you're feeling sentimental towards Shelly, her being your Mama's cousin and all, but don't you think that you've made a few too many allowances for her?" he asked absently, while his mind turned over the fact that the boy wasn't a boy any longer. No, now he was a father, apparently a good one, or Anne-Marie would have made that clear already. "You really do need to hire a temp until Marti gets back."

"Marti's due back this week. I can do three more days."

Still pondering how he felt about Jazz, he said, "I imagine you can—but remember, next time, it is okay to tell family *no*."

She grimaced. "Oh, I've learned my lesson." She didn't pry or mention Jazz again—that was his little girl. She knew him well—as she should. She was just like him. They'd talk about something when they were ready and not a moment before.

Jazz, however, might be an exception. Desmond certainly wasn't ready to talk about his son's best friend yet, and he didn't know that Anne-Marie was either.

"So he's come home," he mused, shaking his head. "How does he look?"

Thinking back, Anne-Marie finally answered, "Tired. Haunted." Gorgeous, she added mentally. She rose, then, wandered over to the window, running one finger over the polished pane of glass, smudging it. "I don't hate him, Daddy. I never thought I did, but I always wondered how I'd feel if I saw him again."

"And?"

"I don't know," she answered, resting her forehead against the glass. "But it still doesn't seem right, after all this time. I can't picture him driving into that tree."

Turning around, she pinned her father with an intense stare. "Daddy, Jazz drove like a demon. Drove fast and always

50

got tickets, but he was never once in an accident. Not once. It just doesn't fit."

Chapter Three

Disoriented, Jazz jerked his head up, looked around him, unsure what had woken him. Still half asleep, he pushed his face back into the throw pillow. The next knock was loud enough to rattle the windows. Cursing, he shoved himself to his feet, rubbing the back of his stiff neck.

Mariah had been up at the crack of dawn, but had fallen asleep around ten that morning and Jazz hadn't been too far behind her. She still slept in a boneless little puddle in front of the TV. Stumbling past her, rubbing at his bloodshot eyes, he muffled a yelp as he stepped on a thumb-sized plastic unicorn, the horn poking straight in the tender arch of his foot. With a scowl on his face, he swung the door open.

Any lingering drowsiness disappeared in a haze of hatred as he gazed into the murky brown eyes of Larry Muldoon, the man who had found him torn and bleeding after the accident sixteen years earlier. The man who gleefully announced, while Jazz was pushed into the back of an ambulance, that he had killed Alex Kincade.

Time hadn't been good to Larry. Always rail thin and short, he had developed a protruding potbelly that hung over the polished belt of his uniform and his pale skin had turned sallow. What little hair he had was thin and sparse, sticking this way and that. The star he wore pinned to his stiffly ironed khaki uniform looked more comical than authoritative. Except for the beer gut hanging over his belt, Larry looked a lot like Barney from *The Andy Griffith Show*.

"Heard you were back here," Larry said, tucking his thumbs into the loops of his trousers. Cocking his head to the side, he asked, "You planning on staying long?"

"You generally don't buy a house if you're planning on just staying the summer," Jazz snapped, reaching for the door.

"You'd best be rethinking that plan. We don't welcome killers around here."

"Only wife beaters and bullies who beat up on kids, right?" Jazz replied edgily, backing away from the door.

"I don't rightly know what it is you're talking about," Larry lied with a sly smile on his face. He knew. Oh, hell, yeah, he knew. Larry had been privy to a beating or two, had even once belted Jazz across the face. "All I know is what I told you that last night is just as true now as ever. I hear tell you're a widower, lost your wife to cancer. You're cursed, boy. I've told you that before and you didn't listen."

Rubbing a hand over his face, Jazz swore under his breath. In town less than a week and folks already knew about Sheri? Why in the hell had he moved back to this small town?

"Now, Jazz, I'm just here to offer some friendly advice."

"Go away," Jazz growled, raising his hand to shut the door in that sour face.

"Just a minute there, son. Got some words I need to say to you."

Keeping his voice low and his eyes level, Jazz calmly replied, "Got a warrant on you, Deputy? If not, then you had best get off my land. I've nothing to say to you."

"You'd be wise to pack up and leave, boy. Listen to your

uncle here."

His hand shot out before he could stop it, locking on Larry's shirt, dragging him forward. Lowering his head until they were nose to nose, Jazz whispered, "You are not my uncle. And that sack of shit was never my father. I'd sooner drink Drano than belong in your family, got it?"

Sweat pearled on Larry's brow, his upper lip and his hands. "You must be wanting to be arrested for assaulting an officer," Larry sneered, reaching up and trying to pry the large, dark hands from his shirt.

A low, lackadaisical voice drawled, "Well, now, Larry. I don't rightly see that he assaulted you."

Slowly, relaxing each tensed muscle, Jazz let go. He turned his head to see a familiar face at the top of the porch stairs. Another blast from the past. Another uniform. And a face that brought, for once, welcome memories and smiles. "Look here. Cousin Tate, aren't you looking important?" Jazz asked, tucking his hands in his pockets.

A smile spread over the dark, lean face, so similar to Jazz's. The only son of Jasper McNeil Sr.'s younger brother, and one of Jazz's only remaining relatives, Tate McNeil had been there in the hospital when he awoke, had stood in the rain at his Mama's funeral, a shy, chubby boy.

Tate's father, Waylan McNeil, had died in a fire trying to rescue a young mother. Tate was left alone with his Mama, much like Jasper. But Tate's Mama hadn't remarried. No, Ella had gone back to school, gotten a degree, and had been running her own real estate business for the past seventeen years.

"Deputy Muldoon, you got any official reason to be here?" Tate asked calmly, staring into the older man's eyes.

"Just came to welcome Jazz back, is all. After all, we are family," Larry said, his eyes sullen.

"A little family reunion, eh? Didn't quite look that way to me," Tate said. Raising his shoulders in a shrug, he added, "Course, I could be wrong."

The hatred simmering in Muldoon's eyes was palpable. "Well, now, Sheriff McNeil. You have been wrong a time or two."

"Yes, I have. Don't make yourself one of my mistakes, Deputy Muldoon," Tate advised in a level tone. One straight, black brow lifted fractionally and a single cool glance from his dark eyes had Muldoon's glare dropping away. "Get on back to work now—and I advise you not to go harassing this man here. History is not repeating itself."

Before he could give release to the venom in his head, Muldoon stomped away, grumbling under his breath. Silently, the cousins watched as the police car pulled down the pitted driveway. Then they turned and studied each other.

"I would suggest, Cousin Jazz, that you watch your step with him. He is a pest, but even pests can cause a good deal of damage if they're ignored."

With a slow nod, Jazz acknowledged the warning. And the assistance. "I reckon I had better watch my speeding around town, as well. Seeing as how pulling me over was his favorite pastime a few years back."

Chuckling, Tate said, "I'd reckon Doc Kincade pretty much paid for the renovations on the station house, with all those tickets of yours he paid." He nodded to the swing across the porch. "Mind if I have a seat?"

"What's mine is yours," Jazz offered, spreading his arms wide. "Gotta admit, I'm impressed. You look a damn sight better than I would have expected."

Stretching long, lean legs out in front of him, Tate leaned back and saluted Jazz. "To my inspiration. I knew if I looked like you did, all the girls would be tripping over me. You up and leaving the way you did, left the field right clear for me once I got ship shape. Thank God for the quarry. Went swimming there most every night that summer, clear up until Halloween. Then I started running."

"Another Briarwood success story," Jazz muttered, shaking his head. "So, there's a new sheriff in town, huh? Your Mama's real proud of you." With a sly smile, Jazz asked, "Does that mean you'll fix my speeding tickets?"

With a quick wink, Tate said, "Well, that just depends on who writes the ticket." Pushing the swing back lazily, he stared off into the distance. "Larry is going to hassle you, you know that, don't you?"

Jazz responded with a grunt, reaching up to scratch his head.

"He blames you for your Mama killing Beau. He muttered and cursed about it left and right at that time. And then when you up and left, he preened for weeks."

"How do you know that? You were still in high school."

"I hear things. When you're a quiet kid, a lot of people don't notice you're standing right there and can hear everything that's being said. And Larry likes to say quite a bit. I'll do what I can, but unless he really crosses the line, my hands are tied."

"I'm not worried about it," Jazz said, shrugging his shoulders. He had dealt with worse than Larry Muldoon, more times than he could count.

"You need to worry some. That man has a lot of hate built up inside of him." Tapping his finger against the side of his head, he added, "There's something wrong up here."

"Their daddy must've worn real tight shorts, that's all I can say," Jazz replied, leaning against the door jam. "I've got bigger things on my mind than some little twerp like Larry Muldoon." Shaking his head, he muttered, "How in hell did he get to be a cop, anyhow?"

"Good question. I inherited him, so to speak, when I signed on. Much as I'd like to fire his pitiful ass, I can't do it until he gives me a reason."

Silence broken only by the squeaking porch swing, they sat staring off into the distance. After some time went by, Tate asked, "Where's the pretty little girl of yours? Mama said she's a sweetie."

"Sleeping. It's exhausting, her watching me work," he said with a smile.

"Is she getting in the way?"

Shaking his head, Jazz answered, "Not the way you'd think. She just sits there and watches, with those big eyes of hers. When I'm done, she asks questions, but it makes me feel like she's grading me. A little woman in that baby's body, I'm telling you."

"Mind if I ask about her Mama?"

"Not much to tell. She was a friend of my editor..." Voice trailing off, he stared hard at Tate. Why hadn't he kept his big mouth shut?

"Your what?" Tate asked, a mile-wide grin on his face.

"My editor, damn it."

"What, exactly, does she edit?"

"What do editors usually edit?"

"Damn it all, Jazz. You expecting me to believe you've been writing? What for? You work for a newspaper?" Tate asked.

"Hell, no," he responded, affronted. "I ain't no damn reporter."

"Then what in the hell are you writing?"

"Action adventure crap."

Tate's grin only got wider. "What kind of action adventure crap? Anything I might have read?"

Jazz sneered. "I dunno. You learn how to read?"

"Come on now, Jazz. Is that any way to treat your favorite cousin?"

Rolling his eyes, Jazz said, "You're my only cousin."

"As your only cousin, don't you think I deserve to know if my cousin might be a little bit famous? What do you write?"

"You're not going to shut up until I tell you, are you?"

Tate, looking satisfied, said, "Nope."

"It's a series about a private detective. Vance Marrone." He spat it out like a challenge, wishing he had never even mentioned his editor. Why couldn't he have just said a friend of a friend?

"Vance Marrone? You write those?" Tate's eyes widened, then narrowed. "You're joking."

Jazz glared at him and turned away.

"No. I don't guess you are joking," Tate muttered as he took this in. "You're D.J. McCoy?"

Jazz ignored him, staring at the woods at the edge of his property. Taking this as an affirmative, Tate jumped up and laughed. "Hot damned, Jazz. You're my hero! I gotta ask, how many of those women were inspired by real life?"

"Get real, Tate. How many men you know of have sex lives like that?" Jazz asked, rolling his eyes.

"But some of it has to be real. Nobody has an imagination that good." With that same wide grin still on his face, he sat on the porch railing and said, "You must be pretty pleased with yourself. Got a ton of money stashed in some Swiss bank?"

"I ain't John Grisham, Tate. Used up most of that money paying Sheri's medical bills after she died. Cancer is pretty damned expensive." It was a sad fact that if Sheri hadn't had that life insurance policy, Jazz would probably be stuck writing the Vance Marrone mysteries for the next ten years just to keep a roof over Mariah's head and food in her belly.

His face sobering, Tate replied, "Yeah. I reckon so."

Moments passed as the tension eased from the air. Tate said, "I'm real impressed though. Vance is one mean sonovabitch."

Face burning, disgust crawling in his belly, Jazz turned and faced his cousin. "I hate them. I hate writing that trash. I wish I had never started it. But, damn it, we gotta eat."

Frowning, Tate asked, "If you hate it, why did you start?"

"I was young and stupid. Always been good at telling a story. At first, I enjoyed it, writing out every guy's fantasy. But every one I wrote, it had to be worse than the previous one."

"If you hate it that much, then quit. Find something else to write."

"I have." Eyes gleaming, Jazz explained, "I'll fulfill my contract with this last book. I'm not renewing it. I've got a book another publisher wants. Vance is almost history."

"Don't be mad if I don't congratulate you," Tate muttered. Shaking his head, he said, "I'll be damned. My own cousin, writing that stuff."

"You forget now that you heard it. Otherwise, I'll stomp that skinny ass of yours," Jazz threatened. Then he paused, cocking his head. "Mariah's awake."

Before Jazz had even pushed off the post at his back, his little cherub had appeared in the screen doorway. Face flushed, eyes puffy and sleepy, she was the most beautiful sight he had ever seen. "Hey, pretty girl. How are ya?" he asked, pulling open the screen door and lifting her for a hug. She smelled of sleep and sweetness and innocence and his heart clenched with love.

Mariah squeezed his neck back, then turned her head and looked at Tate. "He looks like you, Daddy. Are you brothers?"

"No, but our daddies were. This is your cousin, Tate."

Tate held out his hand solemnly, his eyes laughing as the little girl accepted his handshake. "My, my, you sure are a pretty thing, Miss Mariah," he told her, tapping her nose.

She gave him a sweet smile and said, "Thank you." Studying his badge, she asked, "Are you a policeman?"

"Town sheriff. Got any bad guys you need me to arrest?" he asked soberly.

"No, thank you. Why are you here?"

"I came out here to invite you and your daddy to church and Sunday dinner with us tomorrow," Tate said, glancing at Jazz. "My Mama sold ya'll this house. Remember her?"

"Miss Ella is your Mama?" At his nod, she smiled, curling her arm around her father's neck, leaning into him. "Miss Ella is real nice." With sad eyes, she sighed and whispered, "I don't remember my mom. She died."

"I heard 'bout that. Real sorry to hear it, too."

"Daddy had a daddy, too. He died, though. Did yours die?"

Tate stood there, looking a little lost. Jazz almost jumped in to save him, but Tate managed to find his footing well enough. Tate reached out and tapped Mariah's nose and said, "You sure are pretty, Miss Mariah. Will you see if you can talk your daddy into coming tomorrow?"

Smiling, she laid her head on Jazz's chest. "We'll be there, won't we, Daddy?"

With a wry smile, Jazz replied, "Of course. You still go to St. John's?"

"Where else? Ten thirty, sharp." He tipped his hat to

Mariah, causing her to giggle. As he strode away, Mariah looked at her father. "I like him," she said simply.

ℰℭ

He had forgotten that the Kincades also attended St. John's Parish. Jazz hesitated at the back of the church, frozen as memories slammed into him. Desmond rousing them all from their beds, every Sunday, come rain or shine, ordering them into their finest while the cook prepared a hardy breakfast.

Then they'd get to church and go their separate ways, Jazz and Alex in the back with the rest of the high school crowd, Anne-Marie toward the middle with her best friend, Jackie. Desmond would sit in the front, as was befitting a man so well respected. So well liked.

And sixteen years later, Desmond still sat there and his daughter was at his side. Jackie sat about midway, leaning against a bear of a man who had his arm wrapped around the redhead. Jazz couldn't seem to make himself go any farther inside. Behind him, Tate laid a hand on his shoulder and spoke quietly, "It has to come sooner or later. You know that."

If he'd been given a choice, Jazz would have chosen later. Holding Mariah's small hand in his, he entered the church. As he walked, he ignored the whispers and the stares. He'd come back to face this.

And to find out what had really happened that night.

Twice, he glanced over to see Anne-Marie looking his way. He looked away each time, unable to meet her eyes.

It was the longest hour and a half of his life. At least, it seemed that way. As the closing hymn was sung, Jazz stood, a headache the size of Manhattan raging behind his eyes.

Grim, he took Mariah's hand in his and headed to his car, with the fervent hope that he could get out without anybody saying a word to him. He was nearly there when he realized his prayers weren't going to be answered.

"Jasper."

Besides his parents, he had only let one other person call him that. Turning, he faced Desmond Kincade, the man who had helped raise him, been the only father figure he had after his own father died in a freak accident at the mill. Wonderingly, Jazz met his eyes, unable to believe he still looked the same.

The thick, black hair had turned the color of salt and pepper with a wide streak of solid white blazing back from his right temple. Those penetrating eyes hadn't changed at all, they still seemed to see clear through to his soul. Few lines marred his aristocratic features.

"Dr. Kincade."

Those solemn green eyes drifted downward, landing on Mariah. "This your little girl?" he asked, kneeling down in front of her.

"Yes, sir. This is Mariah. Mariah, this is Dr. Kincade, Dr. Anne-Marie's daddy."

Mariah smiled at him and held out her dainty hand. With grave dignity, Desmond accepted her hand and they shook. "Are you a kid doctor, too?" she asked, leaning up against her father's leg.

"No. No, I'm not. I'm a doctor who takes care of people with sick hearts."

"Like broken hearts?" Mariah asked, her eyebrows rising. She glanced up at her father, her tiny tongue darting out to lick at her lips. A gleam lit her eyes and she nibbled on her lower lip as she waited for him to answer.

"Yes, I suppose so."

She left Jazz's side and went to whisper in Desmond's ear. His bushy, black brows rose as the little girl asked, "Can you help my daddy? I think he has a broken heart."

"Now why do you think that?" Desmond asked, looking up at Jazz.

"Because he is always sad," Mariah whispered, glancing up and looking back to Desmond. "Can you help him?"

Before Desmond had a chance to figure out an answer to that, Anne-Marie joined them, with a warning look for Jazz and a concerned one for her father. Bending, she brushed back Mariah's hair, studying the closed wound. "That looks real good, Mariah. Does it hurt?"

"No, ma'am. You did a good job," she replied.

"The highest of praise," Anne-Marie concluded, grinning. She tucked her arm through her father's as he rose. "Are you two telling secrets already?"

"Is he really your daddy, Dr. Anne?"

"Yes, he is. A very good daddy."

"I think he's nice," Mariah said. Just then, Tate came up and asked if they were ready. With a quick look back, Mariah said, "I hope you will, Mr. Doctor Kincade." Then she walked away with her dad and Tate.

"Will what?" Anne-Marie asked.

"She wants me to fix his heart. She thinks it's broken," he mused, shaking his head. "Ironic, isn't it? How old did you say she was?"

"Five. Going on sixty-five, it looks like. Acts like a sweet, little grandmother, doesn't she?"

"She's something," Desmond said. "If his heart is broken, I wonder what in the hell that makes mine?"

"Daddy."

He turned to look at her.

The spring breeze blowing through her hair, she looked so much like her Mama, it sometimes hurt to look at her. Her eyes were big and serious, face solemn. Laying one hand on his sleeve, she whispered, "Jazz lost him, too."

&

Sunday mornings were for church. Sunday afternoons for spending with her father. But Sunday evenings were hers. This particular Sunday evening found Anne-Marie stretched out on her porch swing, a glass of iced tea in one hand and a well-read book in the other. The air was mild and sweet, the scent of blooming flowers on the wind.

She loved spring.

Idly, she flipped a page, eyes skimming over the familiar words. She could probably recite most of the book by heart if she had to, so many times had she read it. But she never tired of it, never tired of the fairy tale it wove.

Without even realizing it, she fell asleep, the tea resting against her chest, the book falling from limp fingers with a muffled thud to the ground.

That was how Jazz found her, head tipped back to the sun, a tiny smile on her lovely face, eyes closed. *Alex, you were right. She became one hell of a lady*, he thought, wishing his friend was there to see her.

He lowered himself into the wooden rocker and stared at her. Natural coloring gave her skin a dusky gold hue, contrasting with her black hair. Her classically beautiful features transformed into something almost ethereal, the clean oval of her face, the slim straight nose, high cheekbones and delicate rosebud mouth.

To all the world, she looked more like a high school cheerleader than a doctor. The clean cut, wholesome girl next door.

The girl he could never have.

Jazz had always known how he felt about her, from the time she was ten, staring up at him as Alex stood introducing his scruffy-looking friend to his family. Jazz had been whipped the night before and limped a bit. Bad tempered and irritable, he hadn't been in the mood for some whiny-faced little brat.

But Anne-Marie had looked up from the book she held clutched to her chest and met his eyes. She studied the bruises on his face, lips pursed, eyes serious. Softly, she had asked, "Did somebody do that to you?"

Humiliated, he had turned away, mumbling a goodbye to Alex. When her little hand caught on the tail of his flannel shirt, he had paused, stiff and rigid, looking down at her. She smiled at him and said, "I'm gonna be a doctor when I grow up. If he ever hurts you again, I'll fix it."

In that second, a fist closed around his heart and it had never released.

After spending the better part of his life in love with only one person, he had learned how to accept the fact that he would never have her. She was never meant to be his. But he hadn't known that seeing her after all this time would be so hard. In all honesty, he hadn't really expected her to affect him quite like this. He'd adored the headstrong little brat but after sixteen years, he would have expected something inside of him to change.

Especially after nearly sixteen years of not seeing her. He wasn't the same kid he'd been when he ran away from town.

He'd grown up, gotten married, fallen in love, even. So how could she still affect him so badly?

Why did just the sight of her sleeping soothe him?

As he watched, she arched her head back, stretching her neck, then tensing her shoulders and releasing them before her lids slowly lifted. She didn't jump when she saw him there, just smiled and said, "I had a feeling you would be here sometime today."

"I wanted to make sure the doc was okay. I hope... I hope I didn't upset him."

Anne-Marie arched a smooth black brow at him and said, "It wasn't easy for him, no. But did you really expect it to be?"

He lifted his shoulders in a shrug, feeling like an idiot. Rising, he jammed his hands in his pockets, staring into the distance. "He looks the same. Sounds the same. Damn it, he even smells the same, of the cigars he sneaks when ya'll know he smokes 'em anyway. The aftershave lotion, Old Spice." He smiled and shook his head. "He could afford any kind he wanted and he wears the kind you buy at K-mart."

"Mama always liked it," she said, her lips curving up. "He's actually gotten better about the cigars. I haven't caught him with one in nearly three months."

"You still make him give you a dollar every time you catch him with one?"

"Of course not," she replied. Amusement lit her eyes as she added, "Inflation, you know? It's now five dollars."

He laughed. "You always were good about getting money out of him."

"That's because he spoiled us rotten."

"No. No, he didn't. He may have given you a lot, he may have overindulged a little. But he did right by you two."

"We were lucky to have him." Rising, she went to stand beside him. Resting her hands on the railing, stained a soft mellow gold, she looked up at him. "He loved you, too, Jazz. He stills does. You were like a son to him."

"Yeah. The black sheep. And look how I paid him back." Closing his eyes, he could still picture the way Desmond had looked at him while he lay in the hospital bed. Shoulders bowed and stooped with grief, eyes tired. "I took his only son away and put him in the ground."

"Did you ever remember any of it, Jazz?"

"No," he answered. "I never remembered anything after we got to the lake. The time between then and waking up in the hospital is a blank, like it never happened."

Shoving off the rail, he turned to look at her. "I shouldn't have come here," he told her, staring at the face, so lovely, so pretty. How could he not have recognized her in the doctor's office? If he hadn't been half-hysterical with worry about Mariah, half-mad with guilt, he would have. Even when he had stared through the window at her, her hair pulled neatly back, all professional in her little white coat, his heart had started pounding, his chest had felt tight. Somewhere inside, some part of him had recognized her.

God, he loved her. His whole life, he had loved so few people. Three had been the Kincades, and he had put one of them in the ground. "I shouldn't have come," he repeated, shaking his head and starting down the stairs.

"Jazz..."

He paused, turning to look at her. "I remember the first time I saw you. Beau had beat me something bad the night before and Alex wanted your daddy to take a look at me. I figured he would be better than the social worker. Not that it did much good. I didn't know that he had to tell her anyhow.

"You asked if somebody had hurt me," he reminded her, the wind ruffling his hair, the sun setting behind him. "Then you told me that when you were older, you'd fix it next time I was hurt."

He sighed, looking past her, past the house, into the distance. Some ten miles away was a lake hidden in the woods, and a long gravel road. It was there that his entire world had shattered around him. Sixteen long years ago, and he had yet to put it all back together.

"I'm hurting now, Annie. But there's not a damned thing you or any other doctor can do about it."

With that, he turned on his heel, climbed into his car and left.

But he stared at her through his rearview mirror until the turns in the road blocked her from his sight.

Chapter Four

Desmond sat in his office, puffing at one of his Cuban cigars. Remembering what his daughter had said to him on Sunday, he sat muttering. Thinking. If Jazz hadn't been driving in the condition he was in, this wouldn't have happened. Alex would still be alive.

Jazz lost him, too.

But it still doesn't seem right, after all this time. I can't picture him driving that car into that tree, drunk or not.

How many times had that boy been cited by cops for speeding? More times than Desmond could count. And how many tickets? Scads. But accidents? Not a one. Accused of wanton endangerment? Zero. Reports of drunk driving? Nada.

Remembering back, he thought of the concealed glee he'd seen in Larry Muldoon's face. Breathing in the heady scent of smoke, he pondered it a moment. He had always thought it was because Larry hated anybody who had more than he did and he saw this as a slap to Desmond.

But maybe it was something else.

Slowly reaching for the phone, he stabbed out his cigar. Hell, the least he could do was some nosing around, see what turned up.

॰ॐ

When the call came in, Larry just happened to be sitting at his desk filing a report on some punk ass who had been hotdogging around town. Otherwise, he may not have learned anything about it. As things happened, he overheard Darla Monroe saying, "Those records being so old, it'll take me a bit to find them. None of the records before 1990 are in the computer. What day was the accident?"

She hummed under her breath, jotting down a date. "Seven-thirteen-eighty-four. Got that, right? Alex and Jazz, right? Well, Dr. Kincade, I'll get that information as soon as I possibly can."

Darla glanced up as she jotted a note down on her huge desk calendar. She met Larry's beady-eyed stare with cool blue eyes. "Is there a problem, Deputy Muldoon?"

"Oh, no. I was just wondering what old Doc Kincade was wanting. Was that about his boy?"

Darla didn't like those eyes. And she didn't like Muldoon. She never had and Darla knew she wasn't alone. With his beady eyes, sallow face and overall sour disposition, there just wasn't much about him to like. But there was something off about him, something that wasn't quite right. Smelling the stench of old sweat on him, Aqua Velva and spearmint gum, she stifled a shudder. Man, did he give her the willies or what?

"What he wants isn't much concern of yours, is it?"

"Don't go getting all hoity-toity on me, girl," he snapped. Across his forehead was a film of sweat and it seemed to Darla he looked nervous. "I was just asking a friendly question."

"I doubt you've ever asked a friendly question in your life," she responded, covering her notes with a legal pad. As the phone rang, she gave the clock a pointed stare and asked, "Aren't you supposed to be on patrol now?"

℃

No toxicology report. Desmond tugged thoughtfully at his lower lip. Why in God's name hadn't there been a tox report? And the investigating officer's report wasn't worth the paper it was written on.

Larry Muldoon, he thought with disgust. He read the report through once. Then a second time. And a third—he might have read it again, but he wouldn't let himself.

There had been no investigation. Who had been sheriff then? Blackie Schmidt. Frustrated, Desmond threw down the report and dragged his hands through his hair. If he hadn't been so grief stricken...

Buddies with the Muldoon family. The Muldoons didn't inspire ambiguity. People either feared them, hated them—or they were cut from the same cloth, like Blackie had been. Fortunately, Larry was the only one left. Beau's youngest brother died in a motorcycle wreck four years earlier. Those three had run wild and loose throughout the county.

Of course, there was a little girl, Marlena? Marlene? Yes. Marlie Jo, a quiet, timid little thing, if Desmond was remembering right. She didn't seem to fit with the Muldoon clan, quiet where her brothers were loud, polite where they were cruel.

Shaking his head, Desmond muttered, "Stop stalling." With a hand that was still steady, he reached for the reports once more, this time flipping through until he found the mortician's report.

The post-mortem... God, reading those words was like driving a dagger into his chest. How could his beautiful boy be dead?

Multiple facial bone breaks, multiple lacerations, cardiac tamponade—bruising to the sternal area.

Cardiac tamponade.

Consistent with bruising noted on victims with a history of blunt force trauma. Blunt force trauma. The sort of trauma one encountered after being on the receiving end of a steering wheel going into your chest.

The bruise going across Alex's chest—he read the description.

Closing his eyes, Desmond leaned back in his chair. *Why didn't I see this sooner?*

Why hadn't anybody else? Had his grief and shock blinded him? Or was it a willingness to believe that Jazz McNeil had done exactly as they'd said he would? Had Jazz ruined Alex's life, just as so many people had said he would?

Or had Alex ruined his?

Desmond pushed back from the desk with a tired sigh, rubbing the back of his stiff neck with his hand. The haunted look in the boy's eyes had never left him. He wondered if he had done the wrong thing in not questioning the report. Questioning, hell, he had downright refused to even look at any of it.

And Desmond knew well enough why nobody else had investigated further. Even after the Kincades had taken Jazz in, most of the town still looked at him and saw the stepfather they had both feared and hated. Hated, yes. Despised, yes. But if Beau had so much as whispered, "Jump," more than half of the population would have done just that.

Why did they remember Beau, and not Jazz's real father?

"Why didn't you remember his real father?" Desmond asked himself.

Rubbing his hands over his stubbled face, he grumbled under his breath. If nothing else, he had to agree with Anne-Marie. It didn't fit.

ℰ

Gripping the steering wheel with sweaty hands, Larry watched as Doc Kincade stepped out of his house. The doctor had a strange, thoughtful look on his face and didn't seem to notice the patrol car. Larry continued on down the street slowly, circled the block, and came up behind Desmond as he entered the heavier flow of traffic on Main Street. Larry dropped back several car lengths and continued to tail the doc's fancy, gun-metal gray Mercedes.

Twice he had to wipe his palms off on his pressed khakis, leaving damp trails down them. As the old man turned off Main Street, headed out of town and hit the highway, sweat started to trickle down the back of Larry's neck. When the doc punched the gas pedal to the floor and hit seventy in roughly ten seconds flat, a grim smile of satisfaction came on Larry's face as he flipped on his flashing lights.

The Kincades liked speed, that was certain. Sure as the sun rose and set, the moment the road opened up, both father and daughter hit the gas.

The wailing siren split the air as he got on the bumper of the German car. *Shoulda bought American, you pissant,* he thought, idly imagining himself keying the side of that expensive piece of machinery.

"What's the hurry, Doc? Gotta a baby to de-liver out here?" Larry drawled.

"I'm not an obstetrician or a general surgeon, Deputy. You know that as well as anybody," Desmond said, teeth clamped around a fat cigar that smelled of foreign, aromatic tobacco. The heady smell of it went straight to Larry's senses and had him yearning for a taste.

"Yeah, it's the daughter that does that sort of thing, ain't it? No, wait. She works with kids. You getting pretty old to still be cutting around in somebody's chest, aren't ya, Doc Kincade?"

"Apparently not or I wouldn't still be practicing." The doctor sucked on the cigar and blew a smoke ring in Larry's direction before saying, "You just write out that ticket, son."

"Where you headed in such an all-fired hurry?" Larry asked, not even reaching for his pad.

"Out to see a friend," Desmond answered, staring straight ahead, drumming his fingers on the smooth, leather-covered wheel.

"That wouldn't be the McNeil boy, would it?"

"He's hardly a boy anymore," Desmond responded. "But, yes. I am heading out there."

"Don't you think it was time to let bygones be bygones, Doc? I know you miss your boy, but it's been near twenty years now." Larry's sweaty hands had to close twice around his pen before he was able to dig it out of his pocket.

With an amused smile, Desmond asked, "Do you really think I would wait sixteen years just to pound on him a little? Have some imagination, Larry." He puffed a little more on the cigar and stubbed it out in the ashtray before raising his eyes to the deputy. "Now are you going to give me that ticket so I can be on my way?"

Mouth slack, skin pale, he looked from his cruiser back to the Benz, at the doc sitting in his high-priced car in his fine clothes. *That damned McNeil brat*, he thought with hatred. *All his damned fault. If he hadn't come back here...*

His hand itched, burned almost and before he even realized it, he was reaching for his gun. He had a moment to watch as Desmond's eyes narrowed. He imagined planting a bullet between those eyes, those smug knowing eyes. A huge blast of air sounded in his ears as an eighteen-wheeler hurtled down the highway, followed by several pickups.

The final car in the procession was a fire-engine red Mustang convertible. The car pulled up behind Larry's cruiser and the muscles in his arm went slack as Anne-Marie Kincade climbed out, her heavy fall of black hair flowing free to her shoulders.

"Hi, Daddy," she said, crouching by the car, unaware of the tension in the air. "I saw you sitting here while I was heading back into town. I was heading out to see you, thought you'd like to go get a late breakfast."

"Miss Kincade..."

She swung her head around and looked up with mossy green eyes fringed with heavy lashes. "Dr. Kincade, Deputy," she corrected, rising to her feet. In her heeled boots, she barely reached five-foot-five but that didn't keep the snooty little bitch from glaring down her patrician nose at him.

He tipped his hat at her and said, "Doc Kincade. I'm in the process of writing your daddy a ticket."

"Go right on," she offered, gesturing with her hand. A lock of hair drifted in her face and she tucked it behind her ear with a neatly manicured hand. She slid her hands in the pockets of her jeans and leaned back against the car with her booted feet crossed neatly at the ankles.

He started to write out the ticket and cursed silently as he saw his hands shaking. The doc's daughter kept standing right there, chatting with her father; it didn't matter a bit that he wasn't chatting back. He mumbled an order for the elder Doc Kincade to turn over his license and after snagging it, stomped back to his cruiser.

Sitting in the seat of his cruiser, he leaned his head back against the headrest and tried to steady his ragged breathing. Godamighty, had he been planning to shoot him?

Already, Larry could see the neat little hole his sidearm would have left, could see a dazed look entering the doc's eyes while his brain died before his heart received the message.

He'd never killed before, but had thought of it, imagined it.

And right now, he was yearning for it. He was going to do it, too, because if he didn't that damned doctor was going to cause a shitload of trouble. All on account of that no-good bastard, McNeil.

Behind him, Anne-Marie watched Larry walk away and she frowned. There had been a weird tension in the air when she pulled up, a tension she could have cut with a knife.

Then she looked back at her father and studied his face. He looked normal—a little tired maybe, but nothing major. It was Larry who was acting odd. Or more odd than normal, at least. The moron had a serious ego issue, all puffed up with self-importance, and he had a habit of bullying people around. Probably an inherited trait. Anne-Marie didn't remember his brother well, or any of the others, but she'd heard the stories. Troublemakers, almost every single one.

"Everything okay, Daddy? Larry sure is acting weird"

"Larry's got a bee up his—" He cut that sentence off before he finished it and gave Anne-Marie a grin. "If she was alive, your mama would skin me if she heard me saying that."

76

Anne-Marie laughed. "I imagine Mama heard worse from you, Daddy."

"Hearing worse from me, and then not caring that I say it around you are two different things," he replied.

She shrugged. "I don't really think it would bother Mama that you tell me that Larry has a bee up his ass, Daddy. It's nothing more than the truth." Pushing her hair back, she rested her elbows on the car door and asked, "So you wanna buy me breakfast?"

Reaching out, Desmond ruffled her hair. "I had something I wanted to do..." Then his eyes closed. "But maybe I'm not ready to do it yet. I'd love to buy you some breakfast."

They heard a car door slam and looked up, watching as Larry came stomping back. "Just let me get my ticket here from this fine officer and we'll meet at the diner."

ᔓ

Her hand in his, Mariah looked around the brightly colored room, filled with laughing, gay voices and women wearing black nylon capes over their clothes. With her free hand, she pushed her long bangs out of her face and asked, "Can I have my hair cut any way I want?"

"Depends on which way you want it," Jazz answered, signing the appointment book.

"Who's gonna do it?"

"Going to," he corrected absently, stroking Mariah's thick cap of curls. Looking around the room, he saw several hairdressers at their stations, all chatting with their customers.

His eyes narrowed on one face in particular, a growl sounding low in his throat. Maribeth Park, her platinum blonde hair falling around her face, sat in a chair, flipping through a magazine. She looked almost exactly the same. Her hair was straight now, the frizzy, big-haired look replaced by a smooth, sleek cut. Her brows were waxed and her skin was a deep gold that probably required many visits to the tanning bed. She looked just a little older, still on the skinny side and still as pretty as a picture. And just as soulless.

"Hello. Are we here for a cut?" a chirpy voice asked.

He looked at the cute, cheerleader-type redhead at the desk, dragging his attention from Maribeth, who had just raised her head and looked at him. A cat's smile was gracing her face as she rose.

"I've got an opening, Laura. Widow Shoemaker canceled. Had to take her cat to the vet," Maribeth said, strolling slowly up to the desk.

"Well, that's fine—"

"No. We'll wait," Jazz said, looking away from Maribeth. He looked up and down the aisle, his eyes landing on a familiar face. "Isn't that Mabel Winslow?" he asked, pointing towards a large, heavyset woman with a wide smile and heavily mascaraed eyes. Mabel had been the only one he had allowed to touch his hair as a child.

"Yes, but she won't be able to do it for a while yet. She's in the middle of a perm," Laura said.

"We'll wait. Let's go sit down, angel," he said, turning away. When a hand landed on his arm, fingers tipped with fire-engine red, he looked at the hand, and then at the hand's owner. "You'd be wise to stay away from me, Maribeth." Eyes narrowed and cold, he added, "Very wise."

Eyes were turning their way and Maribeth removed her hand at the gentle clearing of a throat from behind her. She turned and met the mild gaze of her manager, the little tramp with the authority to fire her. Just as her mama had fired Maribeth's mama several years back. "We keep the customers happy, Maribeth," Laura said before calling, "What's the name, sir?"

"Mariah McNeil," he answered, leafing through a magazine while the pretty little girl at his side neatly lined up her crayons on the arm of her chair.

Although he didn't look at any of them, he felt it as damn near every person in the room turned to stare at him. He focused on the magazine as though it were prize-winning material. Next to him, Mariah smiled at Laura. "I'm getting my hair cut," she said brightly. "It's a rat's nest."

Laura smiled and said, "I don't know about that. How do you want it cut?"

"Like Dr. Anne-Marie's," she answered. "She has pretty hair. Daddy has to get his hair cut, too. He promised." Lowering her voice, she said in a loud whisper, "His hair is almost as long as Dr. Anne-Marie's."

Dr. Anne-Marie.

Maribeth stalked away, flopping down in her chair, ignoring the pointed look from Laura as she lifted up her magazine. Dr. Anne-Marie. Alex's brat of a sister. Oh, she hated the girl, always had. With her rich daddy, protective brother and the brain behind that gorgeous face. Everybody in town adored her, from the little kids to the old folks that sat swapping stories in front of the old-fashioned general store.

And Jazz. Even when they had been kids, his face had softened even at the mention of her name. Maribeth stared at Jazz McNeil over the top of her magazine, hatred for him edging its way in.

God, was he gorgeous. He had been so, even as a boy, but now... Standing at six-foot-two, shoulders broad and strong, his midnight hair falling around his golden face, he looked like a dark angel.

No. An avenging one, she thought as he raised his head and met her eyes. The look in those black eyes was disdain, ice-edged and sharp, and knowledge—the knowledge that she was every bit as responsible for Alex's death as him.

Alex, beautiful, golden Alex. He haunted her at night. It seemed every time her life started to take a turn for the better, he came back into her dreams. And lately, the pitiful cry of a forgotten baby punctuated those dreams.

Alex had told her she would pay.

His final words to her had been a curse, one she was unable to break. Yes, she was paying. Stuck in this dead-end town with no hope of ever getting out. Barely scraping by on the money she earned at the beauty parlor, she supplemented hers and Mama's income by sharing her bed with whoever was willing to pay the price.

Yeah, she thought with disgust. She was paying all right and she was damned tired of it.

છ૭

They were watching him. Flipping through the magazine, Jazz was aware that there were eyes trained on him from every direction.

The old blue-haired lady, possibly Daisy Graham, was being quite subtle about it. Others, like Maribeth and the gum-snapping teenager now washing Mariah's hair, didn't bother with subtlety. Ella McNeil was in for her weekly rinse and she lifted a manicured hand to wave at her nephew before closing her eyes to enjoy this small bit of pampering she allowed herself.

One pair of eyes in particular bored into his neck.

When he raised his eyes, trying to find the one in question, all eyes turned away. Maribeth? No. She wouldn't bother him that much. It wasn't Mabel or Laura, both were busy cutting hair. The girl washing Mariah's hair met his eyes dead on, sizing him up. Barely old enough to drink, he figured. And not in the least bit familiar. But malevolence lingered in the air.

He continued to study each person in turn. The shy blonde doing manicures would glance up at him from time to time and then lower her eyes once more. She was familiar in a vague sort of way, tickling some distant memory. It clicked and he realized why she was so timid. Beau's baby sister, a more meek and cowed woman had never existed. Marlene Jo, he remembered. Marlie with the quiet voice and shy manner, sporting bruises from her daddy nearly as often as Jazz and his mama had.

His eyes drifted over her once the memory registered, focusing on the sharp-eyed brunette sitting in the chair in front of Laura. One corner of her mouth curved up and she raised her hand in a casual wave.

Sandy Pritchard. The girl he had been dating the summer Alex had died. She had come to see him in the hospital, had driven him to the cemetery that one time, the only time he had been there. She had also tucked an envelope with nearly three hundred dollars cash into his pocket when she had taken him to the bus station. Then she had kissed his cheek and told him to take care of himself.

They hadn't spoken since.

He stared at her, their eyes meeting in the mirror.

He remembered Sandy's final words to him, the words that had haunted him, the words that had led him back home, even if the journey took sixteen years.

"You weren't driving, Jazz. If you were, that wreck wouldn't have happened."

Chapter Five

Anne-Marie lowered the brush and stared at her reflection. Dark green eyes, troubled and confused, stared back at her. *Why am I even bothering?* She flicked the make-up on the dresser top a disinterested glance.

What was the point in getting dressed up, putting on her make-up, and going into town to sit on a barstool and watch other people dance, other people kiss, other people in love?

Or just in lust.

Lust.

Pressing one hand against her flat belly, she closed her eyes. Oh, yes. She was familiar with lust, had been since she had awoken sweaty and panting in her bed the night of her sixteenth birthday. It hadn't been the sloppy, badly aimed kiss from Dex Embry that had done it.

It had been from a dream about Jazz. He'd been dancing with her on the deck by the lake. At the time, he'd already been gone from her life but not a day went by that she didn't think of him. She'd written him letters, one a week, faithfully, hoping that somebody would hear from him and she'd get an address where she could mail the letters.

But nobody ever heard a word. On her eighteenth birthday, she had written the last one and then tucked them all in a box. That box was stored in the top of her closet and every spring when she cleaned from top to bottom, she told herself she was going to throw them away.

She never did.

Even after she stopped writing the letters, she dreamed of him. Anne-Marie couldn't even count how many dreams she had about him. Hundreds. Some bare wisps in her memory, others so potent, so real, she had awoken in tears to discover he wasn't there with her.

God, it had always been him.

Could a person be born loving another? It seemed she had loved and needed him her whole life. But she was twenty-three before she accepted the fact that he was gone and he wasn't coming back. Eleven years after he walked out of her life, Anne-Marie finally stopped waiting. She accepted a date from a third-year medical student and after four more dates, she went to bed with him. For all the wrong reasons and Anne-Marie wouldn't deny it.

Rick Monohan had been good-looking, funny and considerate but when he touched her, Anne-Marie felt next to nothing. The thunder and lightning bolts she had been hoping for never happened and when he called to ask her out a few days later, she refused.

For the past sixteen years, she had tried to fill a hole inside of her, a hole Jazz left when he walked out of her life and for sixteen years, she had failed. She was damn tired of feeling so damned empty, too.

So why are you going into town instead of out to his place?

A frown darkened her face and she glanced around the room. The voice seemed too strong, too certain, too *real* to have come from her. If she didn't know better, she'd think that somebody was in the room with her.

But she was alone. As always. Alone or not, though, Anne-

Marie decided it was a very good question.

Why, indeed.

ॐ

Jazz smiled at Mabel and asked, "Are you sure this is okay?"

"Boy, if I didn't want that sweet girl here, she wouldn't be here." Her big voice rang in his ears and echoed on the porch as he knelt to hug Mariah against him one more time. Her first sleepover.

Her newest best friend, Tabby Winslow, Mabel's youngest grandchild, stood by, hugging Mariah's overnight case to her chest. "We're gonna have so much fun," Tabby whispered, her dark eyes gleaming brightly out of her ebony face. "Gonna eat popcorn and stay up until nine, right, Grandma?"

"That's right, sugar. And it's for girls only, so get on with you," she said, shooing Jazz down the steps. "And you keep those appointments next month. I gotta eat, don't I?" As she spoke, she slapped her rounded belly with a ringed hand.

"God knows, Mabel, if you miss any meals, you'd just wither away," Jazz replied drolly, grinning when she cackled out a laugh that scared the birds from the trees.

"Big talk for such a skinny boy," Mabel said, shaking her head at him as the laughter faded from her voice. "Boy, you need to get some rest, some good food in you and a good woman by your side."

As Tabby and Mariah raced around the porch and yard, Jazz said, "I've had a good woman. I had to bury her; I don't want another one."

"Want, maybe not. But you need somebody, Jasper Jr. I

never seen a body who needed another the way you do. The way you've always needed." Her wide, deep red mouth compressed into a straight line, her round, cheerful face uncharacteristically somber, Mabel said, "Jazz, honey, some people are meant to go young. Alex, now, God knows he was a wonderful boy, but it was his time. That's just the way of it.

"And some people are meant to go the distance alone. Me, I buried two husbands. Good men, and I loved them both dearly. And as happy as I was with each one of them, I'd never do it again. And then there are folks like you, so sad, so locked up inside, they're almost dead from it." Her round face softened with sympathy and she reached out, patting his cheek with a gentle hand. "Don't let tragedy ruin your life. That'd be another one. God knows you don't need that. You've had too many already," she finished. She heaved a sigh.

Shaking his head, he headed for the Escalade after hugging Mariah one last time. Five years old, already. Her first sleepover. And if he didn't get the hell away now, he was going to change his mind and Mariah wouldn't ever forgive him. Jazz also didn't think Mabel would be too happy if he decided to sleep outside in her driveway, just to make sure everything went okay. So instead of going back to Mariah for one last hug, he climbed into the car and started it up.

It took less than a minute for it to hit him. He had an entire night to himself. One entire night. With the wind blowing through the open window, Jazz took the turn off to his house at a brisk forty miles an hour. With pleasure, he watched in his rearview as gravel dust filled the air.

An entire night to himself. And he didn't have a clue as to what he was gonna do with it.

How long had it been since he'd had a night to himself? Right before Sheri got sick, Jazz realized. That last weekend

Mariah had spent with Sheri's folks while he and Sheri went out for dinner. The following Monday Sheri had gone to her doctor and learned she had a brain tumor. Such a bright light, put out so fast, just like Alex. He could still hear her laughter, that loud, bawdy laugh, that low raspy voice. How could that fast-living, fast-talking woman possibly be dead?

With a sigh, he ran his hand over his face. She had gone so quickly, in under six months. Jazz was going to miss her until the day he died. Sheri, God rest her soul, had given him his salvation. Rounding the final curve to his house, he decided he'd go home, dig out his wedding album and take a little walk down memory lane, pay his respects to his wife's memory.

But as he crested the hill, he realized that he wouldn't be doing that tonight. There in his drive sat a shiny little Mustang convertible, fire-engine red, the ragtop down. Perched on the hood was Anne-Marie Kincade. One look at her hit him like a punch right in the solar plexus and all thoughts of Sheri faded away, lost in the fog of need that took over as he stared at Anne-Marie.

Her thick, black hair was falling around her shoulders, shoulders left bare by a simple, white camisole-styled top. Long legs were revealed by a pair of neatly cuffed, black shorts and her small feet were shod in a simple pair of canvas tennis shoes.

She didn't look like a doctor; nope, she looked like a high school coed, too young and too damn innocent. Until she turned her head and met his eyes. The look in those misty, green eyes was pure woman and Jazz could literally feel it as the blood drained out of his head, straight down to his cock.

His breath caught in his chest as her gaze locked with his, a small, mysterious smile tugging at the corners of her lips. Sweet God, how had she grown up to be so beautiful?

A soft breeze fluttered her hair around her face, framing it in dense black. She slid off the car and moved towards him, that mysterious, teasing smile still on her lips. "Hey," she said softly, coming to a stop a few feet away. Cocking her head, she studied him in the fading light. "You had your hair cut."

A soft, elusive scent floated to him on the air and an insane desire to bury his face against her neck seized him. Gruffly, he asked, "What are you doing here?"

Her shoulders lifted and fell and she said, "I wanted to talk to you."

"What about?"

"I don't know." She shrugged, again. "So here I am."

Looking at her, he saw Alex. Though they looked nothing alike, he saw his old friend in the arrogant lift of her chin, in the confident way she held herself. The way she offered no explanation for her actions. She was so alive, as Alex had been. So damned alive, and Jazz had felt dead inside for too damn long. He didn't think he could keep his hands off her if she stayed so close.

"Did you forget who I am, Annie?" he asked, moving closer, until his toes nudged hers.

She had to tilt her head back to meet his eyes. "I know who you are, Jazz. I've always known you."

Shaking his head, he scoffed at her, "You don't know me any more than I know you. Hell, you haven't seen me in sixteen years and the last time you did see me, I was laid-up in a hospital bed after I killed your brother."

He wanted to scare her away, and for a second, she paled and her eyes darkened with pain but then her features smoothed out and she shook her head. "Nice try, Jazz."

"Leave, Annie."

Instead, she cocked a brow at him. "What's my favorite color?" she asked.

Blue, he thought, even opened his mouth to answer before he clamped his lips shut.

"My favorite food?"

Strawberry shortcake. "How in hell am I supposed to know? I haven't seen you in years, sugar."

She smiled serenely. "Why do I like rainy days?"

So you can curl up with a book and munch on popcorn. Brows lowered, he stared at her.

She shrugged and said, "You like the color green." *Green, like her eyes.* "You love steak and potatoes, sour cream only. You don't like butter. Rainy days don't bother you but you always liked the sun better. When it rained, you were supposed to stay in out of the rain. And that made it easier for Beau to find you."

Shame slid through him, hot and greasy. He'd always done his best to hide from her whenever he took a pounding. It was humiliating looking at anybody, but it had been so much worse with her. All the years since then hadn't done a damn thing to lessen that shame, either. She caught his shoulder as he turned away. "You think I don't know what he did to you? To your mama? I was young, Jazz. Not blind. I knew. I'm the one who saw you go into the barn that first time after Beau nearly beat the life out of you. I told Alex about it because I didn't think you would want Daddy to know."

Whirling around, he shrugged off her hand. "I don't need sympathy, Annie."

"I haven't any for you," she replied evenly. "If my heart breaks for the little boy who was beaten black and blue, so be it. But what I felt about that little boy has nothing to do with why I am here now.

"I do know you," she whispered, reaching out, laying one small, neatly manicured hand on his rigid arm. "You were my hero, Jazz. And I wanted to talk to you; we were friends, of a sort."

"We were never friends, angel. I was friends with your rich brother and you were the nosy, little brat who had a crush on me," he snapped. "Go home to Daddy, Annie. You want to talk to somebody, go talk to him."

In the fading light, he saw the delicate color wash out of her cheeks and hurt bloom in those green eyes. And then she blinked, and as easily as that, a mask fell. She shrugged, carelessly. "Your loss, Jasper," she told him, turning on her heel and heading for her car. The denim drew tight across her hips as she dug into the hip pocket for her keys.

Before Anne-Marie could reach for the handle, hard hands closed over her elbows, twirled her, pinned her against a heavy, male body. Against her back, she felt the cool, smooth glass of the window and the heat of the metal door against her legs. She raised her head, looked into those deep brown eyes that had haunted her dreams for years on end.

"I don't wanna talk to you," he whispered as he lowered his head to hers.

Oh.

Oh, my.

There really could be thunder and lightning bolts...

The ground seemed to open up beneath her feet, leaving her clinging to Jazz for balance. He nipped her lip and when her mouth opened, his tongue swept inside, tasting her, savoring, diving deep for more. His hands slid down the length of her body, plastering her against him. Against her belly, she could feel the thick, hard length of his erection. The feel of it did something to her insides, turning her all molten and soft—

empty. Too damned empty.

Anne-Marie rose on her toes, pressed against him, and wrapped her arms around his neck. Desperate to get closer, she arched up against him, feeling the heat and power of his body against the softness of her own.

"Damn it, Annie. We shouldn't do this." Dragging his mouth away, Jazz stared down at her. *What in the hell am I doing?* he thought, dazed. He jerked his arms away from her and pulled away. She raised one hand to her lips, touched them lightly. When her tongue darted out, slid over first her lower lip and then her upper, Jazz groaned.

What in the hell was he doing?

Alex would have killed him for even thinking what he was thinking, much less putting his thoughts into action. Desmond would have laid into him with a dull scalpel. By touching her, he betrayed both of them more than he already had.

Awkwardly, he opened his mouth to apologize but then the words froze when she took a single step toward him. And then another, and one more until she was close enough for him to see the wild pulse beating a tattoo under the thin skin of her neck. She pressed one finger to his lips, wrapped an arm around his neck, and leaned forward, pressing her mouth to the vee of skin bared by his simple, cotton button-down.

His eyes closed and his hands came up to cup the back of her neck, holding her against him. *Sweet Anne-Marie. God, I love you.* He had dreamed of her over the years, dreamed of a woman who had been just a child when he had left. Dreams that had kept him company at night, even after he'd married Sheri. Guilty dreams that he had denied having, dreams that felt so real, waking from them was almost painful.

Some people didn't believe in love at first sight, but Jazz always had. He'd fallen for her as a boy and those feelings had only strengthened in their years apart. Now, she stood in his arms, pressing herself against him. Totally and completely willing—and eager. He could see an answering hunger in her eyes, feel it in the way she leaned into him when he touched her. It was every dream he had ever had, and every nightmare. Because finally he could have her, but only for a while.

Jazz would never be able to hold her. He would never deserve her. But damned if he wouldn't take whatever he could get before she walked away. He held her pressed tightly against him as she trailed a line of butterfly kisses up his neck.

"Why shouldn't we do this, Jazz?" she asked, reveling in his taste. He tasted hot, erotic, forbidden. Like whiskey and chocolate. Her hands itched to touch him until with a sigh, she gave in, running her hands down his arms, up his sides, learning the long, lean body by touch.

She hadn't come out here for this. Not intentionally.

But Anne-Marie had fallen in love with Jazz McNeil the first time she laid eyes on him at the tender age of ten. And she had always known there would be no other for her. The one time she had tried to use another man to forget about Jazz had ended in miserable failure.

Nothing had changed that, not the sixteen years of separation, not the knowledge that he had been driving the night Alex had died. Jazz was it for her and he always had been.

Rigidly, Jazz stood in her arms and tried to think of the reasons they shouldn't do this. There were reasons. He just couldn't, for the life of him, think of them as she pressed another kiss to his collarbone, going up on her toes and pressing another whisper-soft kiss to his jawbone. It was torture, the satin-soft feel of her mouth on his skin. He wanted to cradle her head between his hands and kiss her again, taste her, hold her open while he gorged on her.

Then he wanted to lean back and watch as she used that pretty rosebud mouth in other ways. Even the thought was enough to make him go cross-eyed with lust and when he lifted his hands to her waist, they were shaking.

She's so tiny, Jazz thought. Her waist was slender, so narrow he could nearly span it with his hands. Slender, almost delicate, like some kind of fairy princess and yet so strong. He could feel the strength in her hands as she clasped his shoulders, reaching up against him.

"Take me inside," she whispered, lifting her head so she could stare at him.

"Anne-Marie..."

"Don't tell me we shouldn't do this. Don't tell me anything. Just take me inside, Jazz. This is what I want."

Hell. How could he argue with that? Especially not since it was something he'd been waiting half of his life for. Wrapping one arm around her waist, he boosted her up. She weighed less than nothing, and she wrapped her legs around his waist, hooking them over his hips. Through the layers of clothes, he felt the heat of her sex and he groaned. Jazz made one last attempt at sanity, pressing his lips to her neck as he whispered, "Anne-Marie, this is not a good idea."

Brushing her lips against his, she replied, "I think it's a great idea. And I'm always right, didn't Alex tell you that?" Then she covered his mouth with her own, burying her hands in his hair so she could hold him close.

His mind went blank and he couldn't think. There were reasons why they shouldn't do this, he knew there were. But for the life of him, he couldn't think of a single one. Thoughts of the betrayal he was committing fled his mind, chased out by the wonder of a dream come true.

She was here, with him, wrapped around him. With quick, light hands she touched him. With a soft, sweet mouth, she tasted him. No. No, he couldn't let her go, not tonight.

With a groan, he fisted a hand in her hair and tugged her head back, covering her mouth completely. He pushed his tongue into her mouth, seeking out her sweet, addictive taste. She met him without hesitation, kissing him as deeply as he kissed her.

He started up the stairs to the front door, taking them by memory as he lost himself in her. She tasted of home, of cool nights, of long lazy summer days, of innocence and youth.

The bedroom up the stairs was too far away, too many steps. Instead, he wheeled to the right and took her to the couch, sitting on the couch with her in his lap. Molding the back of her skull in his hands, Jazz tore his mouth from hers, angling her head back, exposing her neck, pressing his lips to the pulse beating wildly there. The scent of her rose to haunt him as he lifted his head to stare at her. She smelled like honeysuckle. Jazz found himself craving a deeper taste. He wanted to press his lips to her skin and seek out the pulse points, find out if that teasing scent was stronger there. Perfume? Or was it just her?

His hands were shaking as he pulled her shirt from the waistband of her shorts. Slowly, he pulled the top off of her. She shook her hair back as he threw the shirt across the room. The lacy confection under the simple top made him smile. The white lace was so sheer, he could see her nipples through it. He stroked one and watched it stiffen under the lace. "I knew you weren't as practical as you always pretended to be," he whispered, running a finger along the edge of her bra. The smooth flesh roughed with goosebumps and her nipples strained against the lace.

Hands resting on the tops of her thighs, staring at him out of calm eyes, Anne-Marie smiled and let her head fall back as he cupped her breast in his hand. Delicate, soft, smooth. The rose of her nipples pushed against the lace of her bra and with a groan, he lowered his head and nipped gently at her through the webbing.

She shuddered, her hands reaching up to curve over his shoulders while his raced over her. He settled them on the couch, shifting Anne-Marie around so that he could undress her without completely letting go. In under a minute, she was sprawled across his lap wearing nothing more than a lacy bikini that matched the bra he had tossed over the back of the couch.

"You are so beautiful," he whispered, rubbing his knuckles against the underside of her breast.

Smiling up at him, Anne-Marie murmured, "Thank you." Running a hand through his heavy black hair, as she had always wanted to do, she told him, "You're not too bad yourself." Her head fell back, a tiny hum of pleasure inside her throat as his hands cupped her breasts.

"Anne-Marie…"

Through slitted eyes, she watched as the hesitancy once again entered his eyes. Slowly, she shifted until she was able to stand. And just as slowly, she rose to her feet, her hair tumbled loose around her shoulders, mouth swollen. Her tongue darted out to lick at her lips as she knelt in front of him.

"I can't remember a time when I didn't want to be with you, in some way." She reached for the button of his fly, smiling as his belly jumped under the light brush of her hands. "I didn't come here for this. But I know that I would have, sooner or later." With her head tipped back, she looked at him and traced the length of him through his boxer-style briefs. "I don't believe in wasting time."

His breath whistling between his teeth, Jazz let his head fall back as her small, quick hands raced over him. He jolted when she pressed her lips to his belly and damn near vaulted off the couch when she slid her hands into the back of his jeans. She tugged his jeans and boxers down as far as she could and then she bent over him.

Jazz swore as Anne-Marie took him in her mouth. His field of vision narrowed down as she slid her mouth down and then back up, lifting up just enough to lick the head of his cock. Then she closed her lips back over him and Jazz almost whimpered at the sight as she started to take him in and out of her mouth, smooth, shallow strokes that sent him hurtling towards the edge. She wrapped a hand around the base of his cock, holding him steady. Her mouth, red and swollen, stretched around his flesh and she took him deeper and deeper until the head of his cock nudged the back of her throat.

She hummed a little and the vibration of it had him jerking in reaction. She lifted up just a little and Jazz sagged back against the cushions, trying to catch his breath. Before he had a chance, though, she slid back down and when his cock bumped the back of her throat again—she swallowed.

He arched up with a shout, fisting his hands in her hair. He shuddered, sweat forming on his body and the urge to come burning down his spine and settling in his balls with a heated fury. "Stop, Annie," he groaned when she lifted up and started that same slow glide all over again.

Anne-Marie lifted her head up and smiled at him. Voice husky, she murmured, "No."

This was power. Anne-Marie might not have taken any other lovers since her failed attempt in college, but that didn't mean she was a scared, shy near-virgin. Near-virgin, maybe, but there was no way she would let fear or shyness intrude, not here, not with Jazz. The length of his sex throbbed. Under her hands and mouth, he felt both hard and silky smooth. Iron covered with silk. She scraped her teeth over the tip of his penis and then took him back into her mouth, taking him deeper and deeper. When she lifted back up, her eyes were watering, her mouth felt bruised, and she was riding high on the fact that she was making him shake.

"Witch," he muttered as he looked at her, his eyes dazed. She grinned at him and he growled. He reached for her and Annie didn't pull away fast enough. He growled against her mouth and the sound of it echoed through her entire body. With a pivot, he tumbled her down on the couch, slid his hand inside the waist of her panties and jerked. If she hadn't already been shaking with hunger, that desperate, greedy gesture would have done it.

"Why waste time, you little witch?" Jazz muttered against her mouth. Witch—definitely a witch, Jazz decided as she stared up at him, a sexy, confident smile on her swollen lips and her eyes hot and wild. Looping his hands under her head, he held her still as he covered her mouth with his, as he pinned her hips against the cushion with his own.

Her thighs parted and she shifted slightly under him, staring up at him with a sly little smile. As he pressed slowly against her, her eyes drifted closed and she moaned softly in the back of her throat. The wet warmth enveloped him tightly, snugly as he eased forward.

Snug. Too snug. "Fuck, you're tight," he muttered.

She lifted her hips up, taking him deeper as he tried to pull back. "Been a while," she whispered. Then she smiled. "Waiting for you."

Even if she didn't mean that, it was humbling to hear her say it. "Damnation, Annie," he muttered. "Annie, you, oh, hell..." His words trailed off into a groan as she rolled her hips under his. "Would you slow down?"

Lids rising slowly, Anne-Marie stared up at him, her wicked, green eyes glinting up at him. "Why should I slow down? I've been waiting for this for half my life, Jazz. Don't make me wait any more."

She smiled up at him, a sexy invitation of a smile, as she reached up and cupped his face, urging him to meet her eyes. That confident female smile had every nerve in his body humming; his nerves broke into a chorus when she trailed her fingers up his sides, then slid her hands down, gripped his hips, lifted hers to meet him.

"Jazz," she whispered, her husky, soft voice caressing his ears like silk. "Make love to me. I've been wanting this for as long as I can remember."

With a groan, he lowered his head, buried his face in the smooth, softly scented skin of her neck and thrust deep, planting his length within her body.

Distantly, Anne-Marie realized there was a little more pain than she'd expected. It had definitely been a while but the pain of taking him inside was well worth it and she was in too much wonder to dwell on it. Having him inside her felt like coming home.

She wrapped her legs around his hips, pulling him back to her when he withdrew, rising to meet his hips with every thrust. "Annie..." When he breathed her name against her skin, goosebumps went rushing down her body. How many times? she wondered. How many times had she imagined this?

As vivid as her imagination was, it could never compare to the reality of having him next to her, having him buried inside her, whispering her name while he rained kisses over her face. His length throbbed inside, rubbed against nerve endings so sensitive, that each stroke was an exquisite pain. Blood pounded in her ears and the sound of it almost drowned out Jazz's rumbling groan. Lights flashed behind her closed lids when he slid a hand between them and circled his fingers around her clit.

The first mini-climax hit her hard and fast and her head was still spinning a minute later when he started to move inside her once more. *Thunder and lightning,* Anne-Marie thought, just a little dazed. A lot dazed.

Jazz propped himself on his elbows, dragging air into his lungs. Her flesh, soft, slick and tight, caressed the length of him, pulsing around his cock with every beat of her heart. They fit together perfectly, he realized with some wonder. Slowly, he pulled out and eased back into her. The scent of her filled his head, honeysuckle-scented flesh and sweet, hungry woman. Innocent and seductress combined.

Her inner muscles clenched around him and he gritted his teeth against the urge to take her, mark her and brand her as his own. By God, this may be the only night he ever had.

He would make it last.

He pulled back, resting his weight on his knees. Sliding his hands up the sides of her legs, he cupped the firm flesh of her bottom in his hands and pulled her against him. The shudder that rippled through her drew him deeper inside. "Look at me, Anne-Marie," he demanded, pulling her harder against him.

Her eyes opened, dazed and smoky with need. Every breath she took burned, every pulse of her heart sent fire coursing through her veins. Her skin, super sensitive, felt hot and tight, as though her body was trying to turn inside out on her. An explosion was building within her and when it finally broke free, it was going to make that little mini-orgasm seem like raindrops in the ocean.

She couldn't breathe and she couldn't focus or think. His cock throbbed inside her and instinct had her tensing her inner muscles, tightening around him. That made the ache inside all that much worse. But she couldn't stop herself from doing it again and again. His hands came up, stroking up her thighs and capturing her knees. He pushed them up against her chest and his eyes burned into hers as he rolled his hips against her.

He was so deep inside her she hurt. The way he watched her had her flushing consciously and then he touched her, rubbing his thumb around and around her clit until she bucked and cried out his name. She tried to rub herself against him, but he kept her pinned down so that she couldn't. The loss of control was terrifyingly erotic and Anne-Marie wasn't sure what was going to win out, the terror or the hunger.

"Jazz, please," she gasped out, her torso twisting, arching off the couch. He fell forward, pinning her body to the couch, his shoulders wedged between her knees.

Her muscles were squeezing him tight, clamping around him, holding him. Staring blindly up at him, her face flushed, lips red and swollen, hands seeking. "Come with me, Annie," he whispered. He watched her face as he drove deep within her.

She shook her head, trying to pull away from the storm that was brewing within her. "Yes," he demanded gutturally. "Yes." He surged forward, burying himself in her body over and over, lifting her to him. "Yes."

At his words, she plummeted, falling headfirst inside a seething volcano. There was more lightning—more thunder, more of everything. She felt caught in a maelstrom of pleasure, with heat suffusing her body in waves, washing against her, within her. The pleasure seemed to batter her, going on and on. His cock jerked inside her and she felt the heat of it as he came inside her.

A choked cry tore from her lips and she strained up against him, everything within reach. He pulled out, drove deep within her one more time. She fell apart underneath him, shattered into a million tiny pieces.

And when he pressed a soothing kiss to her temple, he put the pieces back together again. The low moan that rumbled through his chest vibrated throughout her body and she held him close. She smiled slightly, knowing that she had been right about him all along. He made her whole.

With his heart pounding against hers, she slept.

&

"What did you end up doing with yourself, Jazz?" Anne-Marie asked softly, later that night. Her hand traced an absent pattern on his chest, her head tucked against his shoulder. "You never told me what happened after you left here. What you've been doing."

"Whatever I could, for the longest time. I had to delay going into the Marines until I healed up but I ended up only serving a year." A faint, bitter grin tugged at his lips. "Training op went bad and my leg was messed up six different ways to Sunday."

With a frown, Anne-Marie pushed up onto her elbow so she could look at his leg. "Damn," she whispered as she studied the jagged, twisted scar. His kneecap looked a little off center and judging by the numerous neat surgical scars, he'd gone under the knife for corrective surgery a time or two. "Does it bother you?"

He shook his head, not even glancing down. He held a lock of her hair and rubbed it between his fingers. "No. Aches some if it gets too cold and I might limp some in the winter, but other than that?" He just shrugged.

"So you had to leave the Marines?"

"Yeah. But I'm fine with that." Finally, a real smile appeared as he glanced up and said, "I was told I had issues with authority."

Anne-Marie widened her eyes. "Really. You don't say," she said, her voice deadpan. Lying back down beside him, she curled up against him with her hand on his chest. "So after that, where did you end up? Where have you been living all this time?" she asked.

"Around," he murmured. But she wasn't going to let it go at that. She heard the reluctance to talk that lingered under his voice, but Anne-Marie paid it no attention. She was so hungry for everything that had to do with Jazz, had so much time to make up for.

And so many empty days ahead for which she had to prepare.

Jazz wouldn't stay around, and Anne-Marie knew, certain as she knew her own name, he wouldn't let her go with him when he left.

"Buffalo," he finally said on a sigh. "I've lived in Buffalo, New York, the past nine years."

"And what do you do in Buffalo? Are you an arm breaker?" Anne-Marie guessed, smiling against his bare skin. "A professional hockey player? A male dancer?"

Gripping a lock of silky hair in his hand, Jazz gave it a good sharp yank, smiling when she yelped. "You are still every bit as nosy as you ever were, Annie."

Pulling up, rubbing at her scalp, she scowled at him. "Pardon me, but I wasn't aware it was rude to inquire about your bedmate's life."

With a hoot of laughter, Jazz asked, "How do you do it? How can you sit there, naked as a jaybird, and act as regal as the Queen of frigging England?"

Pursing her lips, she primly replied, "It's a gift. And you are trying to change the subject."

Flopping onto his stomach, staring out at the dark sky, Jazz groaned. "I write, Annie. Okay?"

Her lips fell apart in a surprised gasp and she rubbed at her ear. "Excuse me, Jazz. I'm sorry, but it sounded to me like you just said that you write. You mean write as in, writing for a living."

"It hasn't always been for a living. Started out as something to keep my sanity while I was in rehab for my leg. Then for a while, it was to keep food in my mouth and gas in the tank while I wandered around the Bible Belt." He flopped over onto his back and met her eyes, a little reluctantly, it seemed. "My pen name is J.C. McCoy and I write for AdventPub."

"AdventPub. McCoy," Anne murmured. "McCoy. Wait a second, you write that guy, uh, Vince?"

"Vance," he corrected wearily, waiting for the censure.

"Daddy reads those sometimes," she whispered, a frown sitting on her face. With a wrinkle of her pert nose, she added, "Not exactly my taste, though."

"Your dad reads them?" he repeated dumbly.

"Yeah. Every once in a while, he gets tired of medical journals. We both do. He picks up one of those and I pick up a romance." Reaching up, Anne rubbed her temple with her forefinger, still frowning. "I can't believe this. You write?"

Where was the disapproval?

Didn't she know what kind of trash it was?

But Desmond read them. Confused, Jazz sat up, turning to

103

look at her in the soft moonlight. "Yeah, I write. Not exactly Nobel prize-winning stuff, though."

"Nobody calls romance Nobel material, either. But I love to pick one up whenever I have time," Anne-Marie said with a casual shrug. Her eyes narrowed thoughtfully as she studied him. "I don't quite believe it, Jazz, but I think you are embarrassed."

That confused, vaguely blank look still on his face, Jazz asked, "Your dad really reads them?"

"Uh-huh. So does my business partner, Jake. I believe he keeps one on his desk all the time." A smile lighting her face, Anne-Marie sat up and wrapped her arms around his neck. "Imagine that. Jazz McNeil, a big-time author."

"I wouldn't call writing Vance Marrone big time, Anne. You'd hate him. He's a jerk, a bastard and a user," Jazz said in a flat voice, shaking his head.

"He's also just a figment of your imagination, Jazz. One you created and gave life. Not everybody can do that," Anne-Marie said. "I certainly can't. I couldn't tell a story to save my life."

Stroking his stiff shoulders, Anne-Marie said, "You oughta be proud of yourself, Jazz. Most wannabe writers would kill to say they have as many published books as you do."

With a snort, he said, "They're welcome to him. I don't want him any more."

"If you don't like him, then write about something else," Anne-Marie suggested with a casual shrug of her shoulders. "I'm certain you can write anything you want to. A writer. Hot damn, Jazz. That's unbelievable."

Lowering them back to the bed, his arms holding her tight against him, Jazz let the dazed wonder wash over him. She wasn't unhappy about it, didn't disapprove.

Hell, she actually seemed proud of him.

Imagine that.

ℰↄ

Desmond sat in front of his computer, doggedly working to complete an article for the AMA. Why in hell had he agreed to this article anyway?

When the door whispered open, he didn't even hear.

I am supposed to be slowing things down, getting ready to retire. He sat back, flexing his hands, unaware as a shadow moved around the corner of the room to stand behind him. Staring at his hands, he hardly even recognized them any more. They were getting stiff, and every now and then, shaky. It only happened when he was worn out and he was careful to make sure he got enough rest, that he ate right, and did everything else required to keep his energy level up, but there was no denying the inevitable.

Desmond was getting old. No surgeon in his right mind operated with shaky hands. If he couldn't do surgery, then it was time to shut down the business. Or sell it out. *With hope, I'll find some young version of myself.* They needed his skills here in central Kentucky, needed them badly. They were only a half hour outside of Lexington but the small, rural county had many patients that wouldn't make that trip into the city to see a specialist for their ticker. Many of his colleagues had questioned his decision to return home and set up his practice. While dedicated physicians, they were caught up in the business of being a highly regarded doctor with their business luncheons, weekends spent golfing, skiing or a thousand other things that didn't interest Desmond in the least.

He wanted to be a doctor and he wanted to help people. In Lexington, good physicians were a dime a dozen, but here...here he did some actual good. It was time to let it go, though. He knew that and he could even accept it. Mostly. Once more, he opened his fingers and spread them wide before resting them back on the keyboard.

But just as he started tapping at keys, he paused. Something white drifted at the edge of his line of vision. Desmond turned to look just as a click sounded right behind his head. Before he could see anything, his world exploded right before his eyes.

And he felt nothing else.

Hours later, at nearly dawn, Jazz lay awake with her curled against his side, sleeping soundly. *What in the hell have I done?*

As if life hadn't been complicated enough. He turned his head, studying her profile in the pale moonlight. He had spent the better part of his life holding himself responsible for the death of her older brother, a brother she had adored, and rightly so.

Alex had been a golden child, smart, kind, compassionate. He'd had a quicksilver temper and a heart of pure gold. He had died his eighteenth summer, right before he would have started college. There was no sense to it.

Jazz was tired of trying to make sense of it, had spent too much time trying to do just that. But some years ago, it had dawned on him how very little the puzzle fit. He remembered only fragments of that night after leaving Maribeth's, but there was one thing that stood out in his mind.

Jazz hadn't lingered around town long after he'd been released from the hospital and all he knew about the accident was what little he heard in whispered tones—and what Larry had crowed about. Jazz, driving drunk, had killed Alex.

But it didn't make sense. Although the backseat had been littered with empty cans of Miller beer, Jazz hated the taste of beer and wouldn't drink it. Period.

∞

Pleasantly sore and content, Anne-Marie opened her eyes, staring up at the ceiling. Jazz lay in bed beside her, face buried against a pillow. His shoulders rose and fell rhythmically with every breath he took. Reaching out, she traced her hand against the mellow gold of his skin, marveling at how smooth it felt, how firm the muscles were beneath it.

She was a medical doctor. Damn it, she could name every muscle that made up those wonderful shoulders, that long, elegant back, and what purpose they served. But all the knowledge meant nothing, not when she was able to simply lie there and admire him. The human body in itself might well be a miracle, but the miracle of Jazz's body was something else entirely.

Mmm, one thing was certain, if the females in school could use him during anatomy, the drop-out rate probably wouldn't go sky high before they even made medical school.

Anne-Marie sighed and settled more comfortably against him. This was going to complicate things. That was a fact.

But she didn't regret it, not for one instant.

Closing her eyes, she said silently, *You would have wanted this, Alex. You would have wanted me to be happy. And Jazz can do that. I know it.*

She rolled onto her side, just watching him while he slept, while the sun slowly edged up over the horizon. Once the sun's rays were pouring into the room, she sat, studying the long form under the simple, white sheet. It followed the dips and rises of his body, clinging to one particular rise.

With a cat's smile, she threw the sheet to the foot of the bed. For a minute, she sat there and just admired him. The length of his sex jutted upright against his belly, hard and firm. His body gleamed like gold against the white sheets, all sleek, sexy muscle and long limbs. His belly wasn't a perfect six-pack, but it was flat and as he stretched a little, the muscles there rippled, drawing her eye and tempting her to reach out and touch.

She did, but she didn't settle for the smooth, practically hairless expanse of his chest or abdomen. Instead, she straddled him and wrapped her hand around his cock, holding him steady as she took him inside. He was buried deep within her before his eyes opened. She rolled her hips slowly, from side to side, back and forth, until she found the rhythm she wanted. Hands braced against his chest for balance, she rode him slowly, watching his face.

She was just starting to shudder with climax when his eyes locked on her face. "Annie," he muttered. Then he grabbed her hips, flipped and twisted, burying her underneath him, and driving deep inside her. He pressed his lips to her mouth and muttered, "That's one hell of a wake-up call."

She might have laughed but he pushed his tongue inside her mouth, kissing her like he had been starving for the taste of her. Anne-Marie wrapped her arms around his neck, arching up into him. One big, rough hand palmed her ass, lifting her up and holding her steady for each deep, hard thrust. "Scream for me, Annie," he whispered roughly. "Come for me. I want to feel it again."

Like she had been waiting for just that, she climaxed,

clenching around his length, hard and fast. Distantly, she heard his hoarse groan as he followed her into oblivion.

$$\text{\large �&}$$

"I like the way you wake up," he said appreciatively, gliding his hand over the curve of her bare hip.

"Hmm," she murmured sleepily, her mouth curving up in a smile. "I'm hungry."

With a bark of laughter, he raised his head and looked at her. "Now that is one romantic lady I ended up making love with, Annie—did they teach you that in med school, Doc?"

"Nope. I always wake up hungry. I learned that in the cradle," she replied. "Got food?"

Why isn't this awkward? he wondered moments later as he headed downstairs to fix breakfast. Why had it felt so right to go to sleep with her beside him? To hold her throughout the night and know she'd be there in the morning. And waking up inside her...sweet heaven. Nothing had ever felt that right.

Part of him insisted he should feel guilty over what had happened, but he couldn't. As much as he might have wanted to, he hadn't seduced Anne-Marie. She had known what she wanted and had taken it.

Taken him.

Hell, if anything, she'd seduced him. A faint grin curved his lips but it faded as fast as it had come. He'd loved Anne-Marie his whole life. He'd loved women before. His mother and Sheri. He'd cared a lot about Sandy, might have even loved her a little. But it all paled compared to what he felt about Anne-Marie Kincade. Letting her go was going to kill him. Jazz lowered himself onto the bottom step, rubbing the heel of his hand over his heart. How on earth could he let her go?

Why should you have to?

The voice whispering in his mind didn't even seem like his own and he felt an even bigger fool when he jerked his head up, searching for somebody else in the house. Only Anne-Marie, padding around upstairs in one of his shirts, waiting for food and coffee.

But why in hell should he have to let her go?

He was breaking eggs open when he heard the shower kick on. Whistling under his breath, focused on the job of preparing breakfast, he was so preoccupied, he never heard the car drive up.

When the knock came, he frowned. He ran a hand over his bare chest then through his hair before he headed for the front door. They'd never gotten around to locking it, he noticed. Pulling it open, he squinted into the bright sunlight, staring in puzzlement at his cousin.

Hat in his hands, Tate was staring at the little red sports car with a frown on his lean face. Beside him stood Larry Muldoon. It ate at Tate that he'd had to bring Larry along, but being first on the scene...

"Hey, Tate. Little early for visiting, ain't it?" Jazz asked, dismissing Larry with less than a glance.

"Well, Cousin, it seems we have a bit of a problem."

"Is that so?" Looking from Tate to Larry and back again, he leaned in the doorjamb and crossed his arms over his chest. "And exactly what is the problem?"

"Where were you last night?" Larry asked, his chest all puffed out with self-importance.

Sliding Larry a single look, Tate calmly said, "I will handle this, Deputy. If you don't like that, then you know your way back to the station." Turning his gaze back to Jazz, he studied the eyes so like his own and wished to God Jazz hadn't come back home.

"I'm afraid I'll have to ask you your whereabouts for last night, Jazz," Tate said, mouth grim, eyes shadowed and dark.

"What's happened, Tate?"

"There was a shooting, attempted murder. And a witness placed you in the area."

"That would be rather...difficult, considering he was in bed with me all night," a soft, low voice said from the stairs.

Jazz turned, staring at Anne-Marie as she walked down the stairs, one hand trailing on the banister. Her hair was wet, slicked back from her face, leaving it unframed. The shirt draping her body covered her adequately, but there was nothing sexier than a woman wearing a man's shirt. Slim, shapely legs were bared to the mid thigh and the cuffs were turned back to reveal well-toned arms.

All in all, just the sight of her had him hard and ready. And jealous as hell. He didn't want Tate or Muldoon seeing her that way. But he wasn't so stupid to think he could tell her to go get dressed, either. So instead, he held out his hand to her, realizing how very right it felt to do just that. When her hand rested in his, he drew her closer, tucking her against his side.

"Dr. Kincade."

She nodded politely at Tate, glanced at Larry and away again. "Exactly what is the problem, Tate?"

"The problem is that there has been a shooting, an attempted murder. We had a call that Jazz was seen in the area at roughly three this morning." When Muldoon opened his mouth, a steely glare from Tate silenced him once more.

"That would hardly be possible, Tate. Jazz is a talented

man, but it would be difficult, even for him, trying to commit murder at the same time he was on top of me," she replied, silently aligning herself with him. "And that is pretty much how we spent the entire night."

"You'd be willing to testify to that?" Tate asked evenly.

"Of course," Anne-Marie replied, her voice level, her eyes clear and direct.

"Your daddy would be ashamed of you," Larry snarled, poking a bony index finger her way. "Rolling in the sheets with trash like him."

Anne-Marie turned bland eyes his way and smiled. "Oh, hello, deputy. I didn't notice you standing there." Running a languid hand through her damp curls, she aimed sultry, green eyes at him and drawled, "What's the matter? You jealous?"

Witch, Jazz thought once more. Heaven and hell, this woman had been born a seductress.

"Anne-Marie. I've been trying to get a hold of you. Called the answering service and they said Jake Hart was on call. And I couldn't reach you through your pager," Tate said.

Tate's words pulled Jazz's attention away from Anne-Marie. *Murder.* Tate was here because somebody had accused him of trying to kill somebody. He remained silent, thinking, as Anne-Marie leaned back against him.

"I needed a night away from that thing," Anne-Marie said, talking to Tate when all she really wanted to do was turn around and press her face to Jazz's chest. The warmth of his flesh seeped through the shirt she had swiped from his closet. It smelled of him, soap and musk. She smelled of him, she realized with some satisfaction. "What did you need me for, Tate?"

When Larry opened his mouth, Tate turned to him and said in a lethal voice, "Say another word and I will have your badge,

Deputy. I mean that."

Something about the tension in Tate got through to her and she straightened. "Tate, what's wrong? You really are serious? You think Jazz could have actually tried to kill somebody?" she asked quietly, unaware she had reached for Jazz's hand, gripped it tightly.

"No," Tate said honestly. Then he blew out a harsh breath. "But the fact of the matter is, we did receive an anonymous tip, just like I was telling Jazz when you...ah...joined us."

She exploded, shoving away from Jazz and planting herself in front of Tate. "That's nothing but a load of crap, Tate McNeil. Jazz isn't a killer."

"Now, Anne-Marie—"

"Don't you *now, Anne-Marie* me," she snarled, mimicking his coaxing tone. "I can't believe—"

"Anne-Marie."

Jazz spoke quietly, but nonetheless, it cut through her rage more effectively than anything Tate could have said or done. Slowly, she turned to look at him, scowling.

He gave her a lopsided smile. "Why don't we see what Tate has to say before you try to gut him?" He slid his cousin a look and despite his easy tone, she saw the worry in his eyes.

"Thank you, Jazz," Tate said softly. The sheriff looked back at Anne-Marie. "You say you were here all night, Anne-Marie? You and Jazz, you have some troubled history."

She nodded slowly, responding, "Yes. I was here all night. I'm a big girl, Tate. I choose where I spend the night. I chose to spend it here. Our history together was Alex. And we both loved him."

Sullen, Larry stood watching in silence as Sheriff McNeil questioned and reported the things that he should have been doing. Damn McNeils, nothing but a bunch of no good, low account bastards.

And that slut, Anne-Marie, with her witch's eyes and witch's hair tangled about her shoulders, standing there in nothing but a shirt. His eyes locked on the front of that shirt, where hardened nipples pressed against the cloth, licking his lips even as he damned her for being everything he wanted and couldn't have. Wanting her and knowing she had spent the night with the likes of Jazz McNeil, it was enough to make him want to puke. Or slap her. Maybe both. He could see it, the red print of his hand on her face, her lying on the ground in that tangle of hair. He could jerk that shirt off of her and shove inside her and make her beg. Make her plead.

He'd like that. And maybe, just maybe, before he was done, he'd have it, too. That was almost as much fun to think about as it was going to be when Tate told her what happened.

The words passing around Larry barely registered as he sidled a little closer to the door, but as he edged closer, Anne-Marie backstepped and Jazz's eyes focused on him. Deliberately, Jazz urged her a little farther inside and stepped in front of her, shielding her from Larry as he responded to Tate's question.

"Well, this does make things a bit easier, Jazz. But you will have to come down to the station. We need to take a statement," Tate finally said, tucking away the pad he had been doodling on as he jotted down notes.

"Mind if I ask who I supposedly tried to kill, cuz?" Jazz asked, his jaw clenched tight. A sick feeling was spreading through his gut, one that had to do with the odd, strained way Tate kept glancing at Anne-Marie, the way Larry's jaw had dropped when she had come sauntering down the stairs.

"I'm afraid I've got some bad news for the both of you," Tate said slowly. As Jazz wrapped a supporting arm around Anne-Marie's waist, his cousin reported, "Sometime early this morning, at approximately three a.m., somebody broke into your father's house, Anne-Marie. And he was shot. Whoever it was tried to kill him. And it would appear they are wanting to point a finger Jazz's way."

A swirling, black mass rose within Anne-Marie, darkening out everything for just a brief moment. When her eyes cleared, she was sitting cradled in Jazz's lap on the stairs, shuddering wildly.

"That can't be true, Tate," she whispered. "There must have been a mistake. Daddy is home, working in the garden."

"No, honey." Kneeling down in front of her, reaching out, and taking her hand, Tate said gently, "Your daddy is in surgery in Lexington. He took a bullet in the chest."

Surgery.

He took a bullet in the chest.

Somebody tried to kill him.

No. It couldn't be real. Looking up at Tate, she shook her head and said, "No. That can't be right."

"I'm sorry, Annie. I really am," Tate said, clenching his jaw when she continued to stare at him with those weeping, heartbroken eyes.

"Oh, God," she moaned. Tears welled in her eyes and she turned her head to stare at Jazz. "I can't lose him, Jazz. I can't lose Daddy, too."

Jazz wrapped his arm around her neck and pulled her against him, holding her close. "He's strong, Annie. He's healthy." Trite words, meaningless, but he could think of nothing to say to her, no way to help her. "If anybody can make it through, it's the doc."

Himself, he was numb, too shocked to really feel anything just yet. "I'm going to Lexington with her, Tate. You can take that statement there, or you can get it some other time. But I am going with her to Lexington."

Tate sighed, reaching up to rub at his neck. "I can take it tomorrow," he finally said, clenching his eyes shut. "Ya'll best get going. I'll get a deputy to give you an escort."

"Hey! He's been reported at the scene of a crime. You have to take him in for questioning," Larry snapped, gesturing towards Jazz.

"He was reported through an anonymous phone call and he has a damned good alibi. I'll take his statement when and where I choose, Muldoon. Now take yourself off to your cruiser," Tate said quietly, a subtle threat in his voice. "I mean that."

"But he—"

Anne-Marie shot up off Jazz's lap, tears rolling down her cheeks. Face flushed, eyes shining, she moved in a whirl of motion and before they even realized her intent, Larry Muldoon was laying on his back, staring up at her, blood gushing from his nose. For a brief moment, all were quiet. And then Jazz started applauding, Tate was hiding a smirk behind his hand, and Muldoon was cursing viciously.

Hands steady as a rock, face once more composed, Anne-Marie turned to Tate and said, "I'll turn myself in for striking an officer after Daddy is stabilized." Then she held out a hand to Jazz. When he folded his hand around hers, she linked their fingers, raised his hand to her lips, and kissed it. "Let's go. Daddy needs us."

Chapter Six

Desmond could feel himself pulling away, leaving his body. As he drifted further away, he looked around him and was pleased to see that he had been right. There wasn't just some empty maw of darkness. Not dark at all. Desmond could see his body down on the operating table, colleagues trying to pound and force life back into him.

His life was leaching away, but instead of feeling sad about that, Desmond felt just fine. There was a beautiful, golden light glowing just ahead of him and when he got there, he'd be with his boy again. And his wife. His pretty, pretty Anna—dear God, he'd missed her. But he was going to be with her again, and soon.

He liked knowing that he'd been right about what happened when the body died. A lot of his colleagues didn't think there was anything after death, but Desmond had known otherwise.

Death was just another beginning, not an end. He rather wished he had the chance to tell them, but it was time for him to move on. *Useless, old buddy*, he thought fondly as he studied Jeb Munroe's haggard face above the blue surgical mask. His long-time friend barked out an order for epi. They started another IV line and Desmond automatically flinched as he watched, even though he didn't feel a thing.

Their voices came from far off. "Come on, you mean old sonovabitch! Don't do this to Anne-Marie." That was Dr. Munroe there, former classmate and lifelong friend. The other soothing tones were from the anesthesiologist and the assisting M.D.

Drifting further and further away, the voices got fainter and fainter.

And then they were gone altogether, and he was alone, drifting through the gray fog, drifting closer and closer to that warm, golden light. No. Not alone.

A familiar, beloved presence wrapped around him, and there was a voice he could hear only in his heart. But even as he drifted closer, something stopped him, an answer of sorts, to a question he didn't recall asking.

Don't do this to Annie.

೮౩

It wasn't easy being the one in the waiting room, Anne-Marie thought, staring at the clock as the second hand circled the face endlessly. Theoretically, she knew this, but this was the first time she had ever experienced it herself. Her father had been in surgery for nearly eight hours now.

"He can't die, Jazz," she whispered. She'd thought she was cried out, but as she spoke, the tears started again "He can't. I'm not ready to let go of somebody else."

He locked his arm around her neck, pressing a kiss to her wavy, black hair. "He's going to be fine," Jazz murmured.

More time passed as she pressed her face against his neck, taking comfort in his presence, in his strength. Anne-Marie shifted closer, rubbing her cheek against the smooth cotton of his T-shirt. Her mind bounced from one thought to the next, confusing, unconnected thoughts and disjointed phrases.

A phone started to ring, intruding on the silence she had cocooned herself in, and she turned her head toward it with a frown. It was then that she replayed the conversation they'd had with Tate just that morning. An anonymous phone call.

From the circle of his arms, she watched as the receptionist lifted the phone and spoke quietly into the receiver. "Somebody wants it to look as though you did this," she said softly, anger starting to kindle inside.

"I'd have to agree," somebody said from the doorway. Together, they looked toward Tate as he entered the waiting room. In his hand, he loosely held a plastic evidence bag. "It would appear that our culprit left this behind." Dropping into a seat, he held up the bag to display the single hair in the bag.

"I'd lay money that it's yours, cuz," Tate mused, sliding his fingers up and down the seam of the bag. "If it wasn't for your very tight alibi, I'd be taking you to the station for questioning. As it is, Anne-Marie coming down your stairs this morning saved your butt."

With a frown, Jazz reached out, taking the evidence bag and holding it aloft. "The haircut," he murmured quietly, running his free hand through his recently shorn hair.

"At the salon in town? Mama mentioned seeing you there," Tate mused, taking the bag back. "That seems the most likely possibility. Which means the majority of the possible suspects are little, blue-haired ladies, Mama, and Laura."

"And Maribeth. She works there," Anne-Marie said quietly.

Jazz snorted in contempt. "She doesn't have the kind of brains to pull something like this. Cold-blooded enough, definitely. But having the smarts to do it? No way."

With a frown, Anne-Marie conceded he had a point. "Did

119

Larry Muldoon have anything to do with this?" Anne-Marie asked, her brow puckering with worry.

"I doubt it," Tate said, shaking his head. "This takes more cunning than he or Maribeth Park could ever hope to possess. More brains. You were an unexpected addition, one Jazz's secret admirer couldn't have planned on." With a slight grin, Tate added, "I certainly never would have expected it."

With a tired sigh, he rose, shoving his thick hair back from his forehead. "Jazz, have you got any idea who'd want you implicated for murder?"

Jazz held Anne-Marie securely against his side as a tiny whimper escaped her lips. He shot Tate a cold glare before pressing his lips to her temple. "Annie, he's gonna be fine." As he rocked her back and forth, he stared at Tate. "This isn't a good time for this," he said flatly. "It can wait until tomorrow."

"Damnation, Anne-Marie," Tate muttered, slapping his hat against his thigh. "I'm sorry. Punchy. Haven't slept in nearly two days."

She offered a trembling smile before turning to the man who held her securely against him. "Jazz—" Anne-Marie tried to push him away, her eyes bright with unshed tears.

"It can wait," he repeated. "I'm not leaving here until we know if Doc Kincade is going to be okay. And I'm not discussing this here. So why don't you go on home and get some sleep?"

With a slow nod, Tate replaced his hat on his head. "I'd like—" His words faded away as the door swung open a second time. Clad in baggy, blue scrubs, his eyes weary, Dr. Munroe entered.

Jeb Munroe studied the woman before him with tired eyes. This wasn't a colleague before him now, but the daughter of a patient. Never mind the fact that she had studied under him before deciding to pursue pediatric medicine instead of surgical.

"Anne-Marie," he greeted, holding out his hands.

She took them and held tight. "How's my father?" she asked, her voice wavering.

"Hanging in," he said, smiling at her. "We're cautiously optimistic at this point. You know how important the next twenty-four to forty-eight hours are. But he is strong, he is healthy, and he's got an angel on his side. Otherwise, he never would have survived this long."

"How bad was the damage?"

"He has a long groove on his head, along the right side of his skull. My guess would be that he heard somebody coming up behind him and moved. The person shot again, this time in his chest. The bullet was lodged along his spine, but there's minimal damage there." He paused, sighing. "Normally, I don't do this, but Annie, I'm going to sit down."

Dropping his face into his hands, Jeb took a deep breath, fighting back the tears of relief that threatened to overflow. Friend or not, doctor or not, she was the family of a patient right now, first and foremost.

Oh, the hell with that, Jeb thought viciously. *If physicians couldn't be human in front of other physicians…*

"Anne-Marie, your father is one hell of a strong man. We lost him, twice, on the table. And each time, I swear to God, I thought we'd lost him, and he came clawing back. I've seen my share of fighters on the table and I always figured your dad to be one, but I've never seen anything like it, Annie. It's a bloody miracle. The surgeon in me knew he was gone that first time, but I just couldn't give up. Then he came back."

A sob caught in her throat as Anne-Marie's knees gave way. Falling back against Jazz, she stared at Jeb with terrified eyes. "And now?" she asked, her voice breaking.

Raising his head, Jeb stared at her with eyes that still bore traces of baffled wonder. "He's stable, Annie. I've never had a patient undergo a surgery like that, lose that patient twice, and then stabilize so quickly after surgery."

"He's going to be okay?" Jazz asked, rocking Anne-Marie, pressing a kiss to the top of her bent head.

"I think so. We're not out of the woods yet. The problem was that the bullet tore through the left lobe of his lung, pierced the pericardial sac. He had a large amount of internal bleeding. He's undergone several blood transfusions and will need more before this is through."

As he spoke, Anne-Marie straightened, taking deep breaths until her racing heart calmed a bit. Clamping her hand tight around Jazz's, she told Jeb, "We're the same type. I'll donate after I see him."

"What type is he?" Jazz asked.

"O positive," Anne-Marie and Dr. Munroe replied at the same time.

"Me, too. I'll donate, if you think he would allow it," Jazz offered, his voice hesitant, his eyes uncertain.

She offered a teary smile and said, "I'd say it's only fair. He always said you and Alex cost him a lot of blood, sweat and tears. You've already given him sweat and tears, waiting here with me." Forcing herself to take a deep breath, she looked back at the surgeon. "You lost him twice on the table, Jeb. How can he be stable?"

"Because your dad's the luckiest son of a bitch this side of heaven," Jeb replied, only half joking. "Your daddy and I had an angel with us in that operating room, Annie. That's the only thing I can tell you."

ꕤ

Tate settled in at his desk, rubbing his hands across tired eyes. Across from him sat Jazz, his face haggard and exhausted. "How's Doc Kincade?" he asked, picking up his pen and twisting it absently between his fingers.

"Stable. That's all they'll say right now. He's stable. He's healthy, he's strong." He blew out a frustrated breath and said, "Anne-Marie is taking this whole thing too calmly, if you ask me. Shoot, she's had to grab hold of me a couple times to keep me from strangling that damned surgeon."

"The not knowing is one of the worst parts," Tate agreed, pressing pen to pad and doodling absently. "What we have here, Jazz, is a big-ass problem. Somebody went and leaked it already that you were supposedly spotted at the scene of the crime, and that Anne-Marie is your alibi. A particular woman, who shall remain nameless, has suggested that this is a scam you two cooked up for his life insurance money."

Snorting, Jazz shifted in his chair. "Anne-Marie's Mama left her a trust fund. She doesn't need a life insurance policy."

"Nobody's paying much mind to the rumor, except to laugh at it. Nobody believes Anne to be capable of something like that." He rocked the chair back on its hind legs and studied the dog-eared picture of him, Jazz, and Jasper Sr. at the lake, a gap-toothed Jazz proudly displaying a scrawny bass. Tate figured he'd been all of four years old when that picture was taken, the summer that Jasper Sr. died. "But it still creates a problem."

"I'm real sorry about that, Tate. I hate that I'm making your job more difficult."

Tate hurled a brief four-letter word at him as he dropped his feet back to the floor. "Help me out here and tell me who you think is responsible for this."

"I have no idea. If not Muldoon, then your guess is as good as mine." He remembered the eerie feeling in the salon a few weeks back when he and Mariah had had their hair cut. But he said nothing. Tate would just laugh if he went and tried to point a finger at little, old blue-haired ladies.

"Nothing? Nobody? No guys who might hate you for sleeping with their girlfriend back in high school? No girls you dumped and humiliated?"

"I usually waited until after they broke up with the boyfriend. As for the girlfriends, hell, I never had a real one. Well, except for Sandy. I was with her most of senior year and all that summer, but she couldn't do this. I know she couldn't. But she was the only one I actually stayed with for any length of time. I didn't like the idea of just seeing one girl then."

"I suppose that would cramp your style a bit," Tate said with a tired grin. "But just because you didn't think it was serious, that doesn't mean some girl didn't think otherwise." As he considered the possibility, his grin faded.

"Ain't that your job to figure out?"

"I'm going to be working in the dark on this, Jazz," he responded testily. "Pretty much solo. Larry doesn't have too many friends, but too many remember his family. They haven't got it in their heads yet that Larry was the cowardly one of the bunch, the stupid one. Too many people here still act like toadies of his. If somebody overhears something, it may wind up back at Larry's desk. I don't want that."

He shoved the chair back from the desk and rose. "So if you don't mind, I'd appreciate any information you can give me." He threw his pen down on the battered desk surface before dragging a hand through his already tumbled hair.

Jazz dug the heels of his hands against his tired eyes. "Tate, I'm sorry. It's been a really shitty couple of days, you know that?" Slouching low in the chair, he wished it were Saturday night again and he was in bed with Anne-Marie wrapped around him.

"Help me out, Jazz."

"I can't. I can't. I have no idea who could have done it, besides your number one deputy, that is." Throwing his arm over his eyes, he blocked out the light, aching for his bed. "Quite a few people here hated me, Tate. You know that. After Dad died and Mom married Beau, they forgot about Dad, and the fact that he was a good man. I became Beau's brat, and I was a mean bastard anyway."

He echoed Tate's muttered curse silently, forcing his eyes back open before he fell asleep. "If Anne-Marie hadn't been with me, I'd be locked up right now, wouldn't I?"

"Yes."

"So there's a possibility that whoever did this may retaliate," Jazz murmured, sitting up straighter. His sleep-deprived brain cleared immediately.

"I've already thought of that. There's a state boy at the hospital with her." He fingered a tiny scar at the apex of his brow. Doc Kincade had patched that up when he'd just been a boy; never mind that Doc Kincade practiced a specialty. He's always been willing to help out anybody and everybody. Which made this mess that much harder to understand. "The doc's got quite a few friends around here. And in Frankfort. When I requested a couple of state troopers, they didn't even hesitate."

Jazz breathed a sigh of relief, even as he mentally kicked himself. He should have thought of that before now. What would he have done if something happened to her? Even as the tension eased from his spine, it returned, doubled in intensity. "I've got to get back to Anne, Tate."

Tate turned around, his mouth open to snarl at Jazz to sit

back down. But the odd strained look around his eyes had Tate groaning and pointing to the door. "Get the hell out. Call me if anything comes into that empty head of yours," he snapped, but the door was already closing behind Jazz.

&

"We'll be fine, Jasper. Now you go on," Mabel ordered. "Miss Anne needs somebody there with her."

He held Mariah against him, smoothing her silky, corkscrew curls and brushing a kiss across her brow. "Honey, I love you. I'll be back in a few days," he whispered. "Now you be good."

"I will, Daddy. Kiss Dr. Anne-Marie for me." She squeezed his neck tightly and then whispered, "I'll talk to Jesus tonight and tell him to help Dr. Anne-Marie's daddy."

He sighed, breathed in the scent of baby lotion and bubble bath one last time before he placed her in Mabel's large, capable arms. "Give Anne my love, Jasper. And my prayers for both her and her daddy."

Minutes later, he was speeding down the highway that led to Lexington. The thirty-minute drive seemed to take hours as he wove in and out of the midday traffic. He kept his hand ready on the cell phone at his side and gripped it while he alternated between praying and swearing. The wind whipped his hair around his face as he remembered the night he had spent with Anne-Marie wrapped around him, her silky hair caressing his shoulders, her small delicate body relaxed against his in sleep.

"God, I love her," he whispered, his whole body aching with the intensity of it. He hadn't let himself picture the worst, but now, he couldn't control it.

If Doc Kincade died, it would shatter Anne-Marie. She had already lost so much, her mother to leukemia, her brother to a drunken fool's mistakes, and now maybe her father. And that was on Jazz's shoulders as well.

Whoever had crept into the Kincade house in the dead of the night, whoever had put the gun to his head and fired, had done it to punish Jazz.

Hands clenching the steering wheel, knuckles white with rage, Jazz swore he'd make the bastard pay. Oh, yeah. He'd hurt Jazz all right, and nothing could have been more effective.

The phone ringing jerked him out of his reverie. He snatched it up, flicked the talk button and held the phone to his ear, pulling to the side of the road so he'd be able to hear. Emergency flashers on, his head fell back against the headrest as Anne-Marie spoke softly in his ear.

That low, soft, southern drawl caressed his ears, soothed the ache inside him. Anne-Marie told him Desmond was doing better than they could have even hoped for, surprising all the doctors and nurses.

"He opened his eyes and smiled at me, Jazz. I think he's gonna be fine."

"Thank God," Jazz muttered, pressing his fingers against the sockets of his tired eyes. "Thank you, God." He waited until the lump in his throat eased a bit before he asked, "How are you feeling, Annie?"

"Tired. Exhausted." As she leaned back from the bed, her voice took on an edge. "And madder than hell. Who did this, Jazz?"

She rose from the chair, paced to the window of the private room, staring out at the horizon. "Who did this, and why?"

"I don't know the who yet, but I will. And as for the why..." His voice trailed off as he wondered what he should say, how he should say it.

Anne-Marie hadn't forgotten the plastic evidence bag Tate had shown them. "It was yours, wasn't it?" she asked quietly. Leaning her head against the cool pane of glass, she listened to the steady beeping from the machines behind her that assisted her father in breathing while his body healed.

"Technically, I don't know for sure. But my gut says yes."

"Then there is just one more thing this person will have to pay for," she promised quietly. "One more thing, on top of this."

Anne-Marie turned, propping the phone on her shoulder and crossing her arms around herself for warmth. The smells of ammonia, disinfectant and death lingered in the air. Nothing could remove the taint left by death.

She said, "I've always believed that what goes around comes around. I prefer to wait for that sort of justice. I'm usually too lazy to expend the effort that hatred requires. But what I wouldn't give for five minutes alone with whoever did this."

ꝏ

A doctor could no doubt dream up incredible ways of making the human body suffer an undetermined amount of time. As Anne-Marie sat watching her father sleep, waiting for Jazz, she imagined a few, wishing she was cold-blooded enough to actually see a few of the ideas through.

Such as tying the bastard to a bed and opening up one vein at a time. Disembowelment. Shattering each bone in his feet, one by one, and then working her way upward. She choked on a sob.

"Oh, God," she whispered. "He can't die."

Strong arms encircled her, lifted her, and then she was lying against Jazz's chest, crying her heart out in silence. Jazz...he was back. The pent-up emotion escaped once more and she sobbed in his arms, choking on her tears as she tried to keep quiet. She wept until her throat ached, until her whole body ached, wept until she could weep no more. Her hands reflexively gripped and released Jazz's shirt as she cried out her misery, cursed out her rage, and eventually calmed enough to rest against him.

"I think I needed that," she said, her voice rough.

"Any time, darlin'," Jazz offered, pressing his lips to her temple. He reveled in the softness of her, the strength, the miracle of holding her in his arms. Oddly enough, her storm of tears had comforted him as much as it had her.

"I'm glad you came back home, Jazz," she said, raising her head to look at him, her eyes red and swollen, face pale from stress and exhaustion.

"If I hadn't come back, this wouldn't have happened," Jazz told her, brushing her hair back from her tear-stained face. Nobody had ever looked more beautiful, he knew, and nobody ever would.

She shook her head. "Don't blame yourself, Jazz. Whoever did this is the one responsible, not you." She turned her head, resting it against his shoulder as she stared at the figure in the bed. So still, so quiet, he barely resembled the indomitable, formidable, lovable Desmond Kincade. "He wouldn't want that and we both know it."

Wrapping both arms around her, he held her against him, his chin resting on the top of her raven hair. The beeps and hum of machinery were the only sounds as they kept vigil. It wasn't until the sun was dropping toward the horizon that she spoke again.

"Who could have done this, Jazz?"

"I don't know, Anne-Marie. I don't know."

"He went to a lot of trouble to set it up. The phone call, that hair. Could it have been a cop, do you think?"

"It wasn't a cop," Jazz said, unwrapping her arms from his neck. Pressing a kiss to each palm before he released her hands, he turned away. "Somebody who knows how the game is played, yes. But it wasn't a cop."

"How do you know?"

"Gut instinct," he said, lifting his shoulders in a shrug. "For one, a cop would have made certain..." His voice trailed off as he looked at Desmond. He was hooked up to machines to breathe, monitors of every kind imaginable, tubes going this way and that, but none of that mattered. Because he was alive, and therefore a loose end. An officer of the law wouldn't have left loose ends, at least, not a smart one.

Anne-Marie paled as she realized what Jazz was thinking. "Is he safe, do you think?" And then she shook her head. "Of course, he isn't safe. That's why there is a state trooper outside the door. Why no phone calls are patched through to me. He's being watched, isn't he?"

"Tate arranged it. But it's fairly routine. The only difference is that with your dad, there is no shortage of off-duty volunteers."

"But..."

"Tate selected the three himself. I trust his judgment. I—" The door swung open and Jazz smiled. "Well, speak of the devil."

Tate nodded to Anne-Marie, tipping his hat her way before

approaching the bed. "How is he?"

"Stable," Anne-Marie said, her voice soft. "He made it through the golden hours. He's gonna be fine. Just fine." Her drawl deepened as she spoke, a sign of how distressed she was. "He has to be."

Tate averted his eyes as Jazz wrapped his arms around Anne-Marie, murmuring into her hair. Idly, he studied the cards adorning the walls, since flowers weren't allowed for patients under intensive care, private room or not. He hummed under his breath, checked his watch, until out of the corner of his eyes, he saw Anne-Marie pull away, wiping at her eyes with the back of her hand.

"Your daddy is a strong man, a good man. He will be fine," Tate said. Resting a hand on her shoulder, he met Jazz's eyes. "You look beat, old man."

"Not looking too hot yourself, cuz," he drawled. "Is this interrupting your sleep?"

Tate smiled tiredly. "You could say that. Every woman in town, and half the men, are half-hysterical right now, thinking that they will be murdered in their beds. And Mom is a basket case. You know how much she admires your daddy, Anne," he said, shoving a hand through his hair.

Tate really did look exhausted. His normally spotless clothes were creased and wrinkled, limp from the heat, and his face was pale, eyes strained. "Jazz, if you have a moment, I need to speak with you."

Jazz nodded and lowered his head once more to Anne-Marie. Tate left, the door closing softly behind him.

Out in the hall, leaning against the tile wall, he closed his eyes. Marlie. No. He didn't care what in the hell anybody had to say, Marlie Muldoon couldn't hurt a fly. They were the same age, had gone to school together. Marlie was Beau and Larry's youngest sister, a late-life surprise that had nearly killed her Mama when her daddy had learned she was pregnant. He'd beat her so hard, it was amazing the pregnant woman had lived through it.

He had used that girl as a whipping post all her life, until he had died some years back, leaving her to support herself and her mother. Beau and Larry hadn't helped, nor had anybody else. Marlie had to do it on her own.

She was stronger than anybody thought, Tate knew. There was pure steel under that soft voice and silky, pale skin. But there was also a good heart. Marlie couldn't have put a gun to Desmond's head to save her own life.

When the door swung open, Tate looked up at Jazz and snapped, "I hate anonymous tips, y'know that?" Whirling away from the wall, he stomped toward the stairwell. "I hate them."

Falling in step behind him, Jazz asked, "Any particular tip you are talking about? Or did you drive thirty miles just to let me know not to leave you anonymous tips?"

"Somebody left a message on my voice mail, for crying out loud. Said they'd seen Marlie Muldoon near Doc Kincade's quite a bit recently."

Jazz scoffed, shaking his head. "No way. Not Marlene. That girl wouldn't hurt a soul."

"I know that," Tate said. "But somebody wants her to take the fall for this, since you have an alibi. It was a .38 used to shoot Doc Kincade. Marlie owns a .38, but apparently, it's gone missing. She doesn't recollect the last time she saw it."

"Lemme guess; the gun turned up at Doc Kincade's?"

"No. It's not on the property, at least not anywhere we've searched. And we've been pretty thorough." Cursing roundly, Tate leaned against the cool, concrete wall in the stairwell. "We're going to have to question her."

132

Jazz stared at him for a minute before turning away. "Marlie and I have never had any trouble, Tate. The only thing that connected us was Beau, and he's long gone."

"That's true. But it's also true that your Mama killed Beau. Some folks may see fit to believe that she'd do this for revenge."

"You don't buy that."

"No. I don't. But it doesn't change the fact that I'm going to have to question her and spend time clearing her, when I could be looking for the bastard that did this."

Tate turned his hat in his hands idly, shaping the brim, releasing it. His voice was mild, his gestures and stance relaxed, but when he raised his head, the fury he felt inside simmered just below the surface. "And it's not going to change the fact that there is a lunatic out there focusing on people I care about."

Resting back against the wall, Jazz studied the gray, concrete ceiling over his head. "I don't know who could be responsible, Tate. I've thought it out and tried my damnedest. But I keep coming up blank."

"You don't think it's Muldoon?"

A sneer curled Jazz's mouth and he glared at Tate. "Gimme a break. He was the only person I could think of right off the bat. But hell, he's not the only person who hates me. That chickenshit ain't got the guts. Of course, shooting somebody in the back would be just like him. But I doubt he could handle the blood."

The corner of Tate's mouth curved up and he agreed, "There is that." Still turning his hat round in his hands, he focused his eyes on the stairs in front of him. "The thing is, these days, too many people have too much information about how the law works. They know about planting evidence, disposing of the weapon, disposing of clothes and so on. That's going to make things more complicated than they already are."

Wishing vainly he hadn't given up smoking, Jazz dug into his jeans in search of gum. "Well, hell. I may as well go ahead and complicate things even more. I'm worried the lovely, young Dr. Kincade may start nosing around."

"Talk some sense into her, then," Tate snapped. "Can't you talk some sense into her?"

"Well, I could try. But that isn't how her mind works. If you go telling her not to do something, then she'll do it just to be ornery."

"Shit," Tate muttered. Shoving off the wall, he started to pace the narrow stairwell. "That's the last thing I need, her poking her pretty little nose into things. It's a damned mess already."

Raising his shoulders in a careless shrug, Jazz said, "I didn't say she was going to sneak out of the hospital tonight to go play Nancy Drew. But I suggest you offer her some answers real quick, otherwise she may decide to try to figure this out on her lonesome."

"If it was that easy, don't you think I'd have closed the book on this already?"

Jazz shrugged, popping a flattened stick of gum in his mouth. The artificial flavor of cinnamon did nothing to relieve his need for nicotine, or the tension settling in his neck. "I'm just sharing this with you, Tate. She's going to get antsy real quick, once he is out of danger."

"Your girlfriend wants to play Nancy Drew and you stand there blowing bubbles and smiling. You plan on being a Hardy Boy next?" Tate asked sarcastically. "Have you considered that Anne-Marie may be a target, since she screwed up the original plan? Or don't you have a thought in that thick head of yours?"

"I thought of it," Jazz said, straightening and meeting Tate's stare eye to eye. "And I decided I wasn't going to let her out of my sight. If she decides she wants to start nosing around, I'll be right on her back. Nobody is going to touch her, Tate. They'll have to go through me first."

"A bullet can go through both of you!"

"What do you want me to do? Lock her up? Why don't you do that, then? Lock her up for wanting to know who did this," Jazz growled, glaring at the face that was so similar to his. "She's already lost her brother and her mom, Tate. Find who did this so she doesn't lose her father."

Whirling away, Tate swore roughly. "I don't need this. I've got an attempted murder on my hands, damn it."

"Then don't you think you should be working on it instead of trying to boss me around? That's a waste of time anyway, and you know it."

Glaring at him, Tate slammed his much-abused hat on his head, shot him an obscene gesture, and then took the stairs at a lope. "Be where I can reach you tonight, Jazz. We got more to talk about."

Chapter Seven

Anne-Marie arched back, so utterly weary. She hadn't been this tired even back during her internship. Talk about emotional stress...

Shifting her shoulders, she tried to find a more comfortable position in the hospital chair from hell. On the bed, Desmond slept on, healing slowly, but surely. Four days out of surgery and he was doing well. They took him off the ventilator two days ago and he was breathing on his own.

In a few more days, they would transfer him out of CCU and onto a regular floor.

She didn't like his color, though. Gray and thin, he was finally starting to show his years. His head was shaved along the right side of his scalp, the four-inch-long tear covered by a bandage and iodine. The rest of his hair was limp, filthy. As soon as he woke up, she was going to get him a bath.

Of course, knowing him, she'd do better to have a few pretty, young candy stripers do it. With a sad smile, she decided if he would only wake up, he could have those candy stripers by his side doing a striptease, even if she had to get one from a strip joint in Lexington.

Since those first few times he had opened his eyes to acknowledge her, he had done nothing more than sleep. Granted, he was sleeping a healing sleep, one he needed

136

desperately.

When the door opened, she turned her head and met Jazz's eyes. He came up behind her, wrapping his arms around her, resting his chin on the top of her head. "I hate to have to do this, but you are under arrest," he told her, slowly pulling her body up out of the chair.

Rolling her head back against his shoulder, she smiled up at him. "I am? What for?"

"Failure to take proper care of yourself. You've been sentenced to spend the night at the hotel down the street to get some rest, a decent meal."

"I don't want to leave—"

"I know that. But that is what you are doing. Because the doc would want you to take care of yourself. It's not going to help him any if he wakes up and finds out you're in the bed next to him."

"But—"

"No buts, Dr. Kincade. You're getting a good night's sleep in a real bed." Pivoting her in his arms, he cupped her face and raised it to his. Brushing her lips with a gentle kiss, he whispered, "You do the crime, you do the time. And your time is a real meal, followed by some decent sleep."

"You're not a cop, or a sheriff. Isn't it illegal to impersonate one?" she asked, tipping her head back as he trailed a line of kisses down her jaw line.

"I've got a badge right here in my pocket. You wanna see?" he teased, nudging his hips against her middle.

"Mmmm. Okay. I'd hate to have resisting arrest on my record."

Jazz felt her sigh brush against his mouth as she relaxed. She watched him from under her lashes as she said, "You know, speaking of taking care of yourself, you don't have to live at the bedside with me. You've got that pretty, little girl to take care of."

"Heading back tomorrow. Which is why I intend to see that you rest tonight," he responded. "I'll be back in a day or two and if I know you, you'll still be sitting right here. So tonight—you rest."

Linking her arms around his waist, she said, "Then you had better keep a close eye on me. I'm sneaky. If I'm left alone, I'll make a break for it."

"I was going to keep an eye on your dad."

"No need. The nurses will call if anything changes. And he's going to be fine," she said, her voice somewhat shaky. "I know that. He's too strong not to be."

"You know that, huh? Then why is it you have spent the past four nights in this hospital, why is it you use the shower in the doctors' lounge and wear OR scrubs?"

With a quick smile, she replied honestly, "Because I don't like hotel rooms. And I didn't want to be alone in one." Rising on her toes, she bit his lower lip and said, "If you come with me, that won't be a problem."

With that single action, the blood drained from his head and pooled in his groin. Catching her hips in his hands, he pulled her flush against him. "I think you're trying to bribe your way out of your jail time."

Smiling against his lips, she murmured, "Can't blame a girl for trying, can you?" Anne-Marie yawned and grinned up at him. "Okay. I'll do the time. A bed is starting to sound mighty tempting, Jazz."

"Am I still invited?" he asked, grasping one hand and lifting it to his lips.

"Whenever you like," she offered, reaching up with her free hand and brushing his cheek with her fingertips.

As she turned away to gather up her things, Jazz smiled sadly. Just how long was that offer good for? He couldn't imagine a time ever coming that he wouldn't want her. Hell, why would there be one in his future when there hadn't been one in his past?

"Jazz?"

Jerking his head up, he snapped out of his morose reverie. He looked up to see her standing a few feet away, watching him with curious eyes. "Are you okay?"

"I just hate having to leave you alone here," he told her, moving closer. He gave in to the urge to touch her again and ran his hand down her hair.

"I'll be fine, Jazz. Daddy's going to be fine. Besides, your little girl needs you. And you need her. You've been with me since Daddy was shot. It's been four days since you went home."

He knew. That ache in his heart was the only reason he was willing to leave Anne-Marie's side for even a minute. "I'll come back up in a few days—"

"No. Once Dad's stable, we're transferring him to County Hospital until he is ready to go home. I can't stay away from the practice for the time it's going to take him to recover. In a week or less, I'll be home."

She moved to Desmond's side, stroking his cheek. His eyes fluttered a bit as she leaned down and whispered, "I'm going to get some sleep, Daddy. I'll be back in the morning."

Straightening, she smoothed one hand down her limp ponytail and said, "I just need to let the nurses know he needs a bath. And then I need one."

"Don't bother with a nurse for yours. I'll help," he told her, offering her his arm. Tucking her hands in the crook of his elbow, they left the room. Behind them, Desmond lay on the bed, a small smile hovering at his lips.

&

Face turned up to the forceful spray of water, Anne-Marie hummed in pleasure as several days of grime sluiced off her body. Filling her palm up with the shampoo she had insisted Jazz stop and get, she lathered up the length of her thick, black hair, breathing in the scent of vanilla and spice. Twice more, she lathered up her hair before rinsing and reaching for the conditioner.

As she turned her back to the spray, she sighed in satisfaction. Her eyes drifted open, then opened wide and she yelped. Jazz had entered the room, pulled the curtain back a bit and was watching her with a strained smile. "Baby, you know, just looking at you right now is a turn on," he told her, lifting one leg and bracing the flat of his foot against the wall behind him.

"You scared the life out of me," she breathed, pressing a hand to her naked breast, waiting for her heart to return to normal.

Jazz didn't respond as his eyes drifted down from her slicked-back hair to her smoothly rounded shoulders. Trickles of water ran down her torso, clung to the neat patch of hair between her thighs, ran down her long, curved legs. With the heat of the shower making the air thick and dense, she looked like a water goddess come to life. Need ripped through him with vicious intensity.

How long, he wondered again. How long would she want

him?

It would never be long enough. So he had to make what time he had count.

He reached for the buttons on his shirt, pushing off the wall.

Cocking a brow at him, she asked, "What do you think you're doing?"

"I'm feeling pretty rough myself. I thought a shower would help me, too," he told her, shrugging out of the shirt. He shucked his work boots in seconds, unzipped his jeans and shoved them down his legs along with his boxers.

"Hmmmm." Anne-Marie said, "I suppose that would be okay. We should conserve water, you know."

"In the name of conservation, then," he agreed, stepping into the wide shower stall and adjusting one of the showerheads to his height. Using his body to protect Anne-Marie from the spray, he wetted his hair down. Then he moved the showerhead back and stepped closer to her.

Conversationally, she said, "This is really a wonderful suite. I love the bathroom." Her voice shook slightly as his hands closed over her hips and their bodies aligned. "Nice and...big."

Chuckling, Jazz replied, "Yeah. I kinda like it, too." Backing her into the wall, he lowered his head and took a pointed nipple in his mouth. Her breath caught in her throat as he applied a delicate suction. Droplets of water pelting her, the heat of his mouth on her, Anne-Marie felt like she was caught in a wild summer storm.

Raising his head, Jazz caught the nape of her neck in his hand, arching her head up to meet his. He took her mouth desperately, almost violently. Her hands closed over his shoulders, kneading the smooth muscle there as his hands cupped her hips and lifted her. "I can't wait," he muttered, nudging against her.

Locking her legs around his waist, arching up against him, Anne-Marie responded, "I don't want you to." A gasp fell from her lips as he imbedded his length within her, withdrew and slammed into her again. Reaching up, she laced her fingers in the wet silk of his hair, holding him against her.

Jazz reached behind, unlocking her ankles and hooking his arms under her legs, opening her body wide before driving deep inside her. As her muscles started to contract around him, Jazz slowed, nuzzling at her ear. "This isn't gonna last," he murmured in her ear.

Water pounding her from the sides, the cool tile against her back, and Jazz thrusting against her, Anne-Marie fell even deeper into the storm. A soft low moan escaped her lips only to be swallowed by his as he covered her mouth. Diving deep, he stroked the inside of her mouth, withdrew to nip at her lower lip.

Soft, wet silk—sinking inside of her was like sinking his dick into soft, wet silk. Her sheath rippled around him, squeezing little convulsions that would drain him dry. Jazz shuddered at the pleasure that came with each and every move she made. As she gasped out his name, he buried his face in the curve of her neck so he could breathe in her scent. He bit her lightly on the neck and she responded with a ragged, hoarse moan.

"Jazz..." She whimpered, trying to get closer. Held as she was, unable to move, completely vulnerable... Who would have known that could be such a turn on? A helpless thrill shot through her when she tried a second time to move and couldn't.

Her eyes fluttered closed, a long moan escaped her lips.

"You look at me," he whispered. "Open your eyes, Annie. And look at me." As her dark green eyes opened, eyes the color of the forest at dusk, he asked softly, "Who do you see?"

Jazz couldn't control the storm raging inside him any longer. Thunder pulsed in his head, his gut, in his cock. Water pounded him from the outside, waves of longing and love from the inside.

It was her. It had always been her. The need to mark her, to bind her to him gnawed at him. And the hopelessness of knowing it would never happen. But he had now. Now she was his. He asked her again, "Who do you see?"

She stared at his face, a face she had tried to picture time and again over the years. A face she would see in her mind every day for the rest of her life. "You," she told him raggedly. "Just you. Just you, Jazz."

Releasing her legs, he moved closer, until not even a breath of air could come between them. Her hands slid up and locked around his neck. Staring up at him through slitted eyes, she said, "Kiss me, Jazz. Like you did that first time."

Covering her mouth, he let the storm inside him take them both.

ᏽ

Dawn was breaking when Anne-Marie woke alone in the bed. The sheets beside her were still warm. Reaching out, she ran her hand over them, before fisting her hand and pressing it to her mouth.

"Did I wake you?" a low, husky voice asked.

Turning her head, she saw Jazz sitting in the chair by the bed, chin propped on his fist. "No. What are you doing up so early?"

"Watching you."

Self-conscious, she tugged the sheet up as she sat in the bed. Looping her arms around her legs, she asked, "Why?"

"Because you're here. Because you're beautiful. Because I want to," he answered, smiling slightly, as if laughing at some inner joke. "Sleep well?"

Shrugging, she fussed with the sheet, with her tangled hair, her hands, as she waited for the blush staining her cheeks to fade. "Better than I have been. Not as good as I will when I can sleep in my own bed." Then boldly, she raised her head, met his eyes and added, "Or yours."

His eyes widened before crinkling at the corners as he grinned. "Feel free to invite yourself any time you wish, Doc Kincade. Any time at all."

Smoothing the wrinkled sheet over her lap, she smiled primly and said, "I believe I just did, Mr. McNeil." And then her face sobered and she sighed. "It will be some time though, before I can do that." Resting her head on her bent legs, she stared at Jazz. "What's going on, Jazz? Why would somebody want to kill my father?"

Tears welled in her eyes, but only one spilled over. It trickled down her cheek and she brushed it away absently. "Everybody likes him," she said quietly. "He's a good man, a good father. He doesn't drink, doesn't steal, and doesn't cheat." She laughed a little. "Of course, there's this widow in New Haven he goes to visit. He thinks I don't know. Daddy's been alone a long time. I can't expect him to stay alone always just because I can't picture him with anyone but Mama.

"She's been to see him quite a bit. Always after I've left the room," she told him, the corner of her mouth curving up in a small smile. "I leave the room more often now that I know she is out there."

"Why?"

"Because Daddy, for some reason, didn't want me to know. I think it started out as something casual, each one comforting the other, maybe. But I think she loves him. Maybe he loves her. He squeezed her hand, once. I came in that first time, not knowing she was there. And she was sitting talking to him. She's a bit hard of hearing, I think. Anyway, she didn't hear me come in and she was standing up, telling him goodbye. And I saw his hand tighten around hers."

"How do you feel about that?"

"If it makes him happy, then I'm happy for him. Mama has been gone a long time, Jazz. It would be selfish of me to want him to stay alone simply because she was no longer here."

Leaning forward, Jazz traced his fingers down the curve of her cheek. "There's not a selfish bone in your body."

"Yes, there is. And it has your name on it," she told him, taking his hand and holding tight. Lacing her fingers with his, she turned her eyes away, not seeing the intense look in his eyes. "Why did this happen, Jazz? Who would want to hurt my dad?"

Shaking his head, he answered, "I don't know, Anne. But we're going to find out."

Turning her head, she met his eyes once more. "Are we?" she asked, her voice calm, casual.

His was anything but when he tightened his grip on her hand as he rose and settled down on the mattress next to her. "Yes. We are."

∞

Tate had a secret passion. For fairy tales, of all things. Books of folklore, myths and legends lined the walls of his office at home. He loved to draw and had since he was a kid. That was part of the reason he was bullied so much when he was little, not just because he'd been so overweight and clumsy. Hidden in the drawer of his desk was a leather-bound journal, stuffed full of drawings of leprechauns, elves and faeries.

Maybe that was why he had always felt drawn to Marlie Jo Muldoon.

She looked like a faerie, tiny, delicate, pale. She barely stood at five feet in her stocking feet and had yards of pale, silvery-blonde hair that she wore in a neat braid down her back. Quiet, shy, she always seemed to hover at the edges, watching all that went on around her, but never really reaching out and joining.

How she came from something like Jackson Muldoon was something nobody could fathom. Though she looked as insubstantial as a mist, Tate had a hunch that there was more to her than most thought. From time to time, something lively and passionate would dance across her face before being subdued.

Wide, blue eyes, eyes the color of the eastern sky at sunset, deep, dark indigo, dominated her small, pale face. Right now, they were full of nerves and barely restrained temper.

"Tate, what are you talking about?" Marlie asked. Her voice was just as soft as the rest of her, whisper quiet.

Tate had to lean forward and concentrate to hear her. "Marlie, I need to know where you were on May fourteenth, Friday night."

"I was at home with Mama." A sad smile curved her mouth and she spread her hands wide. "That's where I am every night, Tate."

"Your Mama can verify that?" he asked, already knowing the answer.

146

Her mouth firmed and her eyes darkened. "Mama has a hard time verifying her own name, Tate. Much less what I was doing last week." Leaning back in the kitchen chair, she asked, "What is this about, Tate? I think I have a right to know."

A slight grin tugged at his mouth. *Yep, I was right. There is some of that sass I knew existed.* He lowered his eyes back to his notepad, adding faerie wings to his sketch of Marlie. That was what she ought to be doing, he thought with disgust. Flitting through a field of wildflowers or dancing on the limbs of a dogwood. Living in a castle somewhere.

Not sitting here in this ratty, dark, depressing house while he questioned her about an attempted murder.

With a deep sigh, Tate threw down his pen. "You were supposedly seen by an anonymous caller out on Old Bluecreek Road several times in the weeks before Dr. Kincade was shot."

"And what on God's earth would I be doing there?" she asked, her eyes puzzled. "I don't think I've ever been out there."

"That's what I am trying to figure out, Marlie. How do you feel about Dr. Kincade?"

"The older one? I don't know. I've never met him, really. Daddy used to mumble about him from to time, but that was long ago. He seems like a nice enough man. I know he did little Macy Conroy's surgery for free. Didn't charge a penny for his services. And he takes on a lot of patients that can't afford him."

"What about his daughter?" he asked, keeping his voice impassive. Nobody would have guessed that just sitting here was making his gut clench with anger and regret. He hated having to put this woman through this. She'd already taken on so much.

"Anne-Marie?" she asked, her voice fainter than normal. Her eyes darted away from his face and her ivory complexion

147

paled even more. "She's a nice lady."

"You look a bit odd there. You have a problem with Anne-Marie?"

"Larry talks about her a lot. And her father. He hates both of them."

"Is there a reason why?"

She raised her eyes and looked at Tate. *He's so beautiful,* she thought wistfully. *So kind.* Her cheeks flushed a delicate shade of pink and she raised her shoulders in a shrug, forcing her mind back to the conversation at hand. "Because they have money. We don't. People like the Kincades, they don't like us."

Reaching across the table, Tate took her tiny hand in his. On the back of her right wrist was an old rounded, puckered scar, the kind caused by a burning cigarette. Rubbing his thumb over that mark, Tate said, "You're not like them, Marlie. You never have been."

A smile trembled at her mouth before she looked away. All around her, there were signs that she was like them. She was a Muldoon, whether she liked it or not. The dingy kitchen that she could never get clean, no matter how hard she tried. The old linoleum, the stove that barely worked. The small lawn outside was cropped short, emphasizing the bare patches of dirt where nothing would grow.

What little money she had leftover from working at the salon, that didn't go to keeping her and Mama fed, she spent on Mama's medicines and spare parts for the car that always fell apart. She couldn't remember the last time she had gone into a store and bought a dress off the rack. She either purchased most of her clothes from a second-hand store or made them.

Thinking back, she pictured how Anne-Marie Kincade had looked the Sunday past, wearing a simple, yellow sheath that spoke of understated elegance. The strand of pearls at her neck had been real, Marlie was certain, as had the simple diamond solitaire she wore on her right hand. Beautiful, smart and kind. The money, though God knew Marlie had so little of it, wasn't even the thing she envied most. It was the animation that seemed to surround Anne-Marie. She was so full of life, something Marlie doubted she'd ever experience.

With a faint smile, she took her hand from Tate's and folded her hands neatly in her lap. "But I'll never be like her, will I?"

"The only thing you have to do is be yourself," he said, duty and office forgotten. Those eyes were so sad, so empty.

"I doubt this is why you came here, Sheriff," Marlie said quietly, her eyes going carefully blank. *I won't take your pity,* she told him silently. It was bad enough when she had to accept it from others, their pity mixed with derision.

But to take it from him...

How would he react if he knew she wanted nothing more than to sit on his lap and hold him? That she woke every morning thinking of him after spending nights dreaming of him?

He'd be uncomfortable, embarrassed, and most likely, even more sympathetic than he already was.

"So your Mama can't exactly be counted on as an alibi, right?" he asked drolly. In the other room, he could hear Marlie's Mama talking to her eldest son, dead nearly two decades now.

A glimmer of a smile flirted with her lips and she shook her head. "I'd rather it not go down in the books that she was outside chasing my naked bottom around so she could put a diaper back on me."

Tate chuckled, acknowledging with a raised brow that it was a distinct possibility. Just the other week, she had flagged

149

down a deputy on the county road and asked if he could please find her lost chickens.

The Muldoon farm hadn't been able to support chickens for more than five years. The empty pen that had once been Naomi's small pride lay neglected.

"Tate."

Waiting until he looked at her, she asked, "What reason on earth would I have for wanting to hurt him? What could I hope to gain?"

"Marlie, I don't think this is anything more than an attempt to distract me, to waste time and confuse things. I'd no sooner think you were a murderer than I'd think your daddy was a priest." He sighed and rubbed his hands over his face. "Godamighty, Marlie. What in the hell is going on? Things like this don't happen in Briarwood."

"You can't find whoever shot Dr. Kincade, can you?" she asked softly, twisting her hands in her lap. She wanted to walk over to him, soothe the lines worry had put on his face. Instead, she focused her attention on the matter at hand. She sighed, shaking her head. "Do you even know why? It doesn't make sense."

"I think it has something to do with Jazz coming back home," he admitted roughly, dragging his hand through his closely cropped hair.

"You don't think Jazz did it," she guessed.

"No. I know he didn't. He couldn't have. But who in hell would want to hurt Doc Kincade like that? He has got to be the kindest, most generous man in the county. He's like...Santa Claus."

"So apparently the Grinch was out that night," Marlie said, looking down at her folded hands. "Jazz got into a lot of trouble when he was younger, didn't he?"

"Yeah, he did. But nothing major until—"

Until the night Alex Kincade died.

"Uncle Larry isn't smart enough to have done this," Marlie said, her voice matter of fact. "He'd be able to pull a trigger, I think, but not cold-bloodedly. He couldn't concoct a plan like this."

"My thoughts, exactly." With a glimmer of a smile, he said, "Not too bad for a manicurist, Marlie."

Her cheeks tinted a pale pink and her eyes darted away. "I prefer to think of myself as a hand-accessory consultant," she said, so seriously it took Tate a moment to realize she was joking.

When he realized it, he couldn't keep from grinning. He held his own hands in front of him, studying the calluses, scars. The nails were neatly clipped, short and clean, the palms wide with long, agile fingers. Flicking hers a glance, he said, "I'll have to admit your hands look much better than mine."

She smiled again, a little wider this time, as she held one hand out for inspection. The pale pink polish gleamed in the light, the cuticles well tended. Her own hands were small, not much larger than a child's. "You'd look a bit odd with cotton candy pink on your nails, Sheriff."

"I would, at that," he agreed, as he took his notepad and tucked it in his breast pocket. The silver of his badge gleamed against the white, workman's style button-down he wore tucked into a pair of jeans.

At the moment, he almost wished he was anything but the county sheriff. Raising his head, he stared at the faerie sitting in front of him, watching him with wide, serious eyes.

"Damn it, Marlie," he muttered as he rolled the brim of his hat in his hands. "You're going to have to come in and let me take a statement. I hate having to do this."

"But you have to get it over with so you can concentrate on who really did it," she finished as his voice trailed off. "Don't worry, Tate. I'll be fine. I'm tougher than I look."

Tate thought she was tougher than she should have had to be, but he didn't say that. He placed his hat on his head, tipped the brim her way. "Try heading out tomorrow morning before you go to the salon. We'll get it out of the way as quick as we can."

With an understanding smile, Marlie agreed. Moments later, after locking the door behind him, Marlie turned, her hands still clutching the door knob, her back pressed against the door.

Her eyes closed dreamily, a smile curving her mouth.

ꙮ

Three days later, Desmond stabilized enough to move to the county hospital. Anne-Marie knew it was going to be a few weeks yet before he could leave the hospital. But just having him closer to home, closer to her, eased her mind a bit. Chatting brightly about a visit from a mutual patient, Anne-Marie ignored the narrowed stare her father was giving her. For the past twenty minutes, he'd been trying to get an explanation out of her, but she couldn't figure out what to say, didn't know if she should say anything yet.

Her father, though, wouldn't be put off. "I think I know myself well enough to know whether or not I can handle the truth."

Deepening her voice, raising her eyebrows, she quoted, "'You want the truth? You can't handle the truth'."

"Don't go getting cute with me, young lady. I want some

answers."

She turned away from the flowers she was fussing with and raised her hands futilely. "I don't know. I don't know what happened, Daddy. Nobody does. Somebody went into your house and...and shot...shot you," she finished, the ache in her throat making it hard to talk, much less talk coherently.

"I know that. What I want to know is what you aren't telling me."

Sighing, Anne-Marie lowered herself into the armchair next to the bed. Was there any point in trying to lie? No. Absolutely none. He could always see right through her. She closed her eyes, pressing her fingertips against her eye sockets. "He made it look like Jazz had done it."

"Excuse me?"

So that was where she got it from, Jazz mused, standing just outside the door. He had gotten there just in time to hear Anne-Marie tell Desmond, and to hear Doc Kincade's frosty reply. With a change of tone and lift of an eyebrow, he made Jazz feel like a dumb fool, and he wasn't even talking to him.

"You heard me well enough, Dad. They planted some physical evidence and made a phony call, saying he'd been seen in the area at the time."

"Good Lord," Desmond muttered. "How much trouble is the boy in?"

"None. It was a set-up and Tate figured that out quick enough. But he doesn't have any idea who did it." She stared hard out the window, hoping he wouldn't ask any more questions.

"Well, thank God for that," Desmond murmured, running a weak, shaky hand across his eyes. "I... What else is it you aren't telling me, girl?"

"Sheesh. And to think I've always considered myself a good liar."

He grinned widely and said, "You are. Unless you're trying to fool your old man."

Jazz stepped through the door, hoping to divert Desmond's attention. Anne-Marie turned and met his eyes just as he stepped over the threshold. She smiled a sweet, almost ethereal smile at him before looking at her father and replying, "Well, it's not exactly easy to tell your father that you spent the night with any man. Circumstances being what they are, I suppose you can understand why I'm having some trouble with this."

"Doc Kincade—"

Jazz opened his mouth to speak, only to have black eyebrows rise as fiery, green eyes focused on his. And then that stern face softened and Desmond smiled tiredly. Closing his eyes, Desmond said, "I can't say it surprises me. No, it doesn't surprise me at all." He shifted around a little and then shook his head at Anne-Marie when she started his way. "Don't start fussing over me. I got the nurses for that."

"Daddy, you look tired. Why don't you get some rest?"

"Going to be doing plenty of that, sweetheart." He sighed and closed his eyes. "You know, boy. I never thought about it; I guess it hurt too much. But maybe I should have thought about it. Because I have to agree with Annie. It just doesn't fit. I can't see you wrecking that car." And then he sighed, exhausted, and slipped back into sleep.

"He doesn't hate me," Jazz said. He looked over at Anne-Marie and asked, "Why doesn't he hate me?"

"He loves you, Jazz. You were his son from the time you came home with Alex that first night." *I loved you, too,* she thought. *What would you say if I told you that?*

"I killed his son, Anne-Marie. Your brother. I'm alive and he isn't. That is reason enough. But somebody put a bullet in him and tried to make it look like I did it. That there is another reason."

"You didn't put the bullet in him. The blame for this rests on one person, Jazz. And it isn't you."

Jazz stood with his hands tucked in his back pockets, staring at her with a closed expression. Standing with her back to the window, the fading sunlight glowing behind her, she looked too beautiful to be real.

How can I expect to hold onto a woman like that? How can she even want me touching her?

Hugging herself, Anne-Marie stared up at him. "I told myself I wasn't going to ask this; that there was no point in dragging the past up. I know it's been hard for you, Jazz. I was his sister by blood. You were his brother by choice. Losing him hurt you as much as it did me. Even as much as it hurt Daddy. It's taken me some time to realize that."

She closed her eyes, forcing herself to breathe. Then, opening her eyes, she quietly said, "I don't want to think of the other possibility. It hurts, but I have to know. Were you driving the car?"

Jazz sighed, his shoulders slumping. Sixteen years, and she was the first to ask. And he couldn't even give a certain answer. "I don't know."

"But that's why you came back, isn't it? Because you don't know?"

His voice rough, he said, "Anne, it just doesn't feel right. It's logical, it makes sense, and if it had happened to somebody else, I'd probably buy right into it. But it doesn't feel right." Dragging his hands through his hair, he turned and looked at her. "It's like I got halfway through a book and then somebody went and put another book in its place."

155

"I know."

He opened his mouth to apologize for not making sense, to try to convince her he wasn't crazy, he wasn't making excuses. And then when her words sank in, they knocked the wind out of him. "You know?" he repeated dumbly.

"Yes. I know. I was just a kid when it happened, Jazz. I don't remember much of the first couple of days; I think I blocked it out. But one thing I remember clearly is standing in room 116A in this hospital, seeing you lying there on the bed, and thinking, this isn't right."

"I could accept that he was dead, as well as a girl can accept something like that. Death was something I was pretty familiar with, after losing Mom and Grandma. And then your mom dying."

"I accepted his death, maybe a little too easily." She frowned a bit, shaking her head and whispering, almost to herself, "But I couldn't accept the story I was told." Turning back to the window, she rested the flat of her hand against the cool windowpane, staring out at the field of rolling grass. The sun sank lower to the horizon, painting the sky with colors of gold and red.

"I can't remember how many tickets Dad paid for. You drive like you belong on a racetrack somewhere. I've never seen anybody handle a car the way you do. You driving drunk? It's unlikely. But you crashing a car? I just don't see it at all."

He walked to her. In the fading sunlight, they stood at the window, staring out, but seeing nothing.

Taking a deep breath, Jazz decided if he was in for a penny, he was in for a pound. "Anne, there's one other thing. The back seat was full of empty beer cans. There were a few found at the lake."

She stared up into his eyes.

"I hate beer. The taste of it, the smell of it, it makes me sick; always has."

Her body went stiff as she remembered that. How had she forgotten? How? He hated beer, reminded him too much of his stepfather. It had come up one night when Desmond had been drinking a cold one out on the deck. Jazz, in his surly, teenage fashion, had curled his lip and sneered in Desmond's direction.

After skillfully drawing out the reason for that, Desmond had sipped a bit more from the bottle, looked at it and shrugged. "It's an acquired taste, son. But you have to remember, not everybody who acquires a taste for beer acquires a taste for roughing up women and kids."

Jazz had accepted that. For years, Jazz had associated the sight of beer with beatings. After time passed, the smell of beer or the sight of a bottle stopped turning his stomach and his knees no longer went watery. Still, he didn't like the taste of it.

So how had he gotten drunk enough to wreck a car on a deserted road that he could drive blindfolded and half-asleep?

ॐ

Irritated, Jazz stood in the doorway, watching as Maribeth climbed from her car. "What do you want?" he asked.

"You don't look happy to see an old friend," Maribeth purred, licking at her raspberry-red lips.

"I'd be happier to see a cottonmouth," Jazz said flatly, propping his naked shoulder against the doorjamb, eyeing her with acute dislike. "What in the hell do you want?"

She raised her shoulders in a shrug. "I thought we could just talk about old times."

"We don't have any old times to talk about. Alex was the

157

one fool enough to go out with you. I knew you were trouble from the get go," he told her, moving to close the door.

"But you wanted me anyway." She knew it; he had to have wanted her. All men did. In a low, sultry voice, she said, "Why don't you take what you wanted back then? Take it now."

He paused, looking back at her. "I never wanted you. When you're a horny teenager that sees a walking advertisement for sex, you're going to check it out. No matter how cheap or well used it may be."

Jazz ran his eyes over Maribeth from her head to her toes. She wore a form-fitting tank top and a skirt just barely long enough to be legal. Just as she had been sixteen years ago, Maribeth was still a walking advertisement for sex. Her small feet were shod in leather, gladiator-style sandals, her toes painted to match the red of her lips. "You haven't changed much. But I have. I didn't want you then; I may have wanted sex, but it had nothing to do with you.

"And," he drawled, leaning closer, until they were eye to eye. "I'd sooner go to bed with that cottonmouth than you."

"Is your little virgin doctor keeping you satisfied, then?" Maribeth asked in a brittle voice.

He straightened slowly, crossing his arms over his naked chest. Jeans rode low over his hips, and his hair was still damp from the shower he had just finished after putting Mariah to bed. "I don't even want you saying her name, Maribeth. You got that?"

"Sweet Saint Anne-Marie," she cooed, batting lashes thick with mascara. "You and Alex always called her that. Sweet, little girl never got in any trouble at all. Are you having fun corrupting her?"

The sound of a powerful engine drawing close cut off his answer. They both turned to watch the fire-engine red convertible fly around the corner. Top down, her long black hair blowing around her face, Jazz saw the exact moment Anne-Marie recognized Maribeth.

"Maribeth," Anne-Marie said in way of greeting as she climbed out of the car. She paused to grab a bag from the backseat and then slammed the door, walking towards Jazz with a smile. "Car trouble?"

Anne-Marie, her face scrubbed clean and devoid of any make-up, wore a pair of white capris and a blue-and-white-striped shirt. She looked every inch the young, rich girl that Maribeth had always hated. A gold chain gleamed at her neck and discreet diamonds glittered at her ears and on the ring finger of her right hand.

"I was just stopping by to chat with an old friend," Maribeth said, smiling brilliantly at Jazz.

"And who would that be?" Anne-Marie asked, arching an eyebrow at her. "I didn't know anybody lived here besides Jazz."

Narrowing her eyes, she glared at Anne-Marie as the young doctor mounted the steps, black leather bag in hand. Jazz left the doorway to meet her, taking the case from her as he lowered his head to brush her lips with his, ignoring Maribeth for the moment.

It's true, Maribeth realized with disgust. They were together, and in every sense of the word, from the looks of it. Why her? Sweet Saint Anne-Marie. She fought down the venom brewing in her throat.

"Why, Doc Kincade, me and Jazz have been...friends a long time," Maribeth finally drawled, sliding Jazz a suggestive glance. "Why, I lost track of how many times we would all go skinny-dipping at the quarry when we were younger. God, that water was always so cold, remember, sugar? But then you and Alex always knew how to get us warm again, didn't you?"

Jazz opened his mouth to speak but a low chuckle cut him off. He turned his head to see Anne-Marie rolling her eyes. "Alex may have been naive enough not to see right through you, but Jazz knew better."

Linking her hand with his, she eyed Maribeth with something akin to pity in her eyes. "Fantasize about your youth all you want, Maribeth. And about him now, if you must. Because that's the closest you'll ever get to him."

Maribeth tossed her tangled hair back and purred, "Why fantasize when I have memories?"

"What memories?" Jazz asked.

Anne-Marie merely stared at Maribeth as she slinked forward. *Scared little mouse*, Maribeth thought to herself as Anne-Marie continued to watch from eyes the color of the summer grass. Maribeth had to wear contacts to keep her eyes the pale green of her youth. Without them, they were simply hazel.

Testing her, Maribeth reached out and laid a hand on Jazz's chest. "You just let me know when you want to…talk old times." Smooth, hot skin and muscles rippled under her touch. Held in place by Anne-Marie's arm behind his back, Jazz reached up to knock Maribeth's hand away.

But a smaller, paler hand closed over Maribeth's wrist, thumb pressing just against the nerve, small, surprisingly strong fingers grinding the fragile wrist bones into one another. "Just because I let one man I loved touch you doesn't mean I'll let another," Anne-Marie said quietly, moving away from Jazz and stepping closer to Maribeth until she was glaring up at the woman who stood three inches taller.

She wasn't able to see the way his eyes widened, his lips parted when he heard her. Nor did she see the way he blanked his features after his gut told him, *Of course she loves you. She always has, just not the way you love her.*

"He's got better sense than that, but I'll warn you anyway. I'll destroy you if you so much as breathe on him, Maribeth," Anne-Marie promised, all but hissing with contempt. "And I mean that. You destroyed Alex. You won't hurt anybody else I love."

"Destroyed Alex? Whatever do you mean?" Maribeth asked, forcing a gay note into her voice. "We were high school sweethearts that drifted apart. Of course, I always meant for us to drift back again."

"Come off it. I know about the baby and the abortion," Anne-Marie said flatly.

Maribeth paled beneath her sun-lamp tan and her eyes went wide. Mouth twisting with hate, she snapped, "Then you know that it's Alex's fault the baby died." The baby she heard crying at night. "Let me go!"

Alex's fault. Alex's fault, she chanted silently to herself. Maybe if she said it enough, she would begin to believe it and those cries in the night would disappear.

Anne-Marie was no shrink, but she knew enough to recognize guilt. She threw Maribeth's hand down, away from her as if the other woman had the plague. Staring into Maribeth's tormented eyes, Anne-Marie realized, they haunted the woman. Alex and the baby. "No. It's your fault. I knew you were pregnant and when you didn't start showing, I figured out what happened. Dad confirmed it.

"I'm no fool, Maribeth. I can put two and two together. The way I figure, Alex had gone out to your house that night to talk about raising the baby, him and Daddy. They were going to give you money, that I know. But you had already decided: no ring, no baby.

"Alex was upset and he went to his best friend, who

happened to be across the street with his girl, Sandy. What upset him, Maribeth? You aborting that baby? Whose fault was it that he was upset? Upset enough he wanted to go and get drunk?" Anne-Marie asked.

"Damn it, he forced me to get an abortion," Maribeth hissed.

"Don't bother lying, Maribeth," Anne-Marie said dispassionately.

"You whey-faced, little bitch," Maribeth screeched. "Don't call me a liar." Reaching out, she placed her hand in the center of Anne-Marie's chest, muscles bunched, ready to knock the smaller woman down on her butt and stomp on her.

In a blur of movement, Anne-Marie caught Maribeth's hand, twisted, applied pressure at the wrist, and before Jazz could even shove off the doorframe, Anne-Marie had Maribeth pinned to the side of the house, arm twisted behind her back, shoved high between the shoulder blades. "I'd think twice before raising your hand to me, Maribeth," she said quietly, her voice a soft and deadly threat.

Maribeth brow throbbed from where it had smacked into the side of the house and her shoulder and arm were screaming with pain. Struggling, she learned quickly, was futile, causing pain to dance through her arm in hot, fiery licks. Under the vise-like grip of that small hand, Maribeth whimpered slightly. "Let me go," she whispered, her voice shaking.

"You killed my brother, Maribeth. You couldn't be any more to blame than if you had been driving yourself." Throwing her wrist down, Anne-Marie stepped back. "And you know that. So you go live with it. That's punishment enough, I guess. Seeing how miserable you've made yourself."

Turning, her shoulders braced against the smooth, painted wood of the house, Maribeth glared at Anne-Marie. "He won't be happy with you long, little girl. Sooner or later, even virgins lose their appeal. And then, don't be surprised when he comes to me."

Tilting her head, meeting those eyes with amusement, Anne-Marie said, "If he came sniffing after a bitch like you, then I would want nothing to do with him. You think I'd let him come to me after touching you?"

"What makes you think he'd want you after he had me?" Maribeth cooed, straightening, throwing her shoulders back, hip cocked out. Confidence and pure sexuality all but radiated off her.

Anne-Marie stared at Maribeth. "After having me, why in hell would he come to you?" Anne-Marie asked, laughing, the ageless knowledge of woman gleaming in her eyes.

With that, she held out her hand to Jazz and asked, "I was hoping to get invited to a sleepover."

He accepted her hand, turning his back on Maribeth as he led Anne-Marie like she was royalty. With his hand at the small of her back, he guided her across the threshold. Looking back, he met Maribeth's angry eyes. "She always did outclass you, didn't she? Right from the start."

§3

Outclass me?

The bitch, Maribeth thought as she sped down the highway, angry tears streaming down her face, smearing her make-up. "God, I hate her," she whispered. "And him. Both of them.

"This is all your fault, Alex," she muttered. "If you hadn't gone and died..."

Why couldn't he have just married her? All she had ever

163

wanted was to take it easy, not have to struggle. He wouldn't have to be faithful or anything. God knows Maribeth never had any intentions of sharing her bed with only one man the rest of her life.

Dashing at the tears with the back of her hand, she never even saw the car in the middle of the road, until it was too late. And then, she only had time to scream before she hit the Buick head on, going sixty-nine miles an hour.

Chapter Eight

Marlie Jo Muldoon stood at the door of the sheriff's office, nibbling nervously at her lip. *What was I thinking?* She glanced down at the deep blue slip dress she wore. Her one good dress, saved for funerals and weddings, and she was wearing it to make an official statement to the police.

"Too late now," she whispered, closing her eyes and praying for courage. Then she stepped across the threshold and smiled at Darla Munroe.

The clerk darted a glance over her shoulder before beckoning to Marlie. "Did you hear?" she asked in a hushed tone, her eyes wide, shock still lingering there.

"Hear what?"

"Maribeth Park got herself killed last night," Darla whispered, casting another glance over her shoulder. "Was hightailing it down one-sixty and smashed right into Miss Ella's Buick. Her car had stalled and she was going to get Jazz to help her move it out of the road. She was halfway through the woods when she heard the crash."

"Maribeth crashed into Miss Ella's car?" Marlie repeated dumbly. "What on earth was she doing out that way? Jazz is the only person who lives there."

"I reckon she was out to see him. I thought, well, you know," Darla finished in a muffled whisper. Sometimes it seemed Briarwood hadn't yet made it into the twenty-first century. Most of the town still considered it improper to speak of such things in front of a young unmarried woman.

Rolling her eyes at Darla, Marlie shook her head. "No way. Not Jazz. He was always too smart for her. Not that she didn't try."

Casting the small, quiet woman a glance, Darla asked, "What do you know about it? You are years younger than Jazz."

"Only five years younger." Raising one naked shoulder in a shrug, Marlie said, "I just hear things." She shifted nervously from one foot to the other, twisting her hands. "Maybe I should do this later. I imagine Miss Ella is a mess."

"Tate's done got her calmed down, as much as you can expect anyway. You know how he is," Darla murmured, seating herself before her boss himself showed in the doorway.

Yes. She did know. He patted, soothed, stroked. Teased or ordered, whatever it took to calm a woman down, Tate could do it. He had a way with women and always had. It was probably handy in his line of work, being able to handle people the way he did.

Marlie imagined the opposite was also true—he could calm a woman down, but then he could heat her right back up. Shoot, he managed to work her up just by breathing the same air she did.

"Marlie."

She turned slowly, goosebumps racing down her bare arms as she met her brother's chilly gaze. "Larry," she said by way of greeting.

"Girl, what are you doing prancing around town wearing a getup like that?" he asked, puffing his chest out and hooking his thumbs in his belt.

She glanced down at her dress. Though the spaghetti straps were all that held it up, the neckline was modest and the hem fell nearly to her ankles. "I don't think there is anything wrong with the dress," she said, averting her eyes, a faint flush staining her cheeks.

And to think, she'd actually come here hoping to make Tate notice her. She stood there, miserable, while her brother degraded her for dressing like a tramp. With kin like this, it was a miracle decent folk even wanted to be in the same room with her.

"You get on home and change out of that dress," Larry ordered.

She raised her eyes, straightened her shoulders. In her mind, she heard Tate from the previous night, saying, *You're not like them, Marlie.* Then, by God, she had better prove it. "No."

He was already turning away. "What did you say?" he asked incredulously.

"I said no," she repeated, stronger this time.

"Girl, you best do what you're told."

"Deputy, I didn't realize her attire was any concern of yours." Tate stepped across the threshold of the file room and approached the desk. Taking in Marlie's appearance with just a slight widening of his eyes and a faint grin of appreciation, he turned his attention to the man across the counter. "I think she looks right nice myself. But she's a grown woman and she doesn't have to please anybody but herself."

Marlie turned her face aside, a heavy curtain of pale blonde silk shutting out the rest of the world as she wished the floor would open up and swallow her whole. Why did he have to come out now? Why not after she had already finished her piece with Larry?

"I believe this matter is between me and my sister, Sheriff McNeil," Larry drawled, crossing his arms over his chest and meeting the sheriff's gaze.

Tate stepped closer to the chest-high counter, propping his elbows on it, cocking his head as he studied Marlie. He decided that Marlie's eyes would match the deep blue of her dress when angered. Or aroused. "She's over eighteen, a self-supporting woman." He leaned back against the desk and crossed his legs at the ankle. "So I don't rightly see how it concerns you."

"She looks like a tramp. No sister of mine is gonna go around looking like that," he snapped, poking an index finger towards Marlie. He looked away from Tate, narrowed his milky blue eyes at his sister and said, "You git on home and change, girl."

A woman, however meek and mild she may be, could only take so much. After years of abuse, both mental and physical, years of depression, years of neglect, Marlene Jo Muldoon had just about had enough.

Marlie had never been kissed by a man. Because no good man would even approach a woman with the last name Muldoon, not in this county. She shied away from any men that were cronies or cohorts of her notorious family.

And he had the nerve to call her a tramp.

Her eyes narrowed, went dark with anger and humiliation. "Why don't you make me, big brother?" she hissed, a minute trembling starting deep inside her body. A tramp?

The words died in his throat as Tate opened his mouth to send Larry scurrying back to his hole. He had been right, he realized. The soft, dreamy, dark blue of her eyes had turned to a vivid, deep, bluish purple, large and dark in her pale face. Flags of color flew high on her cheeks and the pulse at her neck beat rapidly.

Blood drained from his head straight down to pool in his groin, making speech impossible. Seized by an insane urge to grab her and bury his face against that smooth, slim neck, to taste the skin where that pulse beat so wildly, Tate stood frozen to the spot.

God help me, he thought. Tate had wanted her his whole life, it seemed. But he had never wanted her more than he did at the moment as she stood glaring at her brother, face bright with indignation and anger, blue fire snapping in her eyes.

Marlie said, louder this time, "I look no more like a tramp than you look like an officer of the law." Her gaze ran derisively over him; over his starched uniform, before rising back to his eyes. "Who on earth was fool enough to give you a badge, anyway?"

Larry's mouth fell open and finally, he rasped out, "You watch your mouth, girl, else I'll watch it for you."

Tossing her head back, she sneered, "What, like Daddy did? With the back of your hand and a cigarette? You're just like him, too cowardly to fight somebody who isn't weaker than you. God forgive me, you're even worse than he is. You're too damned cowardly to do a damned thing without that gun at your side. Tell me something, Larry, when you go to bed with a woman, do you have to wear your gun just to feel like a man?"

How many times have I backed down? Marlie wondered, furious. She glared at Larry while he stared at her, shock and fury in his eyes. *How many times did I turn away, or ignore him, or give in?* Too many. Quivering with the rage she had suppressed for years, she whispered, "You don't own me. I don't owe you anything, not my love, not my respect, and certainly not my obedience."

"Girl, you'll do what I say," he roared, his hand flying out and catching hold of her upper arm.

The strength in that hand was surprising. But Marlie hardly took notice as an odd heat engulfed her entire body.

Tate had one hand on the station desk and was leaping over it when it happened. By the time his feet touched the black and white tiled floor, Deputy Lawrence K. Muldoon was already lying flat on his back, blood spewing from his split lip, running down his face to pool on the smooth tile of the floor beneath him.

For the second time in a matter of weeks, he'd been knocked flat on his ass by a woman who barely reached his chin.

Marlie reached up, rubbed at her upper arm. An angry red handprint was forming there and she realized it ached. "Don't you ever touch me, brother. Not ever." Turning her dark eyes to Tate, she said, "I've things to get done. I'd like to get this over with, if you don't mind."

Then she turned on her heel and strode down the hall. Silence had fallen over the small common room and all eyes watched as she turned the corner to Tate's office.

Scratching his chin, Tate muttered, "Well, I'll be damned."

Behind him, Larry lay prone, quivering with fury and shame as blood and mucus ran down the back of his throat. "You're gonna pay for that, Marlie Jo," Larry whispered.

The soles of cowboy boots clicking on the floor had him raising his eyes. Hand pressed against his bleeding mouth, Larry stared up at Tate McNeil with sullen angry eyes.

"No, Larry. I don't believe she will," Tate said as he dropped down to rest on his haunches while he studied the pitiful mess of the man before him. "You see, if you so much as touch her, I'll hunt you down, peel the skin from your bones, and watch while the rats eat you."

Voice dropping to a faint whisper, Tate leaned forward and

whispered, "If you hurt her, that's what I'm gonna do to you. And I mean that."

ॐ

Tapping his pen on the completed statement, he studied Marlie's signature. Neat and small, just like her. He lifted his head and looked across his desk at her. God, she was so pretty, he mused.

Her slim, narrow shoulders left bare by the dress, her elegant collarbone, smooth, graceful neck, all the pale ivory skin was set off by the vivid color of her dress and by the passionate color in her face. Instead of its usual braid, her hair was free, curling around her pixie-sprite face, tumbling down her shoulders.

The dress, cut like a lady's slip, alternately clung to and camouflaged subtle curves. On the sides, a slit just above her knee revealed smoothly muscled, sleek calves, tiny ankles.

To Tate's recollection, he hadn't ever seen Marlie in a dress. At least not in this decade. The last time had been at Alex's funeral and her dress then had been a worn hand-me-down made for somebody thirty pounds heavier.

Subtle color smudged her already exotic eyes, making them larger, darker. A delicate pink tinted her lips, bringing to mind strawberry ice cream. There was nothing Tate liked better at the end of a hot, summer day than a bowl of strawberry ice cream.

He was dying to have a taste of her.

"I'm just a bit curious, if you don't mind, Marlie. Why are you so pretty today? Got a hot date?" he asked, forcing his tone to remain bland.

"No." Marlie studied her reddened knuckles as she spoke

and before she met his eyes, she said, "You know, that felt very good." She flexed her hand gingerly, smiling in satisfaction when it hurt.

"I imagine it's been a long time coming," Tate replied. Even though he had wanted to cheer after she had laid Larry low, it sickened him to see any kind of mark on her. The reddened knuckles he could almost handle, but he had to smother a growl as he stared at the dark ring around her upper arm.

After her noncommittal response, Tate sighed in aggravation. "So why are you dressed so nice?"

Until that moment, Marlie didn't even realize she had been thinking it. But when she raised her head and met those deep, beautiful, brown eyes, she said, "I'm going into Lexington to apply for a job."

"A job?" he repeated slowly, setting his pen down.

"Yes."

"You have a job," he told her. *Careful, Tate. Be careful here.*

"I have a life here that I hate," she said, her voice soft and sad. Turning her head, she stared out at the quiet street. Several doors down sat the salon where she did nails, where she managed to eke out a living. A few miles away was a run-down hovel of a home with a leaking roof and a furnace that rarely worked.

Sitting across from her was a man she wanted with all her heart, a man who looked at her with pity in his eyes, pity and kindness.

"Isn't this a bit sudden?"

"Actually, it's something I should have done years ago."

"How do you figure that?"

She shrugged restlessly, rising to move to the window. Staring out, Marlie said, "I could make better money in town, go back to school. Get away from people who only know me as a Muldoon."

"I only know you as Marlie," Tate said.

A humorless smile curved her mouth. "Really?" Turning her head, she stared at him. "And when you think of me, what is one of the first things to come into your mind?"

"Faeries."

"Excuse me?" When he didn't respond, just stared down at his notepad, Marlie laughed. "Faeries. Well, that is certainly better than 'That no good Muldoon clan sprung out another loser'."

"You're not a loser, Marlie," Tate growled. "Don't talk about yourself like you are."

"That's kind of you, Tate. It really is. But you can't change what is."

Staring into her eyes, helplessness welling in him, Tate said, "This is your home, Marlie."

Her gaze fell away. Crossing her arms around her, hugging herself against a chill, she said, "I can't stay here any more, Tate. I have to make a life for myself."

"Why can't you do it here?" he persisted, shoving back from his desk.

She turned her head, staring at him over her smooth shoulder, naked save for a skinny strap of silky, indigo material. Her eyes were dark and sad and far older than they should have been. "Because there is nothing here for me," she finally told him, a somber smile lifting the corners of her mouth.

Silently, she took her purse from the chair and left.

Leaving.

No way in hell, Tate thought, stomping back to his chair and throwing himself into it.

There is nothing here for me.

"Well, Marlie Jo. I'll just have to change that, won't I?" he said to himself.

When he breathed in, the lingering scent of her filled his lungs, his head, his heart.

Like hell she was leaving.

⇝

Hands clamped around the porcelain mug, Ella McNeil stared into the distance. "I feel so guilty," she whispered for the hundredth time. "If I had made it around the bend, she would have seen me and had a chance to slow down."

"Mama," Tate sighed, stroking his hand down her frosted blonde hair. "Now you and I both know if Maribeth hadn't been driving like a bat out of hell, she wouldn't have hit your car." Hugging her against him briefly, he said, "I'm just so relieved you had already gotten out of the car."

"Still, if I had gone and had that tune-up, maybe whatever made my car die could have been fixed..." She pressed her hand against her lips to muffle her sob. "Oh, that poor girl. She was always so unhappy."

Tate said nothing. He had recently returned from sharing the news with Jazz and learned that Maribeth had indeed been out to see Jazz, and summarily sent along her way when Anne-Marie arrived. His cousin had gotten himself into a world of trouble—the question was, who in the hell was behind it?

"She didn't suffer any, did she?"

"No, Mama. She died instantly," he assured her as she moved away, smoothing her suit. He didn't mention that crashing into a still car while driving seventy miles an hour did nasty things to a body. Particularly nasty things when that body wasn't buckled in. Nasty things that still loomed in his mind.

A fast death had been the only death possible in such an accident.

"Well." Passing a hand over her hair, smoothing it down, she paced the small confines of Tate's office. "That is some comfort. How...how is her Mama handling this?"

"Poorly." She had already insisted Jazz be arrested. *He killed her. I know it, just like he killed Alex.* Hell, what a mess. Scrubbing his hands over his face, Tate leaned back in his chair. "Mama, this is going to take some time. I'll have Darla run you home."

Several hours later, when the fretful voice of his mother finally ceased, Tate studied the hastily finished report.

What in the hell were you doing at Jazz's, Maribeth?

What had she hoped to do?

Coffee long since gone cold, Tate pushed the report aside. It was nearing twilight outside; the dusky hue of the eastern sky reminded him of the deep blue of the dress Marlie had worn.

Had she been to Lexington?

"She can't actually want to leave," he muttered. But he knew there was really nothing here for her. This town held no happy memories for her. Tate doubted she had many happy memories period.

But he'd be damned if she would just up and leave. Lexington was only thirty miles away, but Tate couldn't just let go. What if she met somebody?

ౚ

Not many people came to Maribeth's funeral. The small scattering of people standing at the graveside was almost pathetic. Her mother, alone, of course. Her present boyfriend was home sleeping off a drunk. A few of Maribeth's coworkers, but not many. A few men had awkwardly ducked in and out of the funeral home visitation, but none were here now.

Jazz stood at the graveside, ignoring the accusing stare from Eleanor Parks. At his side, Anne-Marie kept her eyes fastened on the minister. "...guide this tortured soul as she leaves our world for Yours..."

It'll take more than that, he thought darkly. *What a waste.*

Naturally beautiful, canny, intelligent—and none of it had added up to jack, because she had a heart of stone. Now she lay cold in a grave, her body so devastated by the crash, an open casket hadn't been possible. All that beauty gone in a second.

"This isn't your fault, Jazz."

Glancing down at the slight figure next to him, he thought back to another funeral. Sighing, he dragged a hand through his rain-damp hair and said, "I know. I feel bad for Ella, though. She's blaming herself."

Silence fell as the short ceremony concluded. Jazz led Anne-Marie back to the car, glancing over his shoulder. Eleanor Park was still glaring daggers at him, standing there clutching a white rose in one thin, pale hand.

He opened the door to his dark blue Escalade, standing aside so Anne-Marie could slide into the passenger seat. She paused, laying one hand on his arm, resting her head on his chest. "We've been to too many of these things together, Jazz, haven't we?"

Cupping the back of her head in his hand, he lowered his, pressing his lips to the soft cloud of her ebony hair. "Yeah, too many." Grief flickered in his eyes as he stared ahead. Some thirty yards away was a simple monument of marble inscribed with the words "Alexander D. Kincade, Beloved Son, Brother and Friend".

Raising her head, she looked up, following the line of his gaze. Stepping away from the door, she held out her hand. "Let's go see him, Jazz," she said.

"I can't," he said tightly, shaking his head.

"Yes, you can." She reached for his hand, gently tugging him along with her. "Do you remember that summer you two started hanging out together? You both lied to your mom and my dad, saying you were going camping in the woods. What you really did was come here."

"We didn't sleep a wink," he whispered, remembering. "We both jumped at every little sound, then bragged to each other how brave we were."

"The next summer, you two started noticing girls."

He slowed in his steps, pulling her to a halt. "I'd already noticed one." He pressed his thumb against her mouth, shadows in his eyes. "It was always you, Anne-Marie. I want you to know that."

"I was always so jealous of Sandy Pritchard," she told him, pressing a kiss to his hand. "I wanted so badly to be tall and sleek, just like her, with straight brown hair and big boobs."

Stroking her silky, black curls from her face, he said, "I've always thought you were perfect."

She laughed, once more taking his hand. "Not always," she refuted, leading him once more in the direction of Alex's grave. "Remember when I told Dad I saw you two smoking cigarettes? I never could understand why he didn't punish the both of you."

"I wasn't his to punish," Jazz said wryly, no longer resisting her silent urging. His eyes focused on the gray marble as it drew closer.

Casting him a slight smile, she said, "You were always his. It just took ya'll a while to find each other. Anyway, when I was sixteen, I tried once puffing on a cigarette butt. I was so sick, and all of a sudden, I knew why he hadn't punished you."

"We got sick right there behind the barn," Jazz remembered. "He found us lying on our backs, green around the gills, and he offered us another cigarette. I started puking again, but Alex just looked miserable."

Their steps slowed, halted, as they came to the elegant, gray memorial.

June 5, 1966 to July 13, 1984.

Such a short period of time.

"God, I miss him so much," Jazz rasped, holding Anne-Marie's hand in a vise grip. "He was the best friend I ever had. And I killed him."

"Just like you killed my daughter."

They both turned at the dry, brittle voice. The wind whipping her tangled hair around her face, Eleanor stood in her worn, black dress, glaring at Jazz with hatred burning in her eyes.

"Ms. Park, I know you have suffered these past few days," Anne-Marie said diplomatically. "But Jazz had nothing to do with Maribeth's accident. He was with me."

Anne-Marie may as well not have spoken for all the attention Eleanor paid her.

"You've got the blood of two on your hands now, more like three. You're the reason the old Doc Kincade got shot."

Jazz remained silent as he urged Anne-Marie to the car once more.

"You're cursed," she rasped from behind them. "Cursed

from the day you were born and will be until you die. Everybody you touch suffers. Even the golden boy couldn't escape it, could he? Just you being in the car with him damned him."

Eleanor had already turned to walk away when Jazz raised his head. Each looked at the other before turning their heads to stare at Eleanor.

Just you being in the car with him damned him.

"Jazz?" Anne-Marie whispered softly.

"I know, honey," he replied. "Just get in the car and let's go for now."

ℰℴ

Just you being in the car with him damned him.

Anne-Marie threw down her pen and pushed back from her desk. A pile of charts nearly up to her nose waited for her signature, another dozen or so were stacked out on the nurse's station, she had a baby to check on, and she couldn't get those words out of her mind.

In a flurry of movement, she shed her lab coat, grabbed her purse and rushed out the door. "None of these are major emergencies, right, Marti?" she asked the young blonde sitting at the front desk.

"Not unless you consider a case of head lice a national crisis," Marti replied cheerfully.

"I think I trust you to handle that on your own," Anne-Marie said dryly. "Listen, I've got some things I need to do. I'm going to go check on Baby Marsden and then do some running. I'll come back later tonight and finish those charts."

"You're the boss," Marti said, shrugging her shoulders. Propping her elbows on the desk, she looked at Anne-Marie with innocent, blue eyes. "I don't suppose your errands have anything to do with the sexy friend of yours, do they?"

"What sexy friend?" Jake asked, swinging through the door and sauntering over to lean against Marti's desk.

Fluttering long lashes at him, Marti said, "Why you, handsome. Who else?"

Leaning down, he covered her mouth with his briefly, then drew away and looked down at her smiling face. "You're a terrible liar, Marti. That's one of the things I love about you." Then he stood, stretching his hands high overhead. "Busy day, huh?"

"Very. Jake, I need to do some errands so I'll finish up the charts tonight or tomorrow. You don't mind if I duck out, do you? Do we need to talk about anything?"

He shrugged, his broad shoulders straining against the white oxford he wore tucked into a faded pair of blue jeans. "Nothing much, that I know of. Need any help?"

Flashing him a tired smile, she shook her head. "No. Personal things, you know. You ought to take that wife of yours out. Probably going crazy from missing you, she sees you so little."

Chuckling, he reached out, stroking Marti's neck in an absentminded, offhand gesture. "Yeah, she only sees me what, sixteen to eighteen hours a day?"

Reaching up, Marti captured his hand with hers. Pressing a kiss to the back of it, she agreed, "Hmmm, twenty-four a day wouldn't be enough."

Anne-Marie rolled her eyes. "Please, get me out of here before I get a cavity," she joked, heading out the door.

A short time later, she pulled up in front of a small, ramshackle house. This was one of the last places Alex had been at before he died. Staring at the dreary, dismal Park household, Anne-Marie reflexively closed her hands around the steering wheel, muttering, "What am I doing here?"

Looking for answers, she told herself, reaching for the handle. Swinging out of the car, she headed up the cracked concrete sidewalk.

Her steps slowing to a halt, Anne-Marie watched as the door flew open. Studying the drunk woman in the doorway, Anne-Marie figured she wouldn't get any answers here.

"Whatcha doin', rich girl?" Eleanor asked, swiping one hand across her mouth, smearing what was left of her red lipstick.

"What did you mean, Alex was damned just by being in the same car as Jazz?" Anne-Marie asked bluntly.

"Boy's dead, ain't he? Just like my baby," Eleanor asked coldly, smiling as Anne-Marie paled. "Dead's dead."

"Do you know something about the night Alex died?"

Cocking her head, Eleanor studied the composed woman in front of her. "Maybe. You gonna make it worth my while to remember?"

Silently, Anne-Marie reached up and removed the gold swirls she wore at her ears. "I don't keep much money on me. These cost nearly six hundred dollars. They're yours, if you remember."

Greed flickered, battling with the grief and self-pity. With Maribeth gone, Eleanor was going to have to find a way to support herself. Those earrings would be a start. Shakily, she dug a smashed pack of cigarettes from her pocket. After lighting one, she studied Anne-Marie through the haze of smoke. "Maybe I know something," she repeated. "But those aren't gonna buy what I know." With a sly smile, she eyed the diamond ring Anne-Marie wore on her right hand.

"Not on your life," Anne-Marie whispered, closing her right hand into a tight fist. Her mind whirling, she did a mental tally of the accounts she had at the bank. "These earrings, and a check for five hundred dollars."

"I like the ring," Eleanor said. But that five hundred sounded tempting, she had to admit. Of course, the ring was probably worth much more, but she wanted it just because Anne-Marie didn't want to give it up.

"This ring was my mother's," Anne-Marie said, shrugging her shoulders. Reaching up, she started to slip the earrings back on. "I'd sooner see a poodle wearing it around a choke chain than to see it on you. Have a nice night, Eleanor."

"Wait."

The girl was every bit as solid as the boy had been, Eleanor mused. Desmond bred his kids with iron in their backbones. With jerky motions, she dragged deep on the cigarette one last time before stubbing it out. "A thousand and the earrings," she decided.

"If what you tell me isn't worth it, I'll stop the check before the sun sets," Anne-Marie said with a shrug, reaching into her bag for her checkbook.

With a catty smile, Eleanor sighed with satisfaction. "Oh, it's worth it, little girl."

❧

Could she have lied to me? Anne-Marie thought, moments later speeding down the highway. Her hands were shaking and her heart pounded like a runaway freight train as she pulled into the parking lot of the small building that housed the county jail and sheriff's office.

"What brings you here so late?" Darla asked as Anne-Marie strode through the door. She already had her purse slung over her shoulder and was reaching for the desk lamp when Anne-Marie approached her desk.

"I need to look at a few things in the archives."

Eyebrows arched, Darla asked, "What things?"

"My brother's accident report and the investigating officer's report, for starters," Anne-Marie said in a clipped voice.

Slowly, Darla replaced her purse into the drawer of her desk. "You mean the ones I copied for your father right before he was shot?" Darla asked, settling back down in her chair and beckoning for Anne-Marie to join her.

"What?" Anne asked faintly, clutching her purse so tightly her knuckles went white.

Leaning forward, keeping her voice low, Darla explained Desmond's request via the phone a few days before someone shot him in his own library. "Tate already knows about it," Darla concluded with a quick glance around the quiet station.

"Coincidence..." Anne-Marie murmured. Then she shook her head. "No. It was not a coincidence. Who all could have known about Daddy wanting those records?"

"Everybody in town," Darla scoffed, shaking her head in disgust. "Muldoon overheard me taking the call and he asked about it, of course. Then he was over at the tavern talking about it to anybody who would listen. Shoot, the man probably told half the county."

"I need to see those records," Anne-Marie whispered.

"That may not be wise," Darla argued. "Look what happened to your daddy."

"If my dad asking for those records has something to do with him getting shot, then somebody has something to lose, or something to hide," Anne-Marie argued. "And they are public records. Either get them now, when it's just us or I'll come back another time, and who knows who'll overhear."

"Give me a few minutes then," Darla said, sighing.

Ᏸ

She took the records home after Darla promised to lock up the originals in the file cabinet in Tate's office. Not as good as a safe deposit box, but this late in the day, it was the best that she could do. Darla had called her back as she headed out of the office.

"Are you sure you want to go stirring up a hornet's nest that's been sleeping for sixteen years? A lot of people could be hurt. You could be hurt."

Quietly, Anne-Marie had said, "I have to. Darla, I have to know."

Consistent with bruising noted on victims with a history of blunt force trauma.

Multiple lacerations, broken sternum, cardiac tamponade.

Cardiac tamponade, when the pericardial sac was ruptured and filled with blood. The type of injury caused when striking something with such force that the coronary arteries rupture. Something like a steering wheel.

Like what happens to a water balloon when flung with force against concrete.

Shuffling through the papers, she searched for the report filed by the insurance company. The exterior damage had been beyond repair, but some of the interior had been salvageable. The two bucket seats, the dashboard. They had found blood and pieces of human tissue on the steering wheel.

Why hasn't somebody seen this? She set her jaw as she reached for the post-mortem once more. Broken nose, a deep laceration across the brow, internal hemorrhaging.

Slowly, forcing herself to take a deep breath, she laid the reports down. It was all there, plain as could be. If you were searching for something unusual, you would have found it. It just happened to be that nobody had been looking for anything unusual. Nobody had even questioned it. Anne-Marie knew why. Larry Muldoon and Sheriff Blackie Schmidt. For decades, the Muldoon family had the run of the town. Blackie had been one of their buddies, and a bully all on his own. A bully who had somehow landed the sheriff's office.

"Alex was driving," Anne-Marie finally whispered. Tightly closing her eyes, she bit back a sob. Having suspicions was one thing, confronted with proof such as this...

Eleanor Park hadn't been lying.

"What do you mean Alex was driving?"

"Jazz wasn't driving that car, honey. Your brother was."

Anne-Marie shook her head and forced her mind back to the matter at hand. She studied the papers before her and faced the bittersweet truth. Alex had been driving. If Alex had been in the passenger seat, he wouldn't have had those types of injuries. If the impact had thrown him as the report said, his injuries would have been different, head trauma, spinal cord damage. And if both passengers were thrown, there wouldn't have been so much blood or tissue inside.

"Oh, Alex. What were you thinking?" she murmured, pressing her hands to her mouth. Emotions that ran too deeply to be labeled swirled through her as she rocked herself back and forth.

Golden, laughing Alex, gone. Because he'd been driving drunk. For nearly two decades, there was guilt resting on the shoulders of somebody who hadn't done a damned thing wrong.

"My God, Jazz. What have we done to you?" she whispered, burying her face in her hands. Lowering her head to the desk, hot tears poured out of her while her shoulders shook with silent sobs.

It was a long time later when she raised her head and scrubbed at the dried tear tracks on her face. After a quick shot of whiskey and splashing her face with cold water, she felt ready to look at the reports once more.

She already knew, but had to check one more time.

The investigating officer, the first on the scene. Larry Muldoon.

With steady hands, she gathered up the reports and locked them in the safe hidden behind the false back of the medicine cabinet. She locked it, replaced the false back, and closed the mirrored cabinet door. In the mirror, she stared at herself. Pale, with slashes of high color riding on each cheek, her green eyes dark with anger.

Then she turned away, stripping off her clothes as she walked to her bedroom. She needed a good night's sleep and some time before she could think of this with a level head.

If she thought about it now, if she decided how she was going to handle it, chances were she'd be watching the sunrise from the sheriff's office. And Larry Muldoon would never see the sun rise again.

Naked, exhausted, but certain she would get no sleep, she tumbled down on the bed.

Her head had barely touched the pillow when she fell asleep.

&

The following morning, she sat behind Larry Muldoon's desk, feet propped on the corner, hands folded on her flat belly. Even though inside she was churning with anger and grief, her face was calm and composed. After all, a lady never let people see she was upset.

Idly, she studied her candy-apple red nail polish. When the door swung open, she saw Muldoon come through out of the corner of her eye, but she made no move to acknowledge him.

He came to a halt in front of his desk. "Don't you have patients to see, Doc?" he asked after she finally turned her head and met his eyes.

She smiled serenely. "I took a personal day. I had a few things that needed to be addressed." Flicking her watch a glance, she figured she had just a minute or so to kill before Tate strolled through the door. "How has life been treating you, Larry? You look a bit peaked there."

"You mind if I ask what you're doing at my desk?" he demanded, his eyes darting here and there, checking the contents of the desktop.

"I was waiting for you," she replied. "Don't worry. I haven't touched your possessions. What I was looking for was in the archives, records open to the public, you know." As she spoke, the door swung open a second time and Tate came sauntering through, sipping from a steaming Styrofoam cup. He paused when he saw her, and grinned at her when she waved.

"My, what a lovely surprise," he drawled, approaching the desk. "How'd you get so lucky to have a pretty lady like that waiting for you, Muldoon?"

Ignoring Tate, Larry turned his beady eyes back to Anne-Marie.

"I found some interesting reading, Tate," she said, pulling a

187

slim file from her black briefcase. Flipping it open, she removed two sets of documents and handed one to Tate. The other, she threw in Muldoon's direction.

"That case is closed," Muldoon rasped, inching backward.

"No case is ever permanently closed, Muldoon," she said, waiting and watching as Tate's eyes narrowed.

"You've been reading about that crash," Tate murmured, flicking through the small stack of papers. When he came across the post-mortem, he paused. Raising his eyes to her, he said, "This couldn't have been easy for you. Why do it?"

"I had some questions I needed answers for," she said evenly. "Read that report, Tate."

She knew the exact moment he figured out why she was here. Slowly, he shuffled the papers back in the original order. Then Tate raised his head, face blank, eyes shuttered as he focused on Muldoon.

"I got to get out on patrol," Larry mumbled, starting to turn away.

"I don't think so. Don't move a single step, Deputy."

"I got work to do, and you two are interfering," he snapped, jerking a thumb in Anne-Marie's direction. "What in hell's it matter anyway? The boy's been dead years now."

"Maybe you should read the reports, Deputy," Tate said, holding out the copy that Larry had ignored. "It is interesting reading, that's for certain. According to this, that boy died from wounds he would have received had he been driving. But you say you pulled Jazz out from behind the wheel, worried that the car was going to catch fire, dragged him a safe distance, and found Alex laying there, already dead."

"That's the way it happened," Larry mumbled, dashing a hand across his forehead.

Even though inside she quivered with rage and grief, Anne-Marie smiled serenely and said, "I wonder what an outside investigator would think of that story, Larry. One without your prejudices, one without your hate, one who isn't afraid of you simply because your last name is Muldoon. Wonder what a jury would have to say about incriminating an innocent boy."

"You can't do that," he rasped, shooting Tate a desperate look. "Look, the boy's dead. Dead is dead, ain't it? And hell, McNeil never said otherwise. Of course he was driving."

"PTS, post traumatic stress syndrome. He blocked it out, Larry," Anne-Marie replied, raising her shoulders in a lazy shrug. Slowly, she uncurled her body out of the chair, stretching like a cat after a long nap in the sun. "I hope you know a good lawyer."

Larry opened his mouth but his words were blocked out when the door opened and Ella called out, "Why, Doc Kincade. What on earth are you doing here?"

Even as she spoke, all hell broke loose. A stray cat came trotting in through the open door, followed by a mangy-looking mutt who spotted the cat and grinned with manic canine delight. With a petrified meow, the cat took off and the dog went in pursuit, knocking Ella off her feet and onto her backside. Behind her was Darla, juggling an obscenely tall stack of records on their way to filing cabinets.

Paper flying, dog yapping, the two older ladies tittering with amusement and embarrassment, Larry retreated quietly, his eyes on the sheriff. Anne-Marie looked up from Ella's side just in time to see him bolt through the side exit door. He paused only long enough to level hate-filled eyes on her and Tate.

80

A week later, Tate called off the APB put out on Larry Muldoon. Sometime Friday night, somebody had driven his cruiser into the tiny parking lot of the station house and left it there.

They also left Larry's body in the trunk, a bullet neatly planted in the back of his head. Two unrelated deaths a few weeks after an attempted murder had the good folks of Briarwood, Kentucky, nervous. Of course, poor Maribeth Park's death had been a tragic accident, brought on by her wild lifestyle.

Muldoon's funeral was attended by only four people. Tate, standing in for the station, Anne-Marie and Jazz and Marlie Jo Muldoon. Sunlight streamed down on the pitiful crowd as the minister spoke his final words over the hole in the ground.

When it was over, an unheard sigh of relief escaped them all.

In less than ten minutes, Marlie was alone at the gravesite, staring at the coffin with dry eyes. The scar on the back of her hand itched and she rubbed at it, remembering the part Larry had played. He'd held her still while Beau had ground his smoldering cigarette out against her tender flesh. Her brothers had laughed while a nine-year-old Marlie screamed in pain, their father smiling meanly as he watched.

How many times had those two hurt her? Stolen what little money she earned on her own? Trashed any little treasure she managed to get her hands on? She had been six years old the time they had drowned her kitten, right in front of her.

It was a wonder Marlie made it to adulthood with her sanity relatively intact. Now they were all gone. Just Marlie and her crazy Mama left.

She stared into the dark hole and breathed deeply. "I'd like to wish you Godspeed, Brother," she said quietly. "I'd like to be able to express some regret over this, but I can't. You made so many enemies, this was bound to happen."

Raising her hand, she rubbed her index finger over the scar. "It's a wonder I never did it, though. After all you and Beau and Daddy did to me and Mama."

Shifting her purse, she smoothed her skirt with one hand as she held the other over the grave. Her fingers loosened and a single, white rose drifted down to rest on the coffin. "If you see Daddy or Brother down there, don't bother giving them my regards."

Chapter Nine

"Jazz, I had to be sure," Anne-Marie repeated, keeping her voice calm and level, despite the surging emotions within her.

"You should have come to me the minute the thought even entered your head," Jazz snapped, turning away, staring out the window. "Damn it, Annie. He could have hurt you. Hell, most likely that's why he shot your daddy."

Lowering her head, Anne-Marie peered at her nails, a nervous habit. Studying the polish, flamingo pink this week, she carefully said, "I don't think Larry Muldoon did it. He doesn't have the guts or the brains."

"He had a motive."

"Every KKK member had a motive for killing Martin Luther King, Jr.," Anne replied dryly. "Motive doesn't mean jack if you don't have the brain power. Come on, Jazz, you know as well as I do, Larry Muldoon couldn't think his way out of a wet paper bag if he had a map and a blowtorch."

She drew her knees up under her, facing Jazz's angry eyes squarely. "This doesn't really have anything to do with Larry, does it? You are mad at me because I didn't come to you first, instead of looking for myself."

"I've spent the last sixteen years thinking I killed my best friend, Anne-Marie."

"Exactly. I didn't want to give you false hope if I was wrong. Why can't you understand that?"

"You knew why I came back here. I had to find this out for myself."

Anne-Marie blew out a disgusted breath, rising to her feet. She walked over to the window, staring out into the night. "Jazz, if I was wrong, it would have torn you apart. I didn't want to do that. I had to be sure."

"You didn't trust me."

"Oh, that's crap," Anne-Marie snapped, whirling around, glaring at him. Eyes flashing, she marched up to him and poked her index finger into his chest. "In my heart, I never believed you'd been driving. I wasn't doing it to check up on you."

"So you go to my cousin, instead of me."

"He's the sheriff. And for that matter, I didn't go to Tate. I bearded the lion in his den, which just happened to be where Tate works." Staring at him, into those simmering, brown eyes, Anne-Marie threw up her hands. "I give up. You want to be mad at me for this, you go right ahead. But I don't have to hang around." Snatching her purse and keys from the table, she stomped away.

With an arched brow, Jazz watched as she stormed to the door. "This is your house," he mildly reminded her.

Whirling around, face flushed, Anne-Marie said, "Then you get out of it. I don't want to put up with you while you are in this kind of mood."

"I'm not ready to leave."

"I am not ready to have you belittle me for this. What, did I hurt your pride or something? Did you want to come back to town, guns blazing, to clear your name?" she demanded, throwing her purse and keys to the yellow-and-white-striped couch.

Yes.

Watching her, Jazz decided that was the whole problem right there. She had done what he had wanted to do, and in no time flat. Before he had even figured out how he had to get started, she had asked all the right questions, looked in all the right places, and boom, problem solved.

She'd hit a nerve, Anne-Marie realized. She planted her hands on her hips and studied him with cool eyes. "That's it, isn't it?" she asked levelly. When he looked away, she said, "I've got a brain, Jazz. And I have my own sense of honor. Did it ever occur to you that I felt I owed you this, for what you've suffered?"

"You don't owe me anything."

"That's not how I see it."

Turning back to her, Jazz asked woodenly, "So is that what the past few weeks have been about? You trying to make it up to me? I wouldn't take money or anything, so you provided free bed-warming services?"

Her hands fell slackly to her sides, mouth open in a silent 'o', eyes going dark with surprised hurt. Roughly, she whispered, "Damn you, Jazz." Tears rose in her eyes before she blinked them away. Face pale, hands shaking, Anne-Marie turned away. "Get out."

"Anne—"

"Get out," she hissed, whirling around to face him. "If that's your opinion of me, then get out."

Reaching for her, bitter regret burning through him, Jazz whispered, "I'm sorry, Annie. I shouldn't have said that."

She evaded his hands, raising her own to ward him off. "If

you hadn't thought it, you wouldn't have said it. Apparently, these past few weeks haven't meant the same thing to you that they meant to me. We've nothing more to say to each other."

"Annie—"

"Get out!" she shouted, pulling back and turning on her heel. Tears spilling over, she tore up the stairs and threw herself on the bed.

ᖇ

Vindication didn't feel as good as it should have, Jazz was discovering. Not only was Anne-Marie still avoiding him after more than a week, he couldn't go anywhere without being hailed down for a twenty-minute conversation.

Walking down the street was a chore. People he hardly knew and people he did know and disliked, all stopped him to chat, overly friendly and contrite. Jazz stood woodenly, staring into space while Betsy Crane went on and on about how she sensed something was wrong, you know?

Finally, he glanced at his bare wrist. "Oh, look at the time," Jazz drawled. "I'm supposed to meet my cousin in just a few minutes." He took off down the sidewalk at a fast walk, his jaw clenched.

"Jazz."

His rapid stride slowed, and then stopped. Looking in the doorway of Greene County Cardiology, he met the dark green eyes of Desmond Kincade. Eyes that were sad and very tired. Eyes so like Anne-Marie's, it hurt him to even look at them.

"Doc Kincade," he greeted, linking his hands behind his back to keep from fidgeting.

"I've been wanting to speak with you," Desmond said,

reaching into his pocket for a cigar. He gestured with it and gave a half-hearted smile. "You won't go telling Anne-Marie now, will you?"

With a shrug of his shoulders, Jazz remained silent, waiting.

"Oh, that's right. You two haven't been speaking much of late, have you?"

When Jazz didn't answer, Desmond sighed. "Why don't you come inside a bit?"

The refusal that leaped to the tip of his tongue wouldn't come out. After so many years of listening to, obeying and respecting Desmond Kincade, Jazz simply couldn't turn his back on the man. He followed him up the stairs, through the waiting room, down a hall into an office done in blues and grays.

Desmond took his seat behind his desk, shoving a pile of charts to the side. With an absent frown, he jotted something on a sticky note and put it on the front of a particularly fat chart.

"I came in to check on a few things. A colleague of mine has been handling my patients." His emerald green eyes met Jazz's over the tops of his glasses. "Did Anne-Marie tell you I'm selling the practice?"

"Ah, no. No, she didn't."

"Yes. Dr. Moss is taking over in the fall. Grew up about forty miles away from here and wanted to come home to set up his own practice. I took care of him, oh, say about thirty-five years ago. He had a Tetralogy of Fallot, a nasty mess his heart was. Back then, it was considered a miracle if the child made it. His mother, now...she says I was her miracle. But I don't see it that way. He was mine. They all were, in every way, their own little miracles. The boy says I was his inspiration.

"Now he's been a miracle two times over. He's been the answer to my prayers." Desmond's eyes fell to his wide-palmed, long-fingered hands. The fingers flexed and spread before clenching into fists. With a slight chuckle, Desmond looked up. "My hands are starting to shake, you know. It was there for a while, but it's gotten worse since...since that night. I've already done my last surgery."

"I'm sorry."

Sighing, Desmond leaned back into the navy blue leather, his head falling back to stare up at the ceiling. "So am I. I'll miss this. But once a surgeon's hands start to shake, that's it." With a negligent shrug of his shoulders, he straightened in the chair and folded his hands on the desk top. "There was a time when I hoped Anne-Marie would follow in my footsteps, be a cardiologist. But she's found her niche, I must say."

"She's an excellent doctor," Jazz said, remembering the follow-up visit. Anne-Marie had handled the nervous Mariah like an old pro. "Kids love her."

"My Annie is a very lovable person all around," Desmond said, his eyes knowing. "But that's not what I wanted to talk with you about." The humor, the pride, the love all melted from his face, replaced by an achingly sad expression.

"I owe you an apology, Jasper. Not just for not questioning this, but for the crash that my son caused," Desmond said, grief lining his face, weighing heavily on his shoulders.

"You had no reason not to believe an officer of the law," Jazz responded in a flat voice, dropping into the chair in front of the desk.

"Oh, hell. Don't give me that, boy," Desmond snapped. "I've seen cockroaches more capable than Larry Muldoon. And I was an idiot for not calling him out. I knew something wasn't right." Pausing, he ran a shaky hand through his salt and pepper hair.

"I knew it," he repeated huskily. "But I didn't want to think about it. I didn't want to think that Alex was responsible for the accident. It was easier to deal with when I had somebody to blame."

Jazz turned away, focusing his stinging eyes on a weepy watercolor. "Doc, it's all over now. Over and done with."

"But my mistakes are still there. I should have believed in you. Some people did from the start." Desmond looked down at a framed picture of Anne-Marie. Reaching out, he touched his fingers to the image of his daughter's face. "And I should have, as well."

Clamping the cigar in his teeth, Desmond raised his head, met Jazz's eyes. "She did it the way she felt she had to, Jazz. For you. Not for herself, not for Alex. Not even for me. But for you. Muldoon wronged you and she wanted him to pay. Had she gone to you, you would have handed him his punishment. And she felt it was her responsibility.

"Don't blame her for doing the same thing you would have done," Desmond said quietly.

"She won't talk to me," Jazz burst out, shooting up out of his chair. "What in the hell am I supposed to do?"

"How about admitting you're wrong?" Desmond suggested, raising a bushy, black brow.

"Damn it, she should have told me! Sharing my bed—"

Any discomfort Desmond might have felt faded at the stunned embarrassment that filled Jazz's eyes and colored his dark face. Chuckling, he tapped out his half-finished Cuban as he said, "If you think I don't see what's been going on between you two, then you must also think I'm a fool."

Jazz's mouth opened and closed noiselessly and he finally gave up, jamming his hands in his pockets and turning away.

"Sharing your bed, sharing your life, that's all the more reason for her to want to do right by you, Jazz. Your pride may be hurt, you not handling Muldoon personally. But Anne-Marie's a modern woman; she wants a partner, not a man to protect her."

⁋

The door to her office flew open, revealing Jazz standing there glaring at her, brows low over his eyes, hostility radiating from him. "I was wrong," he growled. "You were right about my pride being hurt and I took it out on you."

Leaning back in her chair, her calm face revealing nothing, Anne-Marie said, "Nice to see you, too, Jazz. It's been a while, hasn't it?"

Nine days, twelve hours and forty minutes, she thought. *But who was counting?*

"Don't give me that look," he warned, pointing at her. "You and your dad, lifting that eyebrow, royalty facing the serfs."

"Is that what I'm doing?"

"Damn it, if you don't want my apology, then just say so," he shouted, storming into the tiny office. Eyes narrowed, he leaned forward and planted his hands on her neatly organized desk.

"An apology? Is that what this is?"

"Why in hell else would I be here?" he growled.

"Well, from the looks of it, I'd say you're here to yell at me some more," Anne-Marie replied, her eyes drifting down to the palms on her desk. "Usually apologies aren't handled by barging into somebody's office and yelling at them."

Jazz's eyes dropped to his hands, before glancing behind

him to the interested audience just outside the door. Slowly, he took a deep breath and then blew it out.

"Can we go someplace private?"

Flicking her gaze to the staff that gathered just beyond her door, listening with obvious and unapologetic curiosity, Anne-Marie feigned indifference. "This is about as much privacy as I figure we are going to need. I've patients yet to see."

"We need to talk," Jazz said, keeping his voice low and calm.

She raised her solemn gaze to those outside her door, lifted that regal brow at them. As they drifted away, ears still straining, Anne-Marie lifted a silver-barreled pen and spun it idly between her palms. After a moment, when she was sure her voice would be composed, she said, "I needed you to believe in me, to try to understand."

"I'm sorry."

Looking at him, Anne-Marie said, "I know you are. And I can understand why you were upset, why you were hurt. I know I hurt your pride and I'm sorry it happened. But I did it the way I felt was right. The way that kept you out of jail." Pausing, she nibbled at her lip, thinking, picking her way through her tangled emotions. "You would have gone after him, Jazz. And quite possibly killed him. That wouldn't have gained you anything."

"I was wrong, Annie. That's what I'm trying to tell you," Jazz said.

"Apology accepted." With a sigh, she turned her attention back to the open chart in front of her, the words blurring together while he stared at her lowered head.

"Then why aren't you looking at me? Why don't you stand up and come to me?" Jazz asked.

"There's no reason. You think I spent all that time with you just to make up for the past sixteen years. With you feeling that way, it made me realize we don't have what I was thinking, hoping, we might."

"Don't shut me out, Annie," Jazz whispered, shoulders slumping as he turned away and pressed his hands against his eyes. "That was a damned fool thing to say. I don't believe that's what's been going on between us."

"What is going on between us?"

Raising his head, he met her eyes. "I don't know. But I don't want it to end like this. And I don't want to go on the rest of my life wondering what might have happened if I wasn't an idiot."

She didn't move at first, didn't speak. Then she started towards him and slowly, he felt his heart start to beat again. He could breathe again. She slid her arms around his waist and he finally felt whole.

"I think maybe you should stop being an idiot so we can figure this thing out," Anne-Marie suggested.

He could have laughed with relief, but he was too busy kissing her.

℘

Tate's voice echoed through the station house as he shouted at Jazz. "I've still got an unsolved attempted murder on my hands. And an unsolved murder. I've got to deal with Eleanor Park, and God knows, she is a full-blown lunatic. I ain't got time to sit around babysitting you, Cousin."

Eye to eye, snarl to snarl, Jazz responded to Tate's comment with a sneer. "Babysitting?" Jazz shouted, poking Tate in the chest. "Boy, I hauled your chubby butt out of the fire more times than I can count. I don't need a damned babysitter and I got a damned right to know what in the hell is going on with the investigation."

"The hell you do. You're no blood kin to him, thank God. And you're neither a suspect or a witness. You'll hear something when I have something to say," Tate said, his voice cold and flat.

From the doorway, Marlie bit back a sigh of appreciation as Jazz responded with a rather rude suggestion. Tate's response was, "Is that some sick fetish you picked up in the big city?"

How could there be two men that good looking in one small town?

"They are something, aren't they?"

Startled, Marlie turned her head and stared into the amused eyes of Dr. Anne-Marie Kincade. "Um, well, yes. I guess so."

Chuckling, Anne-Marie said, "Girl, you got eyes. You can do better than that." She propped one blazer-clad shoulder against the doorframe, her eyes resting on Jazz's profile. "I know I've noticed it more than once myself."

"They are gorgeous," Marlie said under her breath, rolling her eyes at Anne-Marie's friendly laugh.

"How long have you been in love with him?"

"I...I beg your pardon?"

With a nonchalant shrug, Anne-Marie said, "I've been in love with Jazz most of my life. I know the symptoms. Does he know?"

"Of course not," Marlie replied, shoulders slumping. "It's too pathetic to even think about."

"I don't think it's pathetic at all."

Turning her head, Marlie stared into kind, knowing eyes. "He's the sheriff, the son of a good, decent woman and a man who died rescuing a woman he didn't know from Eve," Marlie said softly, shaking her head. "I'm the daughter of the town drunk and bully, and Mama, God bless her, was the town tramp. I barely managed to graduate from high school and he's the town sheriff. It's beyond pathetic."

"I doubt Tate sees it that way," Anne-Marie said. Making an impulsive decision, she linked arms with Marlie and called out, "Well, if that sight don't just set my heart all aflutter."

The shouting-getting-ready-to-turn-into-shoving-match halted and two identical, dark pairs of eyes turned their way. Each pair of eyes lit and traveled over the attractive pair in the doorway. All silver and blonde and dark blue eyes, Marlie wore a simple pink blouse tucked into white denim shorts. And Anne-Marie, ebony hair and emerald green eyes, with her confident smile and elegant clothes.

Both men felt their hearts stutter in their chest as they backed away from each other.

"Marlie and I ran into each other and thought you two would join us for lunch," Anne-Marie said, none too subtly dragging Marlie forward. "It's Saturday, after all. Tate, surely you know what they say about all work and no play."

"Now, Doc Kincade, you and I both know the job of serving the public isn't one that runs on a forty-hour work week," Tate drawled before looking at Marlie. *She was so damned pretty,* he thought. *And not a good actress at all.* The nerves and embarrassment in her dark blue eyes was every bit as apparent as the humor in Anne-Marie's green ones. "Marlie, how are you?"

"I...I'm fine, Tate. Thank you," she murmured, apparently giving up on the attempt to free her arm from Anne-Marie's. Her cheeks turned fiery red when Jazz said, "It'll be a cold day in hell before I turn down the chance to spend an afternoon with a couple of lovely ladies."

Marlie's eyes darted away as Jazz captured Anne-Marie's free hand and brushed her cheek with a soft kiss. "How are you holding up, Miz Muldoon?" he asked, raising his head and smiling gently at her.

"I'm fine, thank you, Mr. McNeil," she said softly.

"Mr. McNeil?" he repeated, a smile lighting his face. "Hell, Marlie. We're family, in a distant, convoluted sort of way. You can call me Jazz."

It was the first time that Anne-Marie knew of that he referred to the Muldoon family with anything other than hate and bitterness. But she knew Jazz; he was too kind to dislike Marlie simply because she was unfortunate enough to be born into the Muldoon family. "So, are you two coming to lunch or what?" she asked, tipping her head back and smiling at him.

"Only if I can sit next to the pretty doctor," Jazz answered. Tossing his cousin an irritated look, he said, "You can stay here and work your ass off, Tate. We can finish this later."

"Nothing to finish," Tate responded amiably. "You think I'm going to let you loose on these two ladies?"

ဢ

"What was that all about?" Anne-Marie asked, glancing in her rearview mirror before backing out of the parking space. Just ahead of her, Tate and Marlie were pulling away from the curb.

"What?"

"That shouting match between you and Tate. Or maybe it

wasn't a match. You were doing all the shouting." Looking at him sideways, Anne-Marie asked, "Was it about Larry Muldoon?"

Sighing, Jazz said, "It was about the whole damned thing. Your dad, Larry. I'm tired of being in the dark."

"It's a job for the law, Jazz. Not you."

"It concerns me every bit as much it does Tate. More, because it affects you."

"And why does that matter so much?" she asked quietly.

"Because I love you," Jazz said, turning his head to look at her.

Her foot slammed down on the brake and she stared at him, her cheeks unusually pale.

"Ex...excuse me?"

"You're blocking traffic," Jazz responded mildly.

"What did you say?" she demanded, throwing the car into park and turning to him while cars stopped behind her and a passerby stopped to stare with avid interest.

One shoulder raised and lowered in a casual shrug. "I said, I love you." Turning his head, he stared at her with blank eyes. "Is there a problem with that?"

"How..." She paused, licked her lips, cleared her throat. "How long?"

"Seems like my entire life."

"Are you talking like, real love, or the brother-sister kind of love?"

"You're not my sister and I'm not your brother," he answered. She looked mighty nervous, he decided. Mighty scared. Why was that?

Softly, she whispered, "The real kind?"

"For more than half my life," he told her, reaching out and brushing a stray lock of hair back from her face. "Is there a problem?"

He was unprepared when she launched herself across the console at him, her arms going tight around his neck. "I never thought I'd hear that from you," she whispered, burying her face against his neck. "I spent almost all my life hoping you'd come back home. But I never thought you'd actually love me."

Closing his eyes, Jazz rested his cheek against her black cloud of hair. "I've loved you from the first moment I saw you, standing there in your daddy's kitchen, hugging that book to your chest."

"Oh, God, Jazz," she sobbed, pulling back far enough to see his face. Pressing her lips to his, she stifled a giggle while tears streamed from her eyes. "I loved you before I saw you. Before I was even born, I think. I feel things for you that I've never felt."

"Even when you thought I was driving the car?"

Anne-Marie stared at him out of teary eyes. "I never thought you were driving, Jazz. I was too afraid to say anything, because of what it meant if you weren't driving. You'd never get drunk enough to lose control like that. Not after Beau."

Shaken, he pulled her back against him, cursing the tight confines of the car. *So many years wasted,* he thought as he stroked her hair. "Marry me, Annie," he said abruptly, taking her arms and pulling away from her to stare down at her face. "Marry me."

Her eyes closed and she sighed, a slow smile curving her lips upward. "In a heartbeat, Jazz. Just name the place."

ॐ

"Daddy?"

Desmond looked up from his book, a smile lighting his face as Anne-Marie entered the room. The smile dimmed a bit when he saw Jazz standing behind her, but it didn't fade. "Jasper. It's been some time since you've been inside this house, hasn't it, son?"

"Yes, sir," Jazz replied. It looked the same, painted a dark green with red accents and mahogany furniture; it still smelled the same, of those cigars Desmond pretended Anne-Marie didn't know about.

Even the old man sitting in the chair by the window looked pretty much the same, just a little older, a little sadder. And as he pushed himself to his feet, Jazz added silently, a little slower.

"Still a man of many words, aren't you, Jazz?" Desmond asked.

"A man I knew when I was a kid always told me, 'Better to keep your mouth closed, and look the fool, than to open it and remove all doubt'," Jazz replied, the tension slowly draining from his body.

The old man knew. It was there in the sharp green eyes, in the way he reached out to stroke a hand down Anne-Marie's hair. When Desmond looked at Jazz, he gave a single, simple nod of approval.

"Well, Annie, have you got something you want to say to me?" he asked, leaning back against his desk, arms folded across his chest to keep from reaching out to her. His baby had grown up. And was getting ready to leave him; never mind that she had lived on her own for nearly five years now.

This was different.

"What makes you think that?" Anne-Marie asked.

"Girl, you never were able to keep a secret, especially not from me," Desmond said, wagging a finger at her. "Don't ever play poker. Those eyes can't hold secrets."

"Dad..." Her voice trailed off as she stared at him.

"Anne-Marie." He said her name quietly, a smile lifting one corner of his mouth.

Anne-Marie left Jazz's arms to go to her father, wrapping her arms around him, inhaling the scent of aromatic tobacco, peppermint and Old Spice. "I'm going to marry him, Daddy," she whispered into his shirtfront.

"Somehow, darlin', I already knew that," Desmond said quietly, stroking his hand down the wild tumble of raven curls. "You set your sights on him long ago, and you've always gotten everything you wanted."

Jazz stood in the doorway, hands tucked inside his pockets. He met Desmond's eyes and swore, "I'll take care of her. I'll love her until the day I die."

"Shoot, boy. You've loved her from the minute you first laid eyes on her. I don't reckon that's going to change at this late date," Desmond said, shaking his head, and he leaned back from Anne-Marie, studied her glowing face and damp eyes. "Fool kids, thinking you can hide that kind of thing from your old man.

"I wish Alex could be here," Desmond whispered, drying a damp tear track with his thumb. "He always knew this would happen, you know. He knew it before I did. I just wish he was here to see it."

ॐ

"It ain't fitting, if you ask me," Betsy snapped, folding her magazine and laying it in her lap. In the mirror, she met Laura's eyes. "Why, his uncle's been dead in the ground only a few weeks and here they are planning a wedding."

What bothered Betsy most was the fact that she hadn't been the one to share the news with the women at the beauty parlor. Why, she hadn't even known about it until old Mabel up and announced her granddaughter, Tabby, and Mariah were both going to be flower girls.

Imagine, inviting a colored child to participate in the wedding. It was one thing to invite the Winslow family, but to actually have one of them in the wedding... Betsy shuddered, casting a sideways glance at Mabel.

Well aware of what was going on behind those catty, blue eyes, Mabel ignored Betsy as she described the dresses Anne-Marie had in mind for Tabby and Mariah.

"Why, it's sort of sickening, actually. Those two are practically related, with Doc Kincade raising Jazz on his own and all." Betsy huffed and resettled in her chair while Laura skillfully made allowances for her restless customer. Exchanging a sideways glance with Mabel, she pressed her lips together and pasted an interested expression on her freckled face. "Makes you wonder what was going on in that house before Jazz left."

"Now, those two are no more related than you and me," Mabel said, her dark face creasing as a smile spread across her lips. "I think it's about damned time. Any fool can see that those two should be together. Dr. Anne was just waiting and biding her time for him to come home anyhow."

"Up until a few weeks ago, he was guilty of killing her brother," Betsy responded righteously, admiring the way the new red curls fell over her forehead. She'd need to dye her brows to match, though. "What woman would marry the man guilty of killing her brother?"

"Anne-Marie Kincade never believed Jazz killed Alex," a sultry, low voice announced. Sandy Pritchard stood in the doorway of the salon, eyeing Betsy with obvious disdain. "Neither did I."

"Believe or not, what would people think?"

"I doubt Anne-Marie is overly concerned with what people think," Sandy replied with a casual shrug of her well-tanned, nearly naked shoulders. Smoothing down the front of her lacy camisole-styled blouse, Sandy asked, "Laura, are you able to fit me in?"

"Soon as I finish with Miss Betsy, Sandy."

With narrowed eyes, Betsy looked at her reflections. "The color is too bright, Laura. We'll have to fix that before I could ever leave. It looks unnatural."

With a smirk, Sandy turned away. Any seventy-two-year-old woman prancing around with red hair was going to look unnatural, no matter how bright the color. Settling languidly into a chair, Sandy said, "No rush. I just wanted to get my hair cut before the weekend rolled around."

"What sorta plans you got goin', girl?" Mabel asked. Hands covered with suds, she rinsed the shampoo from Willa Davies' hair.

"If I know Sandy," Willa said from the sink, "we may not need to know what sort of plans she has. I doubt mine or Betsy's heart could handle them."

"Shoot, girl. You'd better tell. Your life is what keeps mine interesting," Mabel said, with a loud laugh.

With a small smile, Sandy looked up from her magazine and said, "I plan on lassoing myself a sheriff this weekend. Gotta look my best."

From the corner, Marlie's hands stilled for only the smallest of moments as she started applying a topcoat to Linda Devane's nails. "I think this shade of pink really suits you, Linda," Marlie said quietly, her eyelids barely flickering as Sandy described her plans for the weekend.

A bittersweet smile on her face, Marlie acknowledged that of course Tate would be interested in Sandy, gorgeous as all get out, funny, smart, brave. She wasn't plain white trash and she had gone to college. Currently, she was the sole lawyer in a twenty-mile radius. They even had the law in common.

But, God, it hurt.

"—true, Marlie?"

Glancing up, Marlie met Sandy's friendly brown eyes. Bad enough she was so beautiful, Marlie thought. She was also as nice as she could be. "I'm sorry, my mind was wandering, Sandy. I didn't hear what you said."

"I'd heard you were looking into moving to Lexington. Is that so?"

With money from Larry's life insurance and the pay they would collect from the state, Marlie and her Mama had quite a nest egg now. Enough to put a hefty down payment on a little house somewhere far away from Briarwood, and everybody who knew the Muldoons. It was only fitting, Marlie decided, for her brother to give her this fresh start.

After all, if it hadn't been for her hellish family, her life might not be such a mess. She might not be such a mess.

"I'm looking into it," Marlie responded, looking down, shaping Linda's nails up just a bit more.

"Can't say I blame you, Marlie. It must be so humiliating for you, you poor thing, after what your family went and did to Jasper," Betsy stated loudly, glancing Marlie's way.

Even as Sandy opened her mouth to respond, even as Mabel's eyes narrowed and Laura's mouth firmed, Marlie laid down the nail file and stood up. Her voice quiet but firm, she said, "Larry did it, not me, not my Mama. Larry, and Larry alone. I feel terrible for Jazz, I truly do, but I had nothing to do with it."

"Now, child, I didn't mean—"

"Yes, you did," Marlie interrupted. "You darned well did mean. And don't bother apologizing. I've had it up to here," she slashed at her neck with an impatient hand, "with people offering me false apologies, false sympathy and false friendships. Don't waste your breath."

Not looking at anybody, Marlie settled back down in her chair, added a final touch to Linda's nails, and said, "There you go. You're set for the dance this weekend."

"Well, I never—" Betsy said, her mouth working silently for a moment before she was finally able to speak. "Girl, you have got nerve, talking to me like that. After all I have done to try and help you out of your unfortunate situation."

"I don't call having your granddaughter send her worn-out rags my way helping out, Betsy. Or telling me that I can have the leftovers from your holiday meals if I'd come over and help you serve," Marlie said in a calm voice, even though inside, she was shaking.

"Just doing my Christian duty, girl—"

"Christian duty has nothing to do with what you do. You merely rub in how fortunate and lucky you are, and how unfortunate me and my Mama have always been. I'll say nothing more on the matter, Betsy."

"Way to go, Marlie, honey," Sandy called out, applauding, approval in her dark eyes.

Marlie ignored her, wished Linda a good day and gathered

her supplies, stowing them under the table. Moments later, she was hurrying down the sidewalk, tears stinging her eyes.

Unfortunate? Marlie thought bleakly.

Pathetic is more like it.

"Whoa, there," Jazz said as he crashed right into the tiny blonde. When she raised her eyes to his, he was somewhat startled to recognize Marlie Jo, her indigo eyes awash with tears, her cheeks whiter than death.

"Marlie, what's wrong?" Jazz asked, guiding her into the doorway of the consignment shop, out of the way of the midday sidewalk traffic.

"Nothing," she whispered harshly, dashing a hand across the tears streaking down her face. "Let me go, Jasper."

He tightened his grip on her shoulders, studying her averted face. "What's got you so upset, Marlie?" he asked again, frowning. "What happened?"

Marlie laughed, a brittle, pain-filled sound. "Happened?" she repeated. "Nothing new has happened." With a sudden jerk, she tore free from his hands. "It's the same damned thing that has been haunting me for years. And you know what? I'm tired of it."

"Marlie—"

"Leave me alone," she ordered, her voice rough. Turning on her heel, she strode away from him as fast as her legs could carry her.

೮೦

Tate sipped at his beer and gave Sandy Pritchard an absent look as she ran her red-tipped nails through her fall of thick russet hair. Her brown eyes were full of appreciation and humor, but Tate was only mildly interested. He knew what she was after; he couldn't say he wasn't flattered.

He just wasn't interested.

Full breasts strained against the bodice of her sundress and her perfume was subtle and sexy, but all Tate could think of was silvery blonde hair and sad eyes.

Just then, that familiar, silvery blonde head crossed his line of vision and Tate's head whipped around, following Marlie as she led her mother across the church grounds. She'd finally gotten the old woman out of the house. He couldn't believe it.

When an irritated sigh came from across the table, Tate turned his eyes back to Sandy's. She had a smile dancing around her full, deep red mouth as she watched him. Tapping out her cigarette, Sandy said, "It's starting to look like a McNeil man is not in my future."

He closed his eyes for a minute and then looked back at Sandy, "I've always liked you, Sandy. But—"

"But, nothing," she cut him off, shrugging. "No harm done. At least, not to me." She was remembering the look in Marlie's eyes several days earlier. "Does she know how you feel?"

"I've never told her," he said, slumping in his chair and staring up at the painfully blue sky.

"I'd suggest you do it and do it quick. That girl is aiming on getting out of this town, Tate. And leaving you and everybody else behind her."

With a laugh, Tate brushed that aside. "She won't leave here. She's been thinking about it for years, and she's never done it."

"Until recently, she didn't have the means available," Sandy said. "With Larry being a civil servant and up and dying, well, it's my guess she has a lot more money than before."

"Sonovabitch!" Tate hissed under his breath as he realized how true Sandy's words were. With the life insurance policy alone, Marlie could live for several years without having to lift a finger, if she so chose.

His eyes darted helplessly in Marlie's direction.

With a self-deprecating laugh, Sandy waved him away. "Go on. Wearing your heart on your sleeve like that, you're a waste of my time, anyway."

ℰↄ

Marlie Jo smiled down at her Mama as the old woman stroked a finger over the silky dress of the porcelain doll Marlie had bought her. "She sure is pretty, Marlie. You sure your daddy won't mind us getting her?"

"Daddy's dead, Mama. He's past caring now," she reminded her mother, aching to see that fear leave her eyes once and for all. But Marlie didn't know if that fear would ever completely go away. "Come on, now, Mama. Get in the car." She opened the door and helped her mother into the car. Marlie bent over and tucked her mother's skirt in so it wouldn't catch in the door.

"Dead?"

Crouching down, Marlie touched her mother's arm. "Yes, Mama. He's dead. He died a while back. Remember?"

"Oh. Oh, yes. I remember now." But she didn't, not really. Yet, she was happy, stroking the lovely Gibson Girl-styled doll. Mama had always liked pretty things, just had never gotten any of them.

Until now, Marlie thought, thinking of the money sitting in the bank. They'd have a pretty, little house, pretty furniture that wouldn't get torn to shreds, and maybe even another pet.

"Marlie."

At the sound of Tate's voice, she didn't respond right away. Instead, she finished helping her mother into the car, bending to put Naomi's purse down in the floorboard. Straightening, she gently reminded, "Fasten the seat belt, Mama."

"Yes. Yes, I will," Naomi promised, her faded, green eyes focused on the doll.

Marlie turned slowly, meeting Tate's eyes only after she had carefully blanked hers. "Hello, Tate. Are you enjoying yourself?" she asked him, taking a deep breath, inhaling the scents of fried chicken, cotton candy and summer.

Tate's scent was there as well, heated male and long cool nights, all blended together. Even as the smell of him sent little darts of heat through her belly, she shuddered and fought against letting him see how much his nearness affected her.

"I've heard you still plan on moving to the city," Tate said, jamming his hands in his pockets, watching her with unreadable eyes.

Checking to make sure Naomi's feet weren't dangling outside the car, Marlie shut the door and walked around to the other side. "That's right. I'm going Sunday to look at a house. I think Mama would like it."

"No, she won't. Neither would you. Briarwood is your home, Marlie."

Opening the primer-gray door to the Ford Pinto, Marlie slid into the car as she said, "This isn't home to me, Tate. And I'd be happier anywhere else besides here."

"Marlie—"

"See you around, Tate," she said, jerking the door closed.

"That was rude, Marlie. The boy likes you," Naomi said softly, still stroking the doll. Her misty green eyes were not as distant and dreamy as usual.

But Marlie was lost, too lost in despair to even notice.

&

She hadn't just driven away while he was talking to her?

Tate insisted that to himself three times before he finally forced himself to admit that the evidence was to the contrary. The dust from her leaving had already faded, he couldn't see the rusty red tail of the car, and most importantly, Tate was standing there in an empty field full of cars, by himself. No Marlie.

"I'll be damned," he muttered to himself, turning on his heel.

&

"Sandy, where did that son of mine run off to?"

Glancing up from her beer, Sandy smiled at Ella. "He went chasing after your future daughter-in-law; at least, that would be my guess."

Those lovely, blue eyes went wide and Ella asked, "Excuse me?"

Lifting the bottle in a toast, Sandy sipped at it before saying, "He went tearing off after Marlie Jo. Unless I am seriously mistaken, he wasn't going to come back unless it was with her."

"Marlie...Jo?" Ella repeated, somewhat numbly. "Tate went after Marlie Jo Muldoon?"

"Yep." Sandy shrugged. "I keep getting thrown over for

217

delicate, petite things. I mentioned something about Marlie Jo wanting to move to Lexington or Frankfort and once Tate realized I meant she was seriously wanting to leave, he took off."

One slim hand rose to fiddle with the strand of pearls she wore at her neck as Ella slowly lowered herself to the empty folding chair next to Sandy. "I never realized he had those sort of feelings for Marlie. She's so fragile."

Sandy chuckled and shook her head. "No, ma'am. Fragile, Marlie is not. Delicate, yes. Quiet, yes. But she's not fragile." After another laugh, she launched into a detailed account of the encounter between Miss Betsy and Marlie just two days earlier.

"So, you think she has feelings for him as well," Ella said after Sandy had finished.

"Powerful feelings, unless I am mistaken. If I'd have known, I wouldn't have mentioned today in front of her. She looked so sad, and it just now dawned on me why."

"But you care for Tate."

"Not like she does." Turning her eyes away to study the crowd, Sandy said, "I'm looking to get married, Miss Ella. I'll be honest about that. But I don't want a husband who doesn't love me. Now if I was in love with Tate, maybe it would be different and I'd want to fight for him. But as much as I care for him, as good a man as he is, I don't want him that much."

"I just don't understand it." Ella laced her fingers over her still-flat belly, pressed her lips together in a frown before consciously making the effort to relax. After all, the years you spend frowning will eventually show on your face. Her face was free of lines, save for the small ones at the corners of her eyes. Ella liked to think they gave her face character.

"Marlie is not at all what I imagined for Tate. She's a sweet girl, but..."

"She's stronger than people think," Sandy said with a shrug of her shoulders. "And apparently, she is what Tate wants."

ॐ

"Aren't you coming in?" Anne-Marie asked, lifting her face to his, studying him in the silvery moonlight.

"Nope," Jazz responded, tucking his hands in his pockets. "I'm not coming in until you make an honest man out of me."

A slim brow rose and Anne-Marie repeated, "An honest man? What an oxymoron."

Assuming an affronted glare, he asked, "Who are you calling a moron?"

Anne-Marie smiled serenely at him and replied, "Any man who turns down the chance to spend the night having wild sex with his fiancée is a moron, in my opinion."

Hooking his hand over the back of her neck, Jazz dragged her forward, taking her mouth roughly, running his hands over her slim back. "The thing is, Doc," he said when he pulled away to breathe, "I'm kinda afraid of your dad. If he knows I'm out here, he's gonna come after me."

"Well, shoot."

With a wide grin, Jazz said, "That's what I'm afraid of...*shooting...*"

Snorting with laughter, her system still humming from his touch, Anne-Marie shook her head. "Well, if a shotgun wedding will get you in my bed, I'll hunt up the gun." Reaching out for his hand, she tugged him closer. Pressing her lips to his neck, she repeated, "Come inside, Jazz."

"Annie," he muttered, groaning when her tongue darted out to lap at his neck. "Girl, behave yourself." Why in hell had he

219

decided not to be with her again until after the wedding? He must have been out of his mind.

"Why?" she asked huskily. "I'm so much more fun when I don't."

Dragging her head back, Jazz attacked her mouth, diving deep, nipping, while his hands raced up and down her lithe little body. Then he pulled away and stepped back. Chest heaving, breaths ragged, he said, "Now maybe you'll sleep as good as I've been lately."

Eyes wide and dazed, Anne-Marie wobbled a little, not completely understanding as he ushered her inside. He lowered his head and Anne-Marie reached for him eagerly, only to have him peck her on the cheek and whisper, "I love you."

The gentle click of the lock brought her out of her lust-induced daze and she stood staring at the door, eyes narrowed as the engine outside revved.

Chapter Ten

A week after the summer carnival, Marlie had forgotten the odd exchange with Tate in the shadowed field outside the high school. So busy, it was somewhat unsettling to discover she hadn't thought of him much at all in the past week. Only five or six times a day, maximum.

As she opened the door to reveal an irritable, rumpled county sheriff, that odd, little encounter came rushing back to her mind.

"What in the world...?"

Brushing past a wide-eyed Marlie, Tate stomped into the tiny kitchen and turned to face her. "Have you found a place in Lexington?"

"Lexington?" she repeated, her smooth brow furrowing. "No. I'm not moving to Lexington."

Tate's eyes closed and the tension left his body.

"I'm moving to Frankfort."

His eyes flew open and he stood ramrod straight. "Frankfort?" he repeated, studying her face.

"Yes. I'm making an offer on a house tomorrow. I've already got a job lined up and—"

"No."

Marlie's eyes went cold. Slowly, carefully, she said, "Excuse me?"

"No." Tate advanced on her, cornering her against the door. "I'm sorry, Marlie. But there's no way you can leave here."

"I fail to see why not," she said, her voice quivering just slightly. Her eyes darted across his face and her thoughts stumbled to a stop at the look in his eyes. She'd seen a look like that before, a look full of heat and promise and need. One full of love. The looks she so envied between Jazz and Anne-Marie.

Slowly, Tate traced the line of her face with his hand as he spoke in an offhand manner. "I always thought I had plenty of time. You weren't going anywhere and you never went out with anybody." Long fingers buried themselves in her hair, joined by his other hand as he lowered his head, brushed his mouth across hers gently.

"Looks like I don't have as much time as I thought." Then, using his hold on her hair, Tate angled Marlie's face up and covered her mouth. *Sweet*, he thought, nibbling at her mouth until her lips parted on a shuddering sigh. As he steeped himself in the taste of her, Tate eased her slim body up until she was pressed against him.

"Kiss me back, Marlie," he whispered, dragging his mouth to her ear. Reaching between them, he laid his hand on her chest, felt the rapid pounding of her heart. "Haven't you ever wondered?"

Oh, my. Her head falling back, all coherent thought gone, Marlie decided that she was dreaming. There was no way on earth that she was standing here, in this tiny kitchen, with Tate kissing her.

When his mouth covered hers a second time, Marlie trembled. At first, she stood there passively, hands clenching tightly at her sides, but need and curiosity overtook her. Rising on her toes, she returned his kiss, shy and quick. Her tongue darted out to taste him before withdrawing. Pulling back, Marlie stared up at him. Those warm, brown eyes weren't warm anymore. They were hot.

Rising on her toes again, she pressed her mouth back to his, nibbling delicately at his lip before tentatively exploring within. His hands fisted in her hair as he pressed her back against the door, his large body leaning into hers.

"Don't go to Frankfort, Marlie," Tate whispered, pulling away and staring into her eyes. Everything he'd always dreamed of seeing was there. The love he had felt for her almost his entire life was returned in hers, along with nerves and disbelief.

Cupping her face with his hand, Tate rained butterfly kisses over her cheeks and eyes before homing in on her mouth for a sweet, innocent kiss. Moments later, Marlie turned her head aside. She had to know. She was dreaming and asking him would shatter the dream and she would wake up and go on with her life, without Tate, as always.

"Why?"

A slow smile spread across his face as he eased her back against him. "Because I'd hate living in Frankfort and so would you. This is your home. Our home."

Voice quavering, Marlie said, "Nobody said anything about you moving to Frankfort."

Her breath left her in a startled rush as Tate swung her up in his arms, carrying her to the table. Lowering himself into the rickety chair, Tate settled Marlie against him, telling her, "I wouldn't have much choice in the matter, Marlie. I'll go where you go."

Okay. I'll wake up any minute now, Marlie thought.

But she wasn't dreaming. No dream could be this vivid. And even as much as she loved him, hungered for him, needed him, Marlie wouldn't dare dream something like this. He was so far out of her reach; a fish flying was more likely.

Tate lowered his head to hers and bussed her mouth with his as a tear welled up and spilled over. "I love you. I have for as long as I can remember. There's only been you, Marlie."

ⅎ

Marlie smiled nervously at Ella as she poured her a glass of wine; it was a pretty, deep red color that caught the light. Raising it to her lips, she sipped tentatively, and then more boldly as a riot of flavors burst on her tongue. "Oh, my. This is wonderful, Mrs. McNeil."

"Ella," she corrected, raising her own glass. Swirling, sipping, approving, she then lowered the wine glass back to the table. "After all, we're going to be family." She smiled at her son as he strolled through the door. "So hard to believe, you getting married."

Tate paused by her chair and brushed her smooth cheek with his mouth before going to Marlie and lowering himself to her side. "It's not hard for me," he said, raising Marlie's hand to his lips. "I've been planning it from the first time I saw her, Mama."

"Since you were all of five years old, hmm? And Marlie was maybe three?" Ella asked, amused.

Seriously, Tate said, "That sounds about right." Nibbling at her knuckles, he added, "That's why we're having a short engagement. Been waiting too long as it is."

Marlie's cheeks colored and she pulled her hand away, casting Ella a glance. *Could this really be happening?* she wondered, raising the wine once more. Over the rim of the glass, Tate's eyes met hers, full of warmth and promises. *Yes.*

It's real.

"Have you any idea what sort of wedding dress you would like?" Ella asked, a faraway smile on her face. "I always dreamed of helping plan a wedding."

"I'd be more than grateful for any help you can give me," Marlie offered shyly. "I have no clue how to begin."

Settling back in his chair, Tate snagged Marlie's wine glass and drank half of it while his mother and fiancée talked of silk and lace. After a few moments, Marlie's face lost its stiffness and she became more animated. She was so beautiful. And his.

Mine, he thought again, his fingers curling around the delicate stem of the glass.

"Just think, this time next week, we'll be at Jazz and Anne-Marie's wedding," Ella mused. "You'd think it was spring, with all these weddings going on."

"I saw her dress," Marlie said. "She looked so beautiful. Pure white, lace and pearls."

Ella's eyes narrowed thoughtfully as Marlie described the dress. "I've seen something similar to that in Lexington."

Flushing, Marlie laughed and shook her head. "That's not for me. I want something simple. Ivory, I think."

"Wise choice," Ella decided after a moment. "Nothing too fussy. Understated elegance, that's what we need for you. Perhaps we could go looking...?"

"Oh, I'd love that. But Mama..." Marlie said quietly, a little worried.

Ella smiled. "She'll go, too. We'll make a day of it. How about the weekend after next?"

Tate's thoughts drifted away as they spoke, his contentment fading as his mind focused on the case. Who had killed Larry Muldoon? Mind spinning, he offered occasional 'hmms' and 'uh-huhs' as he laid it out piece by piece in his mind.

"...your hair?"

His eyes flew up from the wine glass he had been studying without seeing it. Reaching out, he brushed his hand down Marlie's silvery blonde locks. "I'd like it down," he said quietly, twining a thick ribbon of hair around his finger. "You've got the most beautiful hair."

As her future daughter-in-law flushed and flirted shyly with Tate, Ella settled back in her seat with a smile on her face.

ꙮ

Jazz stumbled up the steps, his arm thrown across Tate's shoulders for balance. "How come there's so many stairs?" he mumbled. "I coulda swore there were only three of them earlier."

"There's only three now, cuz," Tate replied, half-dragging Jazz's body up those three stairs. "Damn it, Jazz. Lose some weight."

His drunken laugh ended abruptly as he banged his elbow on the doorjamb when Tate let go to dig out his keys. "Bastard," he mumbled, nursing his stinging elbow and glaring at the shadow of his cousin.

"Sue me," Tate offered, jamming the key in the lock and turning it. "Now quiet down or you'll wake up Mabel and Mariah."

"Not my fault ya'll wanted to throw some hokey party," Jazz said as he stumbled through the door. "Six more days, Tate. And she's all mine."

Shooting his cousin an amused glance, Tate said, "Hell,

she's always been yours. She—"

The drunken cloud faded from Jazz's mind as he laid one hand on the banister. The silence echoed in his ears, unbelievably loud. Something was wrong...

He looked up, his eyes focusing halfway up the staircase to a single bloody red swipe that marred the soft yellow paint. A thick silence filled the house and Jazz could swear he heard his own heart stop.

Tate grew aware of it just as Jazz did, reaching inside his jacket for his gun. "Get out," he said flatly. "Call dispatch."

"Hell I will," Jazz said, shaking his head and scrubbing his hands over his face. "My home, Tate." He tore off up the stairs at a run, Tate's muttered curse and booted feet close behind.

Throwing open the door, he lunged for Mariah's bedside. "She's fine," Tate said low, gripping his arm from behind as Mariah's soft, gentle snores filled the room. "Will you stay here?"

"Where's Mabel?" he asked quietly. "She would have met us at the door. I know her."

"Stay with Mariah. What if he's still here?" Tate ordered, his voice full of authority as he reached for the phone. In a quiet voice, he issued orders before turning and studying Jazz. He still stood there, staring down at the sleeping body of his daughter.

As they watched, her face puckered in a frown and she mumbled something before flopping over on her side, dislodging her little ragdoll, Cherries. Cherries went tumbling to the floor.

The head of the doll was missing, replaced by a gaping hole that spilled white cotton stuffing. Slowly, Jazz lowered himself to his knees and lifted the beheaded doll. "Find Mabel, Tate. Find her now."

227

Tate didn't have to look far.

Sturdy, old Mabel, her smooth, brown face was still and cold. Frozen in an expression of pure shock as she lay on her back in the bathroom just down the hall from Mariah's room. By her outstretched hand was the missing doll head.

Tate's eyes fastened on the little piece of metal protruding from the doll's head. Then his eyes locked on the nail gun lying by the door. Finally, he turned and focused on the macabre sight of Mabel Winslow lying in a sprawl in the middle of the floor, her eyes rolled up, as if trying to see the nail that shot into her skull.

Blood and gore splattered the bathtub behind her from where she had fallen and hit the tub with her head.

Pausing, he closed his eyes and took a deep breath. And then he backed out of the bathroom. "Jazz, I'd advise you to call Anne-Marie to come get Mariah."

Ȣ

The whole town was silent, nervous. People shot each other suspicious looks and glanced over their shoulders often.

Instead of a wedding, the rainy Saturday had a funeral scheduled. Ayeisha Winslow, her daughter Tabby at her side, both of them crying quietly as they stared at the headstone. There was no body. The body couldn't be released yet, but Ayeisha had gone ahead with the funeral without the body.

The body.

Oh, God. Mama.

"You'll find who killed my Mama, Sheriff McNeil," she said softly to the man standing next to her. He stood there, quiet and somber, his hat in his hands and his head bowed. When she spoke, he looked up from the headstone and nodded. "I will find him, Ayeisha. I promise."

Though the minister had spoken his final words some time back, people still crowded around the headstone, out of respect, shock, grief and curiosity. Mabel Winslow had been a fixture in this town, much like Betsy Crane.

Softly, he said once more, "I'll find him, Ayeisha."

Nodding once, her proud chin went up in the air. "I'll hold you to that." Across the grass, she met the tearful gaze of Betsy Crane. Her silly, red hair was covered by a wide-brimmed hat draped with black netting. It didn't surprise Ayeisha to see tears in those eyes. Querulous bigot that Betsy was, Betsy had, in her own weird way, really liked Mabel, liked arguing with her, liked insulting her, liked pretending to dislike her.

Mabel had known, as did Ayeisha.

Tears spilled out of her eyes, trickled down her cheeks as she moved across the wet grass to the headstone. Laying her hand on it, she closed her eyes. "Mama, Tate's gonna find who did this. I promise."

ॐ

Anne-Marie stood in the Winslow kitchen side by side with Marlie, slicing a loaf of fresh-baked bread. "I just don't understand it," she whispered. "Who could kill Mabel? And why?"

"I don't know." Marlie's voice was husky and thick with tears. "It just doesn't make any sense."

Casting a look over her shoulder, Anne-Marie studied Jazz's averted profile. "He's blaming himself. He keeps trying to pull away from me. I think he's trying to protect me. Whoever did this, did it to get to him."

Quietly, making sure nobody could overhear, Marlie murmured, "Tate's stumped. There are no prints, no connection, really, other than Jazz."

Anne-Marie's reply cut off as Ella entered the room, looking ten years older. Marlie went to Ella and hugged her. "It's going to be okay, Ella. Tate will find out who did it."

Reaching up, Ella stroked her carefully tinted hair. "She just did my hair last week," she whispered, stricken. "We went to school together. She was too young...

"It just doesn't make any sense. What in the world is happening to Briarwood, Marlie?" Ella asked, turning away, staring out into the miserable rain.

ॐ

Three weeks passed, three terror-filled, endless weeks. No evidence, no suspects. Nothing. The silence hadn't lulled anybody into thinking it was over. Instead, people became jumpier and meaner and just plain dangerous. Tate raised his head, staring into the cells across the room from his desk. All three were full.

That simply didn't happen in Briarwood, Friday night or not.

The thin, early morning light shone through the windows as the three drunks continued sleeping it off. The damage done at the bar had been light, this time. But one man was in the hospital after Bobby Mason had broken his hand.

Tempers were flying high, fear filled every face Tate saw, and there was no end in sight.

God, he wanted this over.

He wanted to marry Marlie, take her to bed, and wake up wrapped around her, no thoughts on his mind save for making love to her again.

Instead, the weddings, both his and Jazz's, had been postponed.

"What am I missing?" he asked himself, locking his hands behind his neck and staring down at the reports on his desk.

With a sour laugh, Tate admitted there wasn't much to miss. No evidence. No hairs. No fibers. The nail gun had come from Jazz's toolbox out in the garage. The only prints were his. And, thank God, Jazz had a good alibi for that night.

When the phone rang, Tate reached for it automatically. "McNeil here."

"Tate."

The fear in Marlie's voice had him on his feet. "What's wrong?"

"Tate...I need you to come out here."

"What's wrong?" he demanded, the fear filling his gut making him ill.

"Please come."

And the line went dead. He slammed it down and was out of the station house in seconds.

When he arrived at Marlie's, he found her sitting in her twin bed, surrounded by locks of pale blonde hair. Her beautiful hair had been hacked away, in some places leaving it hardly longer than an inch. As her eyes met his, he saw they brimmed with confusion and terror. They were oddly dazed, the pupils wide, not contracted at all when he lifted the shade, letting light flood the room.

"Somebody cut my hair," she whispered, reaching up one hand to touch her scalp. "I was sleeping and they just cut it off."

"Honey." It was hard to remember he had to be a cop now, hard to remember he had a job to do, when it was his woman sitting there, her eyes filled with fear and confusion.

"I called Anne-Marie," she whispered softly, her voice singsong. "I don't know why."

"What in the hell...?"

Tate's eyes turned to see Anne-Marie standing in the doorway. It shook him to discover he hadn't even heard her drive up. "Somebody is going to pay for this," he said, rising, lifting Marlie's shaking form in his arms.

"Mama?" Marlie asked, lifting her shorn head from Tate's shoulder. "Is Mama okay?"

"I'm sure she is," Anne-Marie said quietly. "I'll go check on her."

Tate settled in the living room after making his call to Darla. Anne-Marie found him there, rocking Marlie back and forth while the young woman whimpered in his arms.

"Tate."

He jerked his head around at Anne-Marie's voice, feeling the color drain from his face. Please, God, no.

"Naomi's not there," Anne-Marie whispered quietly, casting Marlie a troubled glance. "Not anywhere."

ဢ

With a jerk, Tate pulled down the yellow police tape and stood aside as Jazz unlocked the door.

"What are we looking for?" Jazz asked as he entered the house.

I don't want to be here, he thought, staring at the red smear on the wall. It was Mabel's blood and brain matter, smeared there by her killer to torment Jazz.

"I really don't know," Tate responded, shaking his head, walking around the living room. "There has got to be something."

"How is Marlie?"

"Holding up. Laura fixed her hair and..."

"You don't give a damn about her hair," Jazz interrupted when Tate's voice trailed off. "I can't make any sense of it. Why cut her hair off? Why let her Mama go off wandering around alone? The woman's lucky she ain't dead somewhere."

"I know. It's got Marlie all torn up inside. I just can't figure out how they connect to you."

"Neither can I." Turning away, Jazz studied the painting that Mariah had picked out at a flea market. In the glass, he could dimly see Tate's reflection as he wandered the room.

"This just doesn't make any sense."

Mumbling, pacing back and forth over the floor, Tate said, "There's a connection here somewhere. I know it. We're probably looking right at it."

It took two days for them to find Mrs. Muldoon, and then she ended up in the hospital for dehydration and exposure. Tate got nothing from her. From the looks of her, she had done nothing more than wander around, until she was seen by a passing truck driver. The trucker had recognized her from a picture in the local paper when he stopped at the small park where Naomi had stopped to splash in the water like a child.

A few more days...she would have likely died. Her mind was too far gone to remember things like food and water, even the basics of shelter.

The killer had most likely known that.

∞

"Anne, I can go home. I'm fine," Marlie insisted, following her down the hall, a frown creasing her face.

Turning on her heel, Anne-Marie studied that pale face dispassionately and decided, "The hell you are."

Determined, Marlie said, "I am not going to spend the rest of my life hiding because some nut snuck up on me while I was sleeping and cut my hair."

"He could have cut more than that," Anne-Marie said, jamming her arms into the sleeves of her jacket.

"Don't you think I know that?" Marlie asked quietly, arms held stiffly at her sides, hands clenched into fists. "Don't you think I've had nightmares about that? My God, I wake up expecting to find my throat slit."

The sheer terror in Marlie's voice slowed Anne-Marie's steps. One hand resting on the newel post, Anne-Marie stared straight ahead. It wasn't a stretch of the imagination, not by any means. The worst thing was that it was nowhere near being over. "All the more reason for you not to be alone," she finally said, turning to study the face of her new friend.

"If he wants me bad enough, he's going to get me, regardless of where I am. I can't spend my life hiding because of this. My God, you and Jazz put your wedding off. Because of this," she said, frowning, reaching up to touch her shorn cap of hair.

"Marlie. Stay here. Please," Anne-Marie said tiredly. Dragging a hand over her neat braid, she sighed. Studying her face in the decorative mirror, she shook her head. "You and your mom are safer here with me and Dad."

"We've been here three weeks already. We can't stay here indefinitely. I want to plan my wedding. I want to dance at yours. Are we going to let this end our lives?"

"They'll find out who is doing this," Anne-Marie responded.

"And if they don't? It's been months since it all started. And Tate, God help him, still doesn't have a clue who did it."

"Don't have much faith in your man, do you, Marlie?"

"I have complete faith in him. But I don't want to put my life on hold, waiting for him to finish this. Anne-Marie, I need to go back to my own house."

"Not yet."

"Anne-Marie—"

"Please, just a bit longer. Something's going to happen soon, I know it."

&

One hand on the wheel, Anne-Marie hissed out an irritated breath while she rooted through her bag for her cell phone. "Damn it!" she muttered, smacking her hand against the console before upending the bag and sifting through the contents.

It wasn't there. Where in the hell had she put it? Gee, Jazz was going to roast her alive. She'd promised she wouldn't leave the house without the cell phone.

She glanced at the clock on the dash. It had only been a few minutes since she took the call from the new nurse at the hospital. "Five minutes. It'll just take me five minutes to go back—

"Damnation!" she shouted, jerking the wheel to the side and slamming on the brakes. The impact was expected. She'd been going too fast to stop completely. Still, when she hit the huge, old oak, her brain ceased to function for a moment, just out of shock.

She teetered for a brief moment at the top of the hill, the passenger's side wedged up against the tree. With a grinding noise of metal on metal, the car careened the rest of the way down the embankment, settling nose first into the creek. She had only a moment to be thankful it hadn't been a wet summer before the shock settled and blackness closed in around her.

The gray mist was receding when a familiar voice spoke from just outside the car door, a few feet away on the bank.

"You really should learn to slow down a bit, Anne-Marie. Be more careful."

∾

"What do you mean, there's no emergency?" Jazz repeated, his voice rising. Hand clenched tightly around the phone, he said through gritted teeth, "Marlie was here when the new nurse called and said she hadn't been able to reach Jake Hart and there was an emergency."

"I'm sorry," the unit secretary said. "I don't know what new nurse you're talking about. There aren't any new nurses here. And there's been no emergency today for any of Dr. Kincade's or Dr. Hart's patients."

"No emergency." Slamming down the receiver, he turned on Marlie. "What time was the phone call?"

"Three thirty," she whispered, her face bloodless. "There's no emergency. No new nurse."

"No." Snatching the phone back up, Jazz dialed Tate's cell phone.

"She's been gone four hours," Jazz said testily after Tate told him to calm down. "She's not at the hospital. Not at her house. I call her cell phone and get a damned 'out of area' message. He's got her, Tate."

"I'm heading out," Tate said. "Stay with Marlie—"

"The hell I will. That's my woman out there..." The heated anger in Jazz's voice died away as he turned to study Marlie Muldoon, standing a few feet away with her arm around her mother, tiny and fragile. "Damn it, Tate."

"Go find my daughter," a soft voice said from the doorway.

"Sir, I can't leave Marlie alone here."

"It's not Marlie he wants," Desmond said. "It never was. All of this has revolved around you, Jazz." As he spoke, he reached down, just out of Jazz's sight, lifting the heavy, well-oiled shotgun Jazz had always seen hanging above the desk in Desmond's study. "Besides, boy. I ain't exactly helpless."

&

It was a wonder he saw it, driving as fast as he was. But that flash of red, all but hidden from sight by trees and brush, caught Jazz's eyes as he sped down the lane. Slamming the car into reverse, he backed up until he caught the glimpse of red again. But it wasn't the red paint that caught his eye this time.

It was the torn and mangled bushes, the tree with huge patches of bark missing, the pale under-skin of the tree marred with black streaks and flecks of red paint and metal.

"Jesus," he whispered as he fought his way through the tangled undergrowth.

It was Anne-Marie's beloved Mustang, the body torn and mangled, all but buried in the deep creek bed that ran just inside the tree line. Only a breath of the trunk was visible from the roadside. Half submerged in the water, it sat empty.

"Anne-Marie!" he shouted, frantically searching the banks with his eyes after a quick glance inside the car confirmed it to be empty. "Anne-Marie!"

Splashing his way across the shallow, drought-depleted creek, Jazz's frantic search came to an abrupt halt.

There, lying on the pebble-strewn bank was Anne-Marie's pearl necklace.

&

Tate stood in the silent living room of his house, the house he'd grown up in—the "For Sale" sign out front next to another sign announcing an "Open House" every Sunday from one to three.

His hand closed convulsively around his cell phone and he lowered his lids, blocking out the room and the pictures on the walls. They hadn't found Anne-Marie. A rain had blown up shortly after dusk and washed away the scent before they had time to utilize the dogs.

Returning home only to refuel and change out of his mud-and-rain-stiffened uniform, he had come to an empty house.

Now, opening his eyes, staring at the pictures on the wall, the missing piece of the puzzle finally fell into place.

&

Jazz rubbed his gritty eyes once more before reaching for the thick brew that passed as coffee on the days Darla wasn't there to brew it. Knocking it back, grimacing at the taste, he willed the phone to ring. Willed the door to open to one of the searchers carrying Anne-Marie.

But when the door did open, it revealed his cousin. The odd, blank expression in Tate's eyes had cold chills running down his spine. *Oh, God, no,* he prayed silently as he rose once more.

"Anne-Marie? Have they found her?" Jazz was almost afraid to ask, and at the same time, afraid not to.

"I think I know where she is," Tate said, his voice flat, his eyes cold. "Come on. We don't have much time."

"Where is she?" Jazz asked, lunging for Tate and seizing him by the collar of his shirt. "Who has her?"

Tate's hands reached up, closing over Jazz's wrists. But he did little more than hold on as he stared into the face so like his own. "My mother," he said flatly.

ॐ

Staring into those calm, gray eyes, seeing no remorse, seeing no regret, seeing no emotion at all, was the most frightening experience of Anne-Marie's life. Her mind was still befuddled, still trying to grasp the idea that Ella McNeil was the one responsible for all this.

Ella McNeil.

Nearly twenty-four hours had passed since she'd crashed into the tree, twenty-four hours since she had, at gunpoint, climbed from the mangled wreck of her car. Ella had been waiting for her, looking cool and chic in a silk, khaki camp shirt and jodhpurs.

"Aren't you going to ask why?" Ella asked, cocking her head, her honey-blonde hair falling around her shoulders. She sat across from Anne-Marie, one leg crossed over the other while she sipped from a tin cup of tea.

"Does it really matter?" Anne-Marie asked. "If I'm going to die, knowing why won't bring me back."

With a shrug of her shoulders, Ella said, "Most people would want to know why. I imagine I would."

"I already know the gist of it," Anne-Marie responded. She flexed her arms again, straining against the steel cuffs on her wrists. "I'm going to die because you are a certified lunatic."

"Now, darling, I'm not crazy," Ella said, her tinkling laugh sounding in the air.

"You're right," Anne-Marie agreed. "You're freaking psychotic."

"I'm sure you think so." A cool smile crossed Ella's face, chilling Anne-Marie clear through. Sipping from her tea, she lifted her shoulders in an elegant, casual shrug. "And I suppose I can't blame you for thinking so. I must say, though, Anne-Marie, I thought you were too smart to fall in love with a man like Jasper McNeil."

"What kind of man is that?"

Ella merely gave her a long silent look. Setting the cup aside, she rose, smoothing her slim-fitting khakis down as she moved across the wooden floor to look out the window. "I'd intended you for Tate, you know. You had no right to give yourself to Jazz."

"Excuse me?" Anne-Marie asked, her voice frosty. "I really don't see how you had any say in the matter."

Brushing her comment aside, Ella continued as if Anne-

Marie hadn't even spoken. "And then to fall in love with the man responsible for your brother's death," she mused, shaking her head and clucking her tongue.

"Jazz was not responsible," Anne-Marie said quietly, her voice trembling with rage and fear.

"Oh, posh. Everything the man touches is destroyed or dead. His parents, your brother."

"My father," Anne-Marie offered, baring her teeth. "Don't forget about the friend you shot simply to hurt Jazz. Why do you hate him so much?"

"Because he had everything that should have been Tate's," Ella returned simply. Her soft gray eyes grew distant, a bittersweet smile curving her mouth. "I begged his father to leave Delia, begged him not to marry her. He laughed at me, said I was a sweet girl, but it was just a crush."

Looking back at Anne-Marie, she said, "His brother was a poor replacement. I wanted to make him jealous, make him realize we belonged together. Instead, he told me how happy he was for us. And that Delia was pregnant. It should have been me."

Those words said, Ella took a deep breath, closed her eyes. The lines around her mouth and eyes faded as the tension left her face. "And everything Jasper gave to Jazz should have been Tate's. And then after Jasper died, she up and married Beau Muldoon, the simpering, little fool. Oh, you'll never know how sweet it was to see her come into town with a black eye or split lip."

Edging closer, Ella leaned down and gave a conspiratorial grin and wink. "Beau was always so certain she'd leave him, that she had another man on the side. And from time to time, I let it slip that I'd seen a strange car in the driveway, or her disappearing inside one of Lem's motel rooms."

Understanding dawned in Anne-Marie s eyes, darkening them. Face pale with rage, she whispered, "How did a good man like Tate come from a witch like you?"

The sharp slap across her cheek whipped her head around, hair flying into her eyes. Eyes trained on the floor, she breathed deep, the stinging in her face, the ringing in her ears all fading in comparison to the sickness in her gut.

"You really ought to watch what you say, Dr. Kincade," Ella said, rubbing the palm of her hand. "I can either make this short and sweet or long and terrible. It's your choice."

℃

"Doc Kincade, Mama's missing."

Desmond's head whipped around, his intense gaze pinning Marlie to the wall. "She went to the bathroom. You were with her."

"She went out the window," Marlie whispered, her eyes wide with disbelief. "The window. My Mama who can barely even climb the stairs without help."

"Oh, Jesus." Desmond pressed his fingers to his eyes, frustration and worry eating a hole in his gut. What in the hell did he do? Half the men in the county were out trying to track down his daughter. Who was going to leave that search to come looking for a crazy, old woman who liked to wander off and dress kittens in doll clothes?

"Any idea where she could have gone?" Desmond asked, forcing his voice to stay calm and even.

"No," Marlie whispered. "Damn it, Doc Kincade. Anything could happen to her. She just got out of the hospital. Her body is too weak for this!"

"Okay, girl. Here's what we're going to do. In my desk, I have a small derringer. It belonged to my wife's Mama and I would have given it to Anne-Marie but she doesn't care for guns."

Only the derringer wasn't there.

Neither were the bullets.

§

"You're out of your ever-loving mind," Jazz said flatly as he leaped into the off-road jeep.

"I hope to God I am," Tate murmured. But the sick feeling inside his gut only intensified. He wasn't wrong.

Siren blaring, Tate sped down the highway, taking a small, dirt access road that led back into the woods behind the lake. "She cut Marlie's hair," he said over the noise of the truck tearing through the woods. "I had just said a few days earlier, right in front of...of my mother, how I loved Marlie's hair. And then it gets hacked off."

"You're condemning your mother on that?"

"Mama has a .38 and she knows how to use it. And she wasn't asleep the night I got the call about Doc Kincade. I forgot about that. And the look on her face when I told her you had an alibi—Anne-Marie."

"None of that means shit, Tate. Why would your mother..." His voice trailed off as Tate stopped the vehicle. He recognized the place, the place where he had gone fishing that last time with his father and Tate.

"Mama and Daddy had a fight that night, about me coming with you. Mama didn't want me to come, said Jasper had no right to spend time with me. It made no sense to me. But Mama

243

grieved more for your daddy than she did for mine. And for the longest time, I thought she hated you."

Leaping out of the truck, Tate glanced back to Jazz. "Any way I can convince you to stay here?"

"My woman," Jazz replied softly, heading down the long winding path that would take him to a tiny fishing cabin nearly two miles away.

ဢ

"What are you planning on doing to me?" Anne-Marie asked wearily as the sun sank closer to the horizon. "You can't stay gone forever."

"Mmm. I'm trying to figure that one out still. Should I kill you and dump your body where somebody will find it? Somebody like Jazz? Should I pin it on him? Or should I just do it here and now, and dump your body in the lake?"

She discussed it casually, like she was trying to decide between a red blazer, or a navy one. Somewhat stupefied and getting weak from hunger and thirst, Anne-Marie stared at her with dazed eyes.

"I could always bring his little girl here and make it look like he was stark raving mad," Ella whispered, arching an eyebrow as she considered that possibility. "We can't have Tate wanting to go and raise her once Jazz is in jail, now can we?"

The fog that obscured her brain thickened and her head spun, heart thudding slowly in her chest. Anne-Marie barely even remembered moving but suddenly, she was on her side, a screaming pain in her right shoulder.

And free of the chair.

Hands still bound behind her back, she rolled to her feet

and lunged forward, knocking the taller woman back. In slow motion, Anne-Marie watched as Ella fell backward, arms pinwheeling for balance. Her head struck the rough, wooden floor with a hollow thunk.

Sagging, whimpering out loud from the pain in her arm, Anne-Marie stumbled back, her weight falling against the spindle-legged table. As she teetered and lost her balance, a crash sounded in her head, lights blazing. Just as she slid to the floor, she heard Jazz call out, "Annie."

&

Jazz leaped forward catching Anne-Marie as she dropped toward the floor. A cry tore from her throat and Jazz saw with sickening clarity the angle at which her right arm hung. Swollen and already discolored, her arm hung limply at her side, dislocated at the shoulder joint.

"Oh, God." Lowering his forehead to hers, Jazz whispered, "It's all right, Annie. You're going to be fine."

"No. She's not."

That voice. Turning his head, Jazz stared in numb stupefaction, watching as Ella McNeil staggered to her feet. In her wobbly hand, she held a .38, pointed directly at Anne-Marie's head.

Curving his body around, shielding her as best he could, Jazz's eyes dropped to the gun. "Put that away, Ella. Your son's right behind me."

"You brought Tate out here?" Ella demanded, the gun rising and focusing on Jazz, right between the eyes.

"He brought me. He knows it's you, Ella. He figured it out. It's not going to be easy for a man to lock up his own mother."

"I'll handle Tate," she muttered, starting to pace. She whirled around, the gun raised and locked, once more, on Jazz's head.

"No, Mama. I'm afraid not."

Instantly, the lines around her eyes smoothed and the veil of sweet sophistication fell over her eyes. Turning, she smiled at Tate and asked, "Honey, whatever are you doing out here?"

"Put the gun away, Mama," Tate said, his voice barely above a whisper. Tortured eyes met the gaze of the woman who had birthed and raised him. "I can't let you hurt Jazz or Anne-Marie."

"I've no intention of hurting them," Ella promised, gun still trained on Jazz. "If you come much closer, honey, I'll have to shoot one of them. This is for your own good. He was always interfering and taking what should have been yours. Even Anne-Marie. I intended for her to be yours and look what he did."

"I don't want Anne-Marie. I never did. She's nothing more than a friend." Keeping his voice level, Tate repeated, "Put the gun down, Mama."

"You should leave this to me, Tate. I know how to handle this mess."

"By killing my cousin and my friend? By hacking off Marlie's hair and scaring her to death? You caused the mess. And you're going to have to go to jail for it." His voice roughened. "Why, Mama? Why in the hell did you do this?"

"Because this is what's best for you. And don't worry, I won't be going to jail. Nobody needs to know what happened to them. We can even take care of Mariah." With a small, pleased smile, Ella focused her eyes on Jazz's averted head. "Everything will be just fine."

"I know what's happened, Mama. I'm the sheriff. Do you

think I can ignore the fact that my own mother is a killer? For God's sake, Mama, put the damned gun down!"

"Don't you swear at me, Tate. Don't you ever raise your voice to me," Ella reprimanded, primly. "I raised you better than that."

A tiny giggle sounded in the doorway. Slowly, all eyes turned and locked on Naomi Muldoon, her worn, pink nightgown stained to the knees with mud. In one hand, she twirled a set of car keys. In the other, she held a small, deadly derringer that was pointed dead center of Ella's chest.

"Raised him better than that? You think you can go around and kill whomever you please, but it's wrong for him to raise his voice or say 'damn'?" Naomi asked, still laughing. "I wonder if I am the only one who sees some irony in that."

"Naomi...?"

"Do put the gun down, Ella," Naomi said calmly, a bright, cheerful smile lighting her face, making her look twenty years younger.

Dumbstruck, Ella merely blinked at Naomi as the woman entered the house. "You're wondering how I know about this place," Naomi guessed, pausing by Anne-Marie to brush her fingers against her forehead. She smiled a sweet, gentle smile and whispered, "Things will be fine."

Then she turned her eyes back to Ella. "Oh, I knew about you and Beau. A mother knows those sorts of things. From the beginning, I knew about it. I couldn't have cared less. As long as he was with you, he wasn't laying his hands on Delia. Poor girl, she never could figure out why he went from adoring her to beating her, overnight. It took me a while to figure out, though, that you were the one planting stories in his head."

"Go on home, you crazy bitch," Ella snapped, face flushed, hands shaking.

Smiling, Naomi said, "It's amazing, the things you can do and see and notice when people think you've lost your marbles, isn't it? Of course, for a while there, it was touch and go." Reaching up, she brushed her fingers over the curve of her cheek, remembering the bruises that had faded years earlier. "It's taken me some time to ground myself again. But with Jackson and Beau gone and Lawrence up and moving away, becoming a deputy...well, things finally started seeming real again. And then my son dies."

"I don't know what you're talking about," Ella said calmly, even though her face was pale with rage and her hands shook. "Delia killed Beau."

"That she did. And he most likely deserved it; he was every bit as cruel as his father was. He would have started beating her sooner or later. You just sped things up." Her shoulders rose and fell in a helpless shrug. "I don't know that I could have done anything about it, but I'm ashamed I didn't try.

"But it's not Beau I'm talking about. It's Lawrence. You killed him as surely as you tried to kill Doc Kincade. Of course," Naomi mused, walking in slow meandering circles around the room. "I could forgive that, maybe. As much as a mother could forgive such a thing, considering how evil he was. I am having some trouble, though, with what you did to my Marlie. And poor Mabel."

Naomi paused by Anne-Marie again, watching her intently. Then she raised her head, focusing those misty green eyes on Ella. "Maybe the young doctor doesn't want or need to know why. But I do. I haven't been waiting outside all this time for my health, you know. Tell me why, Ella. I need to know."

"So do I," Tate whispered.

"For you, Tate. I did it all for you," Ella said, the gun falling slackly to her side. "He took everything that should have been yours, even Anne-Marie."

"I never wanted Anne-Marie," Tate repeated, spreading his hands wide. Dumbly, he stared at the gun he still held in one hand then raised his head to meet his mother's gaze across the room. "You never even wanted me, did you? I was just something else for you to try to hurt Jazz's daddy, wasn't I? And that didn't work, either."

"Of course, I wanted you," Ella insisted, moving closer. "You were the only good thing in my life. Of course, Jasper was supposed to have been your father—"

"My father was a good man," Tate interrupted, backing away from her. "A damned good one. And you hated him, just like you hated everybody else. You hid it, all this time."

"I didn't hide it. But with Jazz gone, you would have been able to take your place in the community, the way you should have in the first place. You would have married Anne-Marie, married into one of the oldest, finest families in Kentucky..." As she spoke, Ella's face smoothed and her eyes took on a far-off look.

Jazz brushed Anne-Marie's hair back, kissed her brow, and rose smoothly to his feet, keeping his body between Ella and Anne-Marie. "And then I came back home, and ruined your plans, huh, Ella?"

"You never did amount to anything," Ella sneered at him. She glared at Jazz, barely aware anybody else was around them. Slowly, she raised her gun, completely unaware of her son shouting, of Anne-Marie's cry, and Naomi's movement.

"Mama, don't!"

But it was too late. Even before the words had left Tate's mouth, a gunshot ripped through the quiet night. And they were left staring at the lifeless body of Ella McNeil, a tiny, almost neat hole in the soft underside of her chin, a spreading

249

pool of blood seeping from under her head.

"Mama..."

Tate's eyes closed and he sank to his knees beside her while Jazz eased Anne-Marie back to her feet. Naomi moved closer, one hand resting on Tate's shoulder. "Tortured souls sometimes can only see one way out, Tate. That's not your fault, but hers."

Without responding, Tate reached for his cell phone, his eyes full of rage and grief while he dialed out. Woodenly, he spoke into it. "This is McNeil. I'm out at the old Jenson place. I'm gonna need some medics and..."

Blood roared in her ears as Anne-Marie sagged against Jazz. "It's over, right?" she whispered.

His murmured agreement barely registered before she gave in to the gray that beckoned.

⁃

"He's not here," Jazz whispered, reaching up and rubbing at the back of his neck. Staring out at the full sanctuary, he searched uselessly for a face similar to his.

"Tate's having a hard time right now," Desmond murmured, even as he searched the crowd for the third time. Sighing, he ran a hand through his salt and pepper hair. "I've got to get to Anne-Marie."

As Desmond moved away from the pulpit, Jazz searched the final crowd of faces that had rushed into the sanctuary. But Tate wasn't there. "I can't believe he won't come," Jazz muttered, clenching his jaw tight and turning his head away from the door.

When the strains of *Ave Maria* rang out, Jazz turned his

face once more to the doorway, this time looking for his bride. Marlie appeared in the doorway, a smile curving her mouth, almost hiding the sadness in her eyes. Her dress, a deep blue, sleeveless sheath, clung to her willow-slim figure and in her hands, she carried a spray of white and lavender roses.

Then he saw Anne-Marie come around the corner. Her eyes sought his instantly and he felt the tension drain away. In her eyes, he saw a mirror of his own sadness, and a love he had never hoped to have.

She moved to join him at the altar, and all thoughts of time, regrets and Tate fell away as he stared into liquid green eyes.

"I, Jasper Wayne McNeil Jr., take you, Anne-Marie Kincade, to be my lawful, wedded wife..."

"...and do you, Anne-Marie Kincade, promise to love and honor him, forsaking all others until death do you part?"

"I do."

"And do you, Jasper Wayne McNeil Jr., promise to love and honor..."

"...anyone here who knows why these two should not be joined together, let him speak now or forever hold his peace."

Automatically, Jazz and Anne glanced around before looking back at each other. As Reverend Matthews opened his mouth to conclude the ceremony, Anne-Marie smiled at Jazz.

"Wait."

Black tuxedo jacket flapping around him, shirt half untucked, Tate sprinted up the aisle. "I was supposed to be the best man," he panted, coming to a stop and staring at his cousin. "Am I still welcome?"

Staring into that flushed face, into eyes so like his own, Jazz felt the last of the grief drain from him. "Always," he simply said, holding out his hand.

"Can we make it a double?" he asked, sliding Marlie a sidelong glance.

Tears filled her dark eyes, spilled down her pale cheeks as Tate moved closer. "Am I still welcome?" he asked again, lowering his head until his brow rested against hers.

A smile broke out on her face as she reached up, laid one hand on his cheek.

"Always."

About the Author

To learn more about Shiloh, please visit www.shilohwalker.com. Send an email to Shiloh at Shiloh_@shilohwalker.com or join her Yahoo! group to join in the fun with other readers as well as Shiloh! http://groups.yahoo.com/group/SHI_nenigans or

http://groups.yahoo.com/group/ScampsVampsandSpicyRoma nce.

Caught in the sights of a killer,
David and Miranda fight for life—and the chance to love again.

Love on the Run
© *2007 Marie-Nicole Ryan*

Miranda Raines thinks she has found a safe haven in Oxford, England, until Scotland Yard DCI David French knocks on her door with terrifying news. Her ex-husband, a convicted murderer, has escaped from prison and he's coming for her.

Miranda, who for years has harbored a secret love for the driven Chief Inspector, has no choice but to trust him. She just hopes she can guard her own heart at least as well as he guards her.

After thwarting her ex's first attack, David spirits Miranda and her young son out of England and the three of them end up on the run across Europe. David has no intention of falling in love again, but with each passing day Miranda awakens passions he thought long dead.

Could this be their forever love? With a killer on their trail, they may not live long enough to find out.

Available now in ebook and print from Samhain Publishing.

Enjoy the following excerpt from Love on the Run...

After dinner on the flagstone terrace, Randi helped Mina clear away the dishes and load the dishwasher.

"I'm glad you came back," Mina said. "Jamie would've been quite all right, but I'm not sure *you* would have."

Randi stopped in the middle of folding a towel. She shook her head. "No, I was a wreck. I don't think we went ten kilometers on that bike, and I bawled like a baby the whole time."

Mina smiled and placed her strong arm around her shoulder. "You are losing that pinched look you had when you first came to us."

"That bad, huh?"

"Not bad, but still it was there."

"I do feel safe here," Randi admitted.

"You must relax because David will protect you and your son. It is very obvious to these old eyes how important the two of you are to him."

Mina's words gladdened Randi's heart, but surely the older woman was exaggerating. "He's been absolutely wonderful, but..."

"Time will tell, my dear. Be patient." Mina removed the towel from Randi's trembling hands. "Let's go outside and enjoy this nice fall evening. The men shouldn't have all the fun."

ॐ

On the terrace Randi eased down into a lounge chair and

watched David and Jamie wrestle in the grass. A sensation of pure contentment stole over her and wrapped her in easy comfort.

She turned to Mina. "Dinner was wonderful, Mina. Thank you for having us. For everything."

"It is my privilege. I'm so glad that David thought of us. So rarely do we have visitors from the U.K.—at least none we are so happy to see." Mina turned to her husband. "Jean-Luc, why don't you play some music for us?"

Randi's ears pricked. "Music? Oh, yes, please."

Jean-Luc grumbled, but with good nature, "She doesn't want to talk to me, so she asks me to play. I am wise to her tricks." The older man hauled his cumbersome self out of his chair and ambled into the house, returning a moment later with an old violin.

David turned to Randi, a wide grin spread across his handsome face. "Did you know Miranda plays?"

"*Bon!*" Jean-Luc declared. "You will play for us, Ran-dee?"

"Yes, but you must go first. I warn you I'm very rusty."

Jean-Luc drew the bow across the strings, then frowned at the sound. "Just a little adjustment." He tightened the E string and drew the bow again. "*Parfait!*" he pronounced, and then launched into an old folk tune which Randi immediately recognized as *Sur le Pont d'Avignon*.

After the rollicking tune which had young Jamie up on his feet, dancing, Jean-Luc paused and extended the violin toward Randi. "Now you must play us something from your country, *s'il vous plaît.*"

Randi nodded her assent and took the violin from Jean-Luc's gnarled hands. "I'll play you our state song." She drew the bow across the violin, the melodic strains of *The Tennessee*

Waltz filling the night air.

After she completed the waltz, Jean-Luc stood and clapped. "*Bien*, Ran-dee! *C'est bon.*"

"Mummy, play *Rocky Top*. Jean-Luc, you'll like that one. It's bouncy."

Randi looked from Mina to Jean-Luc to David whose eyes were actually closed. It was the first time she'd seen the taut lines of tension erased from his lean face.

"*Rocky Top, Tennessee* it is," she said with a nod, then launched into the sprightly tune. Jamie sang, charmingly off key, "Once I had a girl on Rocky Top," then fell to humming when he didn't know the words, but intoned, "Rocky Top, Tennessee," during the chorus.

Randi lost herself in the energy and rhythm of the country tune, until it came to an end.

"*Encore, encore!*" Jean-Luc prompted.

"Something classical, dear?" Mina suggested. "I believe David told me that you play with chamber groups as well."

"All right." Soon the lyrical strains of the second movement of Beethoven's Violin Concerto rose through the valley, soaring into the night. Swept up in the mood and imagery of the music, Randi became the violin, the music. When the last note faded, she heard a collective sigh of appreciation.

"That was simply lovely, dear," Mina told her, pulling her sweater tighter around her shoulders. "Why don't we go in? It's getting too cool for these old bones. Besides, I think your son has fallen asleep."

Randi nodded. "He's been conditioned. Whenever he has trouble going to sleep, I play for him until he does."

৪১

Randi tapped on David's door. She heard sounds of his moving about through the door, then it opened. Apparently he'd been getting ready for bed. His shirt was unbuttoned and pulled out of his jeans. Her breath caught in her throat when she caught sight of his broad, muscular chest and washboard abs. She felt his arms surround her, pulling her into his strong embrace.

"You played beautifully," he murmured in a voice so soft and seductive it sent ripples of desire to the pit of her belly.

"Thank you," she said, as he maneuvered her into his bedroom and kicked the door shut behind him.

"It's paid a few bills," she quipped before she could stop herself. Lord, why was she so nervous? David would never hurt her, not physically anyway.

"Is Jamie asleep?"

"Yes, he's all tucked in."

"Have you come to tuck *me* in?"

She bit her lip and tilted her head to the side. "You're a big boy. Do you need to be tucked in?"

"I might do." He closed the short distance between them, his gaze never leaving her eyes. "Depends on who's doing the tucking."

"And would it be presumptuous to assume the *who* would be me?" she asked, trying to keep her tone light so he wouldn't know how scared she really was. She was just no good at sex.

Stefan had told her so countless times.

"No, you'd be right on target."

His lips brushed across the top on her head. "Miranda, will you stay with me tonight?"

She pulled back and looked up into his warm gray eyes and

swallowed hard before answering, "Yes."

Oh Lord! Had she really said yes?

His lips, warm and demanding, descended against hers. Every bone in her body liquefied with the heat of his kiss. He wanted her. The reason didn't matter. She wanted him, too.

Together they fell backward onto the bed, his hands skimming under her sweater and caressing her breasts though her bra. His kisses were hungry and demanding. She opened her mouth to his. His tongue swept into her mouth. He tasted of the strong French coffee he'd had at dinner.

One expert twist, then his hands, warm and gentle, were all over her again. The memories of their earlier bathroom tryst flooded back. Too late to stop, even if she'd wanted. And she didn't. Her ex had never been this kind or gentle. Forcing the bad memories and fears far, far away, she gave her trust again to David.

Suddenly they both were tugging at her sweater. Over her head it went along with her bra, tossed somewhere. He rolled her nipples between his thumbs, then applied his lips and teeth, raking them ever so tenderly, teasing them into taut buds of screaming sensation. An unfamiliar heat spread down her belly and centered between her thighs.

She gasped, "Oh." Hands shaking, she slipped his T-shirt over his head, taking care not to disturb his bandage. She gazed into his eyes and saw the passion and desire burning there. She shivered. Her fingers splayed over his chest. His flat male nipples drew into tight nubs. She kissed one, then the other.

He let out a groan and her name, soft as a sigh. He pressed against her, his rigid erection straining against the confinement of his jeans. His hands worked at the button and zipper of her jeans, easing them apart. She raised her hips, allowing him to slip her jeans and panties down over her hips.

She kicked off the jeans, giving him access. He quickly found the warmth between her legs, his caress gentle, yet urgent.

"You're lovely," he told her, kissing her inner thigh. Shivers ran through her, fanning the heat of her desire into a blaze.

He pulled away. "No, don't go," she protested as he stood.

Glancing down at his jeans, he grinned. "I'm not going anywhere." He unzipped and shucked his jeans in record time.

He stood before her, his lean-muscled body tense. More excited than ever, she reached out and touched him, marveling at the texture of his arousal—rigid steel covered in the softest of silken skin.

"Easy," he gasped, his lips claiming hers again.

Their bodies matched, warm skin to warm skin, lips to lips.

Again, his fingers were at her feminine core. Two entered her while his thumb circled the sensitive spot above. Delicious waves of heat spiraled up from her center, setting her entire body ablaze.

"You're so beautiful." Kneeling between her thighs, he kissed her, circling the sensitive part of her body with his tongue. The fire grew and spread until, swept along, she lost all control and cried his name.

He could be everything she's hoped for.
Or everything she fears.

A Desperate Longing
© *2007 Brenda Williamson*

Two years after Kacy Carwell eluded kidnapping by a serial rapist, she still lives with nightmares and panic attacks on her painstakingly slow path to recovery. When a mysterious new neighbor moves in next door, her tenuous hold on her mental stability spirals out of control. She thinks she sees her attacker everywhere she goes, and no one believes her.

Only the new neighbor, the patient, kind and handsome Gulliver Knight, prevents her from sliding into mental deterioration. He alone feeds her desperate longing to feel normal again. His gentle, attentive care calms her frazzled nerves, while his passionate lovemaking quickly sends her tumbling from attraction to deep love. His affections work like a balm to her wounded spirit.

Then Kacy discovers that Gulliver is not all he appears to be. Her world crashes around her just as danger—this time real—threatens not only her sanity, but her life. Before she can untangle the web of deceit from her own broken emotions, someone will get hurt.

And someone will die.

Available now in ebook and print from Samhain Publishing.

hot stuff

Discover Samhain!

GET IT
NOW

MyBookStoreAndMore.com

GREAT EBOOKS, GREAT DEALS . . . AND MORE!

Don't wait to run to the bookstore down the street, or
waste time shopping online at one of the "big boys." Now,
all your favorite Samhain authors are all in one place—at
MyBookStoreAndMore.com. Stop by today and discover
great deals on Samhain—and a whole lot more!

GREAT
CHEAP
FUN

Discover eBooks!

THE FASTEST WAY TO GET THE HOTTEST NAMES

Get your favorite authors on your favorite reader, long before they're
out in print! Ebooks from Samhain go wherever you go, and work with
whatever you carry—Palm, PDF, Mobi, and more.

9 781599 988306